The Elders' Universe:

Shard Agnor's Book

The Elders' Universe:
Shard
Agnor's Book
By: Keith Imbody

Preface

My friend Adam and I set a goal for ourselves this year, 2024. We were both tasked with writing and publishing a book greater than fifty thousand words by the end of this year. This is my book! A loose sequel to The Elders' Chronicles. If you haven't read it, no worries! These stories are designed to stand alone. But for returning readers, you will notice many connections to The Elders' Chronicles.

I present to you: The Elders' Universe: Shard. Agnor's Book.

Keith Ambody

For my mom.

You would have gladly listened to every word I wrote if you were still with us. Unfortunately, stories do end. I hope you can somehow see the words I've written in this book.

Acknowledgements

I would like to thank my sister, Alecia, for designing the book cover, formatting, and editing.

Thanks to dad for listening to me read the entire story out loud.

Fun fact: it took about eight hours to read the entire book.

The Elders' Universe:

Shard

Shard
By: Keith Imbody

Table of Contents

Chapter One
Faer

In order to understand my story, you first need to understand how I got here.

Hello. My name is Faer.

I was lost. I didn't have much to live for. After losing my best friend, I was so sad all the time. She was my everything. My wife. I didn't have much family. None that cared about me enough to even check on me. But the way my best friend left this world was nothing but a mystery.

These days I just got by. That is, until I got the call. I was sitting in my house, when I heard a phone ring. I went to answer it, the cell phone I had in my pocket, but that's not what was ringing. I stood up to check the landline. Who even has a landline these days? Well, me. But once I reached my other phone, that wasn't what was ringing either.

Now, the fact that the phone was still ringing at this point was weird. No phone would ring that long. I started to wonder if my neighbor had left their phone somewhere in my house when he came over to watch the game earlier that week. I searched. For five minutes. To my dismay, the phone was still ringing!

I walked out the back door. The ringing was instantly louder. That means wherever this phone was should be out here.

So I should mention that I have a pretty big back yard. About an acre of land back there. I started walking out into my yard, which was full of different plants, flowers, trees, anything you could imagine, could probably be found here. My wife was a gardener, so this was her life's work. After losing her about three months ago, I dedicated my life to the upkeep of this garden.

But that ringing was so relentless, it wouldn't stop. I started to really listen to it. I had to find it. And if it was back here, I had to figure out who this phone belonged to.

I walked by the daisies, tulips, and lilacs. Nothing. I checked around the big oak tree my wife and I used to have picnics under every Saturday morning. Nothing. I slowly scanned every inch of the ground as I made it to the tomato plants. We always had so many of those things every year. But still, nothing.

I made it to the edge of my acre of land, and began to turn back around. I was beginning to think I was going crazy with this ringing. I followed the outer path my wife had made that was one giant square around the entire garden. But in the back left corner, something caught my eye.

I had never seen this arrangement of flowers before. But I had been tending to this garden for months now! How were these over here?

Orchids. A bunch of bright, beautiful orchids. I went over to them to see their beauty up close. But that ringing was irritating! It took away from their beauty.

I turned my head and saw a second patch of unrecognizable flowers. Dahlias. Who planted all these

14

flowers? Was I just going crazy? And that ringing was about to drive me mad!

I turned away from the new additions and kicked something by mistake. I looked down, and saw a phone. I checked my pocket, and I still had my cell phone. So I had no idea whose phone this was. It was a simple looking cell phone, with a picture of an analog clock on the back. Somehow, the picture was moving, even though it was completely flat. I checked the time on my phone, and sure enough, the picture of the clock on the back was accurate! Now that's an impressive phone cover. The second hand ticked on, as I stared in amazement at this phone on the ground.

But wait! I listened as the ringing continued. This was the phone! I picked it up to finally solve this ringing mystery. The screen's caller ID said 'unknown', so I had no idea who could be on the other end of this call. But something was weird about all of this. This phone was ringing for ten, twenty minutes straight.

I instinctively answered the phone, and held it to my ear.

"Hello?" I said.

I heard an automated voice on the other end.

"Hello! Welcome back. To reach the main office, press one."

Main office? For what? The voice continued as I wondered.

"To talk directly with your director, press two. To speak with someone else at the agency, press three. If you're confused, and have forgotten your mission, press four."

Director? Agency? Was this some sort of business phone or something?

"If you believe this phone has fallen into the wrong hands, if the mission is compromised, or for any further questions, please stay on the line."

"Mission?!" I yelled. "What sort of game–"

"Faer?" a familiar voice said. "Faer, is that you?"

"Hello?"

The person on the other side of the call, it couldn't be.

"Faer, you've forgotten the mission? Again?"

Tears welled in my eyes as I heard her voice for the first time since I lost her.

It was my wife.

Chapter Two
Remembrance

"Is this a joke?!" I cried.

"Faer! This mission was simple!"

"What mission?!"

"Do you not remember anything from the past three months?"

"No! As a matter of fact, I don't! I've been tending to your garden for months now, missing you like crazy! I thought you were gone! Where are you?!"

"Faer. No. Not again."

"What do you mean?"

"I'm not your wife."

"W–what? You sound just like her!"

"Yes, I do. But I'm not her. Faer, you need to pull yourself together. I understand what you went through to get here. And I'm genuinely sorry. But if you want to save the timeline, you need to focus."

"Save the timeline? What am I, a superhero or something?"

"Faer. You were a very broken man. A man who stumbled upon a phone with a clock on it. The phone you are currently talking to me on. I am not your wife. And this is the fifth time you've been confused like this since you chose to become an agent with us."

"Who is us? Who are you? Wait, who even am I? Why can't I remember anything?"

"The side effects of using this technology have been known to cause confusion like this. You just need to think. But also, get out of your own head. Your wife could be out there somewhere, and you won't ever find her if you keep forgetting everything."

"Just tell me why you sound like her."

"A side effect of the technology."

"WHAT TECHNOLOGY?!" I screamed.

"Faer, the phone! The time phone!"

Right when she said that, everything came flooding back to me. Three months ago, my wife mysteriously vanished. I had no idea where she was or where to look. But she vanished right in front of me. Literally. She faded away before my eyes. It doesn't make sense. About a week after I lost her, I was in the garden, and I found this phone. Much like I did, again, today. I must have dropped the phone yesterday, only to find it yet again today. But where it originated from, I'm not sure I'll ever know.

After picking up the phone back then, I remember so vividly now, I was recruited via this exact phone to help this agency, whoever they were, to keep the timeline safe. This phone was powerful. Magic, even. But the only reason I agreed to help them was because they said they might be able to locate my wife. But these forgetful side effects were very persistent.

I've never been to this agency's building. The only communication I've had with anybody regarding this, was on this time phone.

Somehow, this agency could see the past, present, and future. But they weren't omnipotent. They needed help from people like me. There are many of us that work to constantly stabilize the timeline. It sounds silly and even impossible.

There's always another mission, though. I've only completed a dozen or so over these months, but there was always something else to do.

Simple things like helping out a stranger at a grocery store were the kinds of missions I was tasked with. That sounds silly, but I do what I'm told. They say I can move up and start working on bigger missions soon. But, not if I keep forgetting like I do.

If you're wondering how helping out a stranger at a grocery store could stabilize a timeline, let me put it this way: If a very powerful and important man of the future gets botulism from an unfortunately placed can, the future, well, the future's future, would be in grave danger. So I do what I can. It's all for her. Yes, saving the timeline does feel good, saving all those people, that's also amazing. I just wish I could see her again.

"Faer?" a voice on the time phone said.

Strange. It no longer sounded like my wife.

"Yeah, I'm here, I'm sorry."

"Maybe this technology, this mission, and all this stress is too much for you."

"No, it isn't! I remember my current mission now. I'll get right to it."

"Faer. Try to keep the phone on you at all times. You tend to have these episodes when you're away from it. The technology is powerful, but eventually, your forgetful bouts should cease. Do you have any further questions for me?"

"No," I said. "Thank you for calling the phone, and reminding me who I am. What I'm here for."

"That's why we like you, Faer," she said. "You're a valuable asset to the agency. Now get out there, and save the timeline!"

I heard a click as she hung up the phone. Oh, by the way, that was my director. The woman I always report to. Her name is Nadia.

This current mission was going to be a tricky one. But I was ready.

Now that you understand how I got here, and now that I remembered myself, hopefully the future, and the past, and even the present, can be a lot more clear.

Chapter Three
Gala

The agency I work for is called Shard. I'm guessing because some of our missions are so minuscule, they're kind of like a shard of glass. It seems unimportant, but trust me. As even more memories of the past three months are brought to the front of my mind, I believe so strongly that this is all for the greater good.

My current mission from Shard is a little dangerous. I have to sneak into an event that is held by some billionaire of a neighboring city. People from all around the world are going to be there. It's some gala that celebrates advancements in technology and science. I was told that I had to make sure two specific people met. Without an agent there, Shard claims that these two people, who invent some very important technology in the future, would never meet. And that technology would never get invented otherwise.

They sent me pictures so I knew who I was looking for.

Sasha Kiyla, an up and coming inventor. She is actually giving a presentation at the event, so this could be tricky.

And Albert Heron. His ideas help later generations perfect time travel. That's what Shard tells me anyway. I guess time travel could be possible, but I kind of want to see it myself. Maybe then I can find a way to save my wife.

They also told me they would be sending a car to bring me to the event in style. I have to blend in.

I was ready. I was dressed in a black tuxedo. I felt important. But I began to wonder what I was going to say to get Sasha and Albert to talk to each other.

A car pulled up outside. It was a limousine. I grabbed my phone off my nightstand and headed outside. The driver opened my door for me. I got into the car, and we drove on for miles. I was so anxious but knew I had to hide those feelings. After what seemed like an eternity, and nothing but silence from my driver, we pulled up to the gala.

The driver got out of the car and opened my door for me again. I got out of the car, and Immediately saw Sasha. She had gorgeous long black hair, just like the picture Shard sent me. Maybe if I go introduce myself now, she'll be more open to listening to me later when I find Albert.

I walked toward her, and was about to speak, when someone else stopped me.

"Hello!" he said. "Welcome to the Gala! Have you signed in yet?"

"Signed in?" I asked.

"Why of course…" he paused as he didn't know my name.

Now I was never allowed to give my actual name during missions. That would put me, and the agency, at risk. So I always had to come up with something new.

"Sir, my name is Alan," I said.

"Well, Alan," he said, while looking through a book of names. "Alan, what is your last name?"

I began to panic. I didn't know there would be a guest list. How could I guess a name that was actually in that book?

"Alberts," I said, without thinking.

Alan Alberts? Now why did I say Alberts? I need to find Albert, not be him!

"Ah, yes, Mr. Alberts, I unfortunately don't see you on the list of names…"

Sasha walked over to this man to ask him a question. I couldn't hear what she said. She walked away, but stood nearby.

"Well, Mr. Alberts, it seems there are a few names missing from this list. If you don't mind following me, we can get this squared away."

The man went into the building, and had me follow him. I was going directly where I needed to go. I just had an uneasy feeling in my stomach, as I followed this man past the main hall, past a bunch of socialites that were already gathering, and into a secluded room. The man told me to sit down. I obeyed.

"What do you want with us, Mr. Alberts? If your game is to steal important information, I could have you sent to a deserted island where you could live out what is left of your miserable life."

I had to be confident. People like this were full of themselves. They think the world is theirs, and we're just living in it. Well I was about to show some confidence that I didn't know I even had.

"Now how can you talk to me like that when I don't even know your name?" I asked.

"Excuse me, sir?"

"You heard me," I continued. I stood up. It's all about confidence. "And another thing. I don't think Mr. Heron would appreciate you treating me like this!"

"Mr. Heron? You know Mr... I'm so sorry, sir. I think there is a misunderstanding."

"You bet there is," I said, confidently. "Now let me out of here this instant!"

"I don't think so," a woman said. She walked into the room, and to my chagrin, my confidence was immediately drained.

As I recognized her, and as she came into full view, I realized this mission was going to be more complicated than I thought.

It was Sasha.

Chapter Four
Presentation

"Who do you think you are?!" Sasha demanded.

"I am Alan Alberts!" I tried to say with confidence.

"Alberts. Like the man you claim to know, Albert Heron?"

Wait, she already knows of him? Why was I here to make sure they met?

"You've heard of him," I said, softly.

"Who hasn't?!" Sasha scoffed. "Do you not know?"

"Know what?!"

"This is Albert's event," Sasha said, sternly. "And the fact that you didn't know that solidifies what I originally thought. You're an imposter or spy of some sort."

I was taken aback. Why would Shard send me here to make sure the two of them met? The host of the gala and someone who was giving a presentation and clearly looked up to Albert were bound to meet without me here. I was puzzled, and beginning to get frustrated. Shard holding back information like that made me question the real reason I was sent here.

"So who are you, really?" Sasha asked me.

Without thinking, I blurted out the first sentence that came to my head.

"I'm Albert's butler," I said.

"Why would a butler show up in such a fancy limo?"

"Oh, you know Mr. Heron. He is quite the showman."

Sasha looked at the man that brought me into this room, then back at me.

"It took me months to line up this presentation. If you do anything to mess this up, I will find you, and take care of you."

"Understood."

"You're lucky Mr. Heron couldn't make it tonight," Sasha said, staring at me as if trying to see into my soul.

"Quite right," I agreed. "Mr. Heron is a very busy man, and he only allows the best. That's why I have full confidence that your presentation will go well."

Sasha fought back a slight smile, and remained serious. "Of course it will. I am the best."

Sasha and the other man escorted me out of the room and into the main hall where everyone was now gathered.

Sasha stared at me one more time.

"We're both watching you, Mr. Alberts. Alan. I don't believe that's your name. But my friend here won't hesitate to take care of any issues you may cause. Don't try anything."

They both walked away, leaving me in a room full of socialites that I had never met.

But how was I even supposed to complete the mission now? With Albert Heron himself not being here… wait a minute. If Sasha was speaking at this event, Albert's event, then he must know she exists. So why was I sent here to make sure they met? None of this makes sense!

"If I could have everyone's attention!" a voice could be heard saying through a bunch of speakers. They were on a stage. It was the man that escorted me earlier.

"My name is Albert Heron, and I am here to introduce this new technology to you!"

The crowd erupted in confusion, as everyone knew that was not what Albert looked like.

"And they thought I was an imposter," I mumbled.

"You are not Mr. Heron," a voice from the crowd shouted.

"Oh, on the contrary," the man claiming to be Albert said.

He revealed a small device on his arm.

"This is my latest invention!" he smiled.

He pressed a button on the device, and his appearance completely changed. He pressed it again, and he looked like Sasha.

The real Sasha gasped from the audience.

He pressed it one more time, and looked exactly like me. He looked directly at me and winked.

Well he would know I'm not his butler, so maybe it was time for me to get out of here. Clearly Shard lied to me, and I can't complete a mission if I don't even know what it is.

The man took the device off his arm, revealing the truth. He was, in fact, Albert Heron. And honestly, that was an amazing, spectacular entrance.

The crowd of socialites started cheering for Albert. Sasha walked on stage and everyone continued cheering.

Albert smiled as she now stood next to him. He looked over at her, then back at the crowd. "Sasha, I think they like your presentation so far!"

Even more confused as to what my mission was, I stared in disbelief.

"This technology is still in development," Sasha began. "Mr. Heron here was so excited to use it to make such a grand entrance. It won't be available to the public for many years, if ever. Such technology is never meant to go mainstream. The reason it was invented is two fold: the first is obvious, and a little selfish, but necessary. It's so we can profit off of it!"

Wow. Of course it's about money. I'm in a room full of rich people. Why would I think otherwise?

Mr. Heron began to speak. "When Sasha and I met to discuss her advancements in science, I was shocked at her results. She is an amazing inventor, and I'm proud to say that Sasha Kiyla, and I, Albert Heron, are here to announce Kiyla Heron industries. KHI will be hiring as soon as tonight, so if anybody wants to be a part of history, advancements in technology like you've seen tonight, talk to Sasha or find me. Only the best will be accepted. Sasha, would you care to tell them where your heart was when you created this technology?"

"I'd be glad to, Mr. Heron!"

"Call me Albert!"

Oh this sounded so staged. It was a little sad, actually.

"Okay, Albert!" Sasha laughed. "This technology has the power to offer closure to those that have lost someone they loved."

My eyes widened, as I forgot my entire mission for a moment.

"Imagine your loved one, taken from this world too soon. Maybe you didn't get a proper chance to say goodbye. With this technology, and of course, a couple hundred dollars, you can meet with someone from KHI. They will have access to this technology, so you can have those final closure moments you would never get otherwise. We can mimic anybody's image. As long as it is somewhere on the Internet, it is in our database. And for those few moments, it's as if you're talking to the loved one that you lost. Closure. It heals. And KHI is all about healing, and advancement."

I couldn't believe what I just heard. And I didn't understand why Shard would lie to me. But in this moment, I was imagining seeing my wife one more time. But, she wasn't dead, to my knowledge. This technology was more for people who had no hope of seeing their loved ones again. So I quickly snapped out of that thought.

"Thank you all for joining us tonight," Albert said. "Now, let's all chat about what we've seen, and let's change lives! Enjoy the refreshments, and remember: KHI needs you!"

Everyone cheered. Albert and Sasha walked off stage. And I was left standing there, confused as to what Shard's angle was, and worried that Albert and Sasha would come find me and question me.

My head began to hurt. I fell to the ground, then stood back up. I managed to walk outside unnoticed. I walked away from the building to regain my composure. I wanted answers. Now. I pulled the phone out of my pocket, and everything began to look blurry. I began to feel dizzy.

I was going to call Shard.

I went to unlock my phone, when I had a horrible realization. I meant to grab the time phone on my way out. But, in haste, I must have mistakenly taken my personal phone. I checked the back for the magic clock, and of course, it wasn't there. This was my own personal phone. And that's why I started to feel this way. I was beginning to forget who I was to Shard, again. I'm guessing the other times I forgot like this weren't while I was on a mission. It sounds like that time phone technology has some nasty side effects. It might even explain why I found the time phone in the garden today. Maybe I forgot who I was, and dropped it by mistake. I tried to return to my normal life, until I heard it ringing again. But, I'm nowhere near it. So I'm not sure what's going to happen to me. I have to get home, fast!

Alone, not sure where to go, and with no way to contact Shard, I was overtaken by my nausea, as I saw two headlights pulling toward me. I saw a silhouette of someone as I closed my eyes. I felt someone carry me into a vehicle. I wasn't sure who it was, or where they were taking me.

Chapter Five
Truth

I woke up to a ringing sound. I guess the Shard limo driver had found me, and brought me safely home. Luckily, I remembered who I was. Maybe the longer I work for Shard, the more immune I become to the side effects. I was still in the limo, but close enough to hear the time phone ringing. The limo driver opened my door, and I carefully got out. After a second of losing my balance, I was stable. I thanked him for keeping me safe, and I walked into my house. I immediately went into my room, and saw the time phone.

I angrily picked up the phone, and started talking.

"Are you people serious? How am I supposed to follow through with a mission if you don't tell me the truth?"

"Hello! Welcome back. To reach the main office, press one."

"Oh, we are not doing this every time."

"To talk directly with your director, press two."

I pressed two. I hate automated menus. Why would such an agency even use them?!

"Faer?" Nadia, my director answered.

"Nadia!" I exclaimed. "Nadia, why did you lie to me?"

"What are you talking about?" Nadia asked.

"That gala! Sasha Kiyla! Albert Heron! The mission was to make sure they meet, in order to advance future technology, up to, and including time travel!"

"What are you talking about, Faer?! That wasn't your mission at all!"

"What do you mean?! You sent me images of Sasha and Albert!"

"Yes, so you could locate them. Oh Faer, maybe this is all too much for you! I think the side effects of the time phone may have altered your memory!"

"Then what was my mission?!" I demanded.

"To get that technology away from that gala. What KHI is proposing–"

"That! How do you know that name?! That was just announced tonight!"

"Past, present, and future," Nadia said softly.

"But, my mission seemed so clear and–"

"And then you forgot the time phone," Nadia interrupted me. "You were going to the right place. But once your driver saw you get escorted inside, we tried to call you. You didn't answer the time phone, so we realized it wasn't even with you. We told the driver to stay close, but out of sight. He saw you stumbling out of the gala, so he brought you home safely. I'm worried about you, Faer. We might have to reconsider your involvement with the agency."

"But it isn't my fault!" I rebutted.

"But ignorance isn't bliss. You forgot the time phone. You forgot the mission. I don't even know where you got such a wild idea to make sure those two meet.

They've been friends for a while now. And if KHI begins to use that technology, pure chaos will ensue. I promise. I've seen it. We have to stop it."

"I'm sorry," I said with tears in my eyes. "Why don't you have my personal number? You could have called that."

"That's a safety risk and you should know it!"

"Well, I don't really have any friends or family so what if I just got rid of the other phone altogether?"

"That's all your decision, Faer. You just need to pay attention. The mission of retrieving that device was your biggest one yet. You need to go back."

"Go back?! But, but…"

"Faer. Make a decision. The timeline is in danger. I'll send another operative if you're uncomfortable with this. But this is your last chance."

"I'll go," I conceded. "I wish there was a way to get rid of these side effects."

"Just take the phone with you," Nadia advised. "You're becoming stronger and your body is getting used to having this technology near. I'm confident that was your last episode. I really hope it was. Because if it happens again, I'm afraid we'll have to let you go."

"I understand," I sighed. "I'll retrieve that device."

"It will be dangerous, but just make sure you have the phone. Trust me. After you retrieve it, the driver will bring you to the closest headquarters. After a detour, of course. We have to make sure no one is following you."

Nadia hung up.

I guess the driver was waiting for me the entire time. After putting the time phone in my pocket, and leaving my personal phone at home this time, I walked outside. He was standing by the limo, holding the door.

"Thank you," I smiled slightly.

He said nothing.

I can't believe I have to go back to this gala. Then somehow find a way to retrieve this device. Maybe Albert or Sasha will believe I just want a job at KHI? I could tell them I was embarrassed so I lied. Maybe they'll believe I'm a rich millionaire's son. Or maybe I'm the millionaire. An unknown recluse that heard whispers of such great technology.

If Shard gets ahold of this technology, and stops KHI from developing it further, can't they just rebuild? Maybe it's time sensitive? Or maybe they need it to develop some sort of counter technology? So many questions.

I also hate that my mind was so jumbled. How could I make such a silly mistake? Thinking the mission is something it's not.

I took the time phone out of my pocket, and looked at the back of it. That moving clock was so cool. That tech alone was just so impressive. And if they offer that to the ones that work for them, imagine the good they can do to keep the timeline safe? I was pretty sure I was on the right side of history. I was just nervous.

Now, back at the gala, it was unfortunately showtime. I got out of the car after my driver held the door for me. I began to walk back into the building. No one was outside anymore. Now inside the building, I looked around for signs of anybody. As I got closer to the main hall, I heard the chatter. Everyone was still celebrating.

I took a deep breath as Albert and Sasha themselves saw me walking into the crowd. Albert was still wearing the shape shifting device on his arm.

They both began to walk toward me.

This was it. I had lost my wife. I basically had no friends. I was pretty miserable. But even though I'm not always in agreement with their tactics, Shard was becoming more important to me. I started to realize the importance of saving the timeline. For everyone.

With this being basically the only chance I might have to see my wife someday, for real, not a chameleon knockoff, I couldn't, no, I wouldn't, let Shard, or the entire timeline, down.

Chapter Six
Gala Redux

"Bold move," Albert said to me.

"Welcome back," Sasha said, sarcastically.

"My butler, eh?" Albert smirked. "I would like to know who you actually are, and why you're here."

The crowd began to notice the commotion, as everyone looked toward me, Sasha, and Albert. Sasha whispered, "I think we have to make an example of him. Everyone is watching."

"Now don't be so hasty," Albert replied. "Everyone! Look who we have here!"

Albert took my hand and brought me up on stage. I had no idea what was going on in his mind, or what he was about to do.

"Say hello!" Albert demanded.

Hesitantly, I obeyed. "Hello."

"This man is some sort of infiltrator," Albert admitted. "Unless any of you recognize him. He came in tonight pretending to be my butler."

No one said a word.

Sasha walked up on stage next to Albert. "Is this not making an example of him?" she said quietly.

Albert laughed. "Sasha," he said loudly, "what should we do with such a spy?"

"Well," Sasha laughed, "I want to make sure of something. None of you know this man, correct? Even if you didn't bring him. You won't be in trouble with us, we just need answers."

"I actually recognize him," a voice in the back said.

"Oh you do?!" Albert gasped. "Who are you? Come on up here!"

Remember, Albert was quite the showman. He was loving every minute of this. But I had no idea who, in a crowd of socialites, would recognize me.

As the man who spoke got closer to the stage, I recognized him. But I couldn't quite remember where I had seen him before.

"It is you!" the man cried as he got on stage. "Do you not remember me?! How did you get into such a fancy gala? Just a few weeks ago, you were working at a grocery store! Do you not remember?"

Wait… could this be the man I think it is? I took a close look at him and realized. This was Mircea Evander. The man I had saved from getting botulism. The man that would someday become a household name. And unfortunately, today, the man that might get me in trouble.

"I still don't quite understand why," Mircea admitted. "You came out of nowhere, and took the can I was about to take. Come to think of it, I've never seen you at the store since. Do you even work there?!"

The crowd started murmuring among themselves. Albert looked angry. "Why is a grocery store employee sneaking into my party?!" he demanded. "What purpose could you have? Who do you work for, really?!"

Sasha looked at Albert. She winked at him, then turned toward the crowd. She yelled, "SPY!"

The crowd began to chant, "SPY! SPY! SPY!"

Albert yelled, "ENOUGH! You have five seconds, whoever you are. Explain yourself. Grocery store employee? Butler? One final chance. Tell us who you are, or you will be escorted out of here."

I had no idea what to say. I couldn't admit to everyone that I worked for an agency that saved the timeline. They would either think I'm crazy, or somehow believe me. And if knowledge of this agency became semi-public, the consequences could be deadly. Imagine someone like Albert or Sasha trying to find and take over Shard? I'd probably lose my job. I had to act fast.

Just before I could open my mouth to speak, I heard a weird noise. I quickly realized it was the time phone. But it wasn't the normal ringtone I usually hear. The melody was haunting. Everyone stared at me. I took the time phone out of my pocket, and everyone immediately noticed the clock on the back.

"What is that?" Mircea said, eyes wide.

Albert and Sasha got a close look at it, and were intrigued.

"Is that a moving picture on an inanimate object?!" Albert cried. "That's brilliant! Let me see!"

Albert was about to snatch the time phone from me, when the device on his arm began to spark. He screamed as another spark made his arm twitch. I looked at the time phone, then at his device. This tune was somehow interfering with his device. Wait a minute.

I glanced at the screen to see a message from Shard: "Get the device! Now!"

Finally realizing what was happening, I brought the time phone right up against the device on Albert's arm. It began to malfunction, as Albert's appearance changed to look like Sasha. Then it changed again to look like the man that escorted me into the building earlier. Then it changed to look like me.

The crowd watched in horror. Security came charging at us.

The device fell off his arm. I grabbed it, as Albert's appearance changed back to look like himself. The time phone immediately stopped ringing.

In all the confusion, I managed to evade the oncoming security. Sasha was tending to Albert. The crowd was in full panic mode. I only had this one chance to escape. If they caught me, I would never see the light of day again.

I flew off stage, and charged through the hall. I quickly found the exit door where I had entered moments before. Someone was chasing me, but I couldn't turn around to see who, or how many people were pursuing me.

Finally outside, I located the limo, and my driver was already at the wheel. He had already opened my door. I hopped into the car, and yelled, "I HAVE THE DEVICE. GO!"

The wheels screeched, as we drove quickly away from the building. I looked back and saw five people watching us. I'm sure they would try to pursue us by vehicle. But for the moment, I was glad to be able to breathe.

Chapter Seven
The Chase

As the gala, and everything behind us, faded out of sight, I tried once again talking to my driver.

"Thank you again for saving me," I said.

Nothing.

"Sir, why don't you talk to me?"

As the silence continued, I noticed something from behind. A small black car slowly came into view, and quickly gained on us. I'm pretty sure they could overtake this limo.

My driver hit a switch, and we seemed to be going faster. We took corners that were so sharp, even with my seatbelt, I felt I was getting tossed about. As we kept driving, it felt like this car behind us was constantly just there.

The time phone rang.

"Hello?" I answered.

"Faer!" Nadia cried. "Great job on retrieving the device. You'll be at the nearest HQ soon. It might be a while, as you need to lose your follower."

"Nadia, I have so many questions. Why won't the driver talk to me? Once I deliver this to Shard, what is our next move? Where am I–"

The limo swerved off the road, and the small black car got closer.

"Oh no!" I screamed.

We were headed directly toward a forest. A forest that wasn't meant to be driven on.

"Faer, we'll answer your questions when you get to HQ," Nadia assured me. "I just don't want you to be alarmed with what you see on the way here."

"What is that supposed to mean?!"

"Faer, you may have been confused, and you've been through a lot... but the following hours will change your life. Be ready for everything."

"Wait..."

Nadia hung up.

As we narrowly missed tree after tree, and as I wondered how such a vehicle could be driven with such... grace? I saw a second car pursuing us behind the black car. It was a green truck. This was ridiculous. Yes, we took their device. But this was for the timeline!

I saw a tree that had fallen down. And we were headed right toward it. There was no way this limo could get by that.

The driver sped up. We were about to slam into this downed tree, which was huge.

"Driver!" I yelled. "What are you doing?!"

I looked back behind us, the black car, and green truck were just at our backs. As the driver reached the tree, and I thought we were about to crash, the driver threw a couple switches, and we began to fly off the ground.

A limo with wings? No. It wasn't that elaborate. What I could gather was there were somehow thrusters in the bottom of the vehicle that allowed us to safely clear that tree. We went right over it and landed on the other side.

I heard a slam, so I could only assume the other two crashed into it. As we continued on through this forest, I saw some random animals. A deer went prancing away. A rabbit was watching us from the bushes. I saw some birds up in the sky.

"Are you okay?" I asked the driver.

I wasn't shocked to get no response at all.

After a few moments went by, I finally took a deep breath. I thought we were in the clear. I would soon see Shard HQ.

All of a sudden, out of the corner of my eye, I heard a loud screech. Something was still chasing us. I looked everywhere, but saw nothing. The driver remained calm, but I don't think he could see what it was either.

SLAM!

Something drove straight into us. But we couldn't see anything.

SLAM!

It hit us again. We started to see a silhouette of the small black car. It glitched in and out of sight.

"Give me back my device!" someone screamed.

Still unable to see what was going on, I started to piece together what might be happening.

The driver began pressing numerous buttons. This limo must be just like something straight out of a comic book.

We were hit one last time, and the moment of impact revealed the black car, driven by Sasha herself.

Whatever cloaking device she had on her vehicle was now completely damaged. I'm sure the limo wasn't unscathed, but it seemed to me it was only cosmetic damage that we suffered.

Sasha opened her car door and screamed, "ALBERT COULD HAVE BEEN KILLED!"

She started banging on my window. "What have you done? Where are you going with my creation? I had to leave Albert on stage, on the ground, at his request! And he told me to stop at NOTHING to get our device back."

She pulled a weapon on us. It was silver, lit up blue, and it was powering up, as I heard a slight hum from it that got louder. Sasha trained the weapon directly on me, through my closed window.

The driver looked over at her, then at me. He took his hands off the wheel, and placed them in his lap.

"What are you doing?!" I cried.

"I will fire!" Sasha threatened. "I'll fire right at you, just to get my creation back."

I said nothing.

"It's YOUR fault," Sasha continued, angrily. "All of this. My friend in the green truck slammed into that tree. He didn't have time to stop. He just wanted to help, and because of you, he is lying unconscious in the back of my car now. As his truck went up in flames, I had to move him to my small car! YOU NEARLY KILLED MULTIPLE MEN TODAY. Do you really think whoever you're working for is good?! Give me my device, and I'll let you live. I, unlike you, offer mercy."

The driver looked back at me and winked. I didn't quite understand why. Sasha noticed.

"That's it!" she yelled, tears in her eyes. "You two don't care about anything or anybody. I rescind my offer of mercy. You're a waste to society. Both of you. I'm getting my device back. Now."

Fully charged, and still trained on me, albeit with a window in the way, the weapon that Sasha held was ready to be fired.

As I stared directly at her, blue light filled my view, and I heard someone screaming. As the blue light from the blast vanished, I could see Sasha flying through the air away from us. The blast didn't phase the window like she thought it would. Instead, it sent Sasha into the air. The driver put his hands back on the wheel, and slowly drove away.

Quickly picking up speed, we drove on for hours. I said nothing. He said nothing. And once we were finally sure we weren't being followed, we were finally able to drive to Shard HQ.

Chapter Eight
HQ

The building itself was elaborate. Beautiful. But also hidden. Unless you knew the exact route to get here, finding it would be basically impossible.

Even after all this time, the driver still hadn't said a word to me. We pulled up to a gate, and the driver took out a card. He showed it to a camera. Then, the car itself was scanned. I think that was to check for passengers. I guess they recognized us because we were allowed access.

We drove through and were met by another gate. A man was waiting for us. The driver rolled down the window, and the man looked into the car. He saw me and the device.

"They have the device," he confirmed.

I could hear another voice from somewhere that said, "Let them in."

The second gate was lifted, and we drove on. We were met by half a dozen security officers, who guided us to a parking spot. I got out of the car. The driver didn't. I looked back at him, then at one of the security officers.

"He has another mission," the security officer said to me. "He has to go help someone else. Don't worry. We have other drivers if you need to leave. But I think you'll want to be here for a while."

I slightly nodded, and waved to my driver. Why doesn't he talk? Like at all? It was a little weird, but I was about to see HQ, so I let that thought go.

I watched as the limo drove away. You could barely tell that we were hit by another car. That limousine must be quite industrial to withstand everything we went through.

The security officer looked at the device in my hand, and motioned for me to follow him. I obeyed.

I wondered if Nadia would be here. It would be cool to meet my director. As I followed security, we reached yet another gate. This place must have a ton of secrets. Security began to walk through what looked like something straight from an airport. A big metal structure with a door cut out in the middle. He stopped inside, and a shiny green light scanned him. His name popped up, along with a check mark. "Varon." He walked to the other side, and motioned for me to do the same.

I walked toward it. I hesitated for a second, but knew it would be okay. I stepped up into this structure, and let out a sigh. The green light scanned me, as I held the device. I looked over at the screen inside, and saw my name. But there was no check mark. I looked over at Varon, who nodded.

After what felt like an eternity, and seeing a series of three dots that made me think something was loading, a check mark finally appeared by my name.

"Sorry about that," Varon said. "It always does that for first time visitors. They need to make sure everything is okay."

"Oh no worries," I said, even though I was definitely worrying. "Maybe this device also messed with the system."

"True," Varon admitted. "It does scan all technology you carry in as well."

I walked through to meet Varon on the other side.

We continued on, following the side of the building for about five minutes. Did this building even have a way in? I hadn't seen any doors or windows so far.

Varon walked up to the building, but there was still not a door in sight. He walked up to a blank wall and put his hand on it. The space around his hand began to glow, and a door appeared right by it.

"Welcome to HQ," Varon smiled.

He opened the door, and I followed him inside.

I was immediately disappointed with what I saw. It looked nothing like I thought it would. It made me think of a dentist's office, not a time agency. There was a tall plant in the left corner. Chairs to the right. And a window to talk to someone. Maybe a receptionist? Was this actually a dentist's office? Was this all a joke?

Varon walked up to the window, and whispered some sort of code. The girl behind the counter picked up a phone, and Varon looked over at me.

The time phone began to ring. Was this girl seriously calling me? Why? Maybe it was the final security check to make sure I was legit? I picked it up, and simply said, "Hello?"

"Hello! Welcome back. To reach the main office, press one."

You've got to be joking right now.

"To talk directly with your director, press two. To speak with someone else at the agency, press three."

I pressed two. Nadia would tell me what was going on. After all this time, she was the one I trusted the most. I'm not quite sure how she felt about me, as I've been forgetful off and on. But this time, I had the device Shard needed, I was standing in an underwhelming Shard headquarters, and as she picked up on the other side, I finally realized something.

"Faer!" Nadia said, excitedly. "It's nice to finally meet you!"

I looked over at the girl behind the window. Smiling back at me, on the phone, with me, was Nadia herself.

I hung up the time phone, put it back in my pocket, and walked over to the window.

"Nadia?"

"Yes Faer, it's me!"

Nadia looked at Varon. "I'll take it from here. This is him."

She looked at the device I was holding, then back at me.

"Why do you look disappointed?" Nadia asked me. "Is this not what you were expecting?"

"Of course not!" I admitted. "This looks like a doctor's office or something!"

"Now Faer," Nadia smirked, "do you really think this is HQ?"

"What do you mean?"

"Let's just say we take security protocols seriously."

"So this isn't actually HQ?"

"This right here? No. But follow me."

Nadia hit a button from behind the window, and a door materialized. I walked through, and Nadia hit a button to make the door disappear.

A big metal gate slowly descended, blocking any potential infiltrators who somehow managed to get this far. If they got to this, dentist's office, it would look like a dead end now.

Taking in my surroundings yet again, there wasn't much to see. It really did look like a place where you would check someone in for some sort of appointment.

Nadia walked through a door that led to a hall. Nadia looked back to make sure I was still following. I caught up to her.

"What do you think of these security measures?" she laughed.

"A bit much," I said.

"We're nearly there," she assured me.

At the end of the hall, there was a keypad by yet another door. Nadia entered a twelve digit code. She was met by a message and a loud computer voice that said, "Access Denied."

I became a little nervous after seeing that.

Nadia nervously chuckled, and looked at me. "I must have hit the wrong button. Gotta love technology."

"Yeah but what if you input the wrong code too many times by mistake?" I asked.

"Oh, this sector blows up," she said, with a serious look on her face.

My eyes widened and she laughed as she entered the code correctly this time.

We heard the computer voice say, "Access Granted." The message was also on the keypad.

"Faer," Nadia beamed, "Welcome to Shard HQ!"

The door opened automatically, and what I saw was amazing. This is what I thought everything should look like.

Chapter Nine
Software Update

Imagine a laboratory. But one that is the size of a warehouse. People everywhere, working. Not quite a call center, but you could hear some phones ringing. Wait, was that my phone? My time phone?

Nadia looked at me.

"Who's calling you?" she asked. "Because it isn't me."

Confused, I took the time phone out of my pocket. The caller ID said 'unknown'. I showed it to Nadia.

"Don't answer that," Nadia warned me.

I wanted to question her, but I decided to just put the phone back in my pocket. I had other things to think about right now.

"So," Nadia began, "some of the information you're about to get may be alarming. There is a lot to take in here."

She brought me to a sort of main desk for the entire HQ.

"You also need to update your phone," she smiled.

"Update my phone?" I asked.

"Yes," Nadia said. "You only have the basic software on there. But the time phone is so much more. Trust me."

"Hello Nadia," a girl behind the desk said. "Is this Faer?"

Nadia nodded. "Faer, I would like you to meet my boss, Zyanya."

"You can call me Zy," Zyanya said.

"Hello, Zy," I smiled.

"I've heard a lot about you," Zyanya began. "Your director, Nadia, speaks very highly of you."

Well that actually shocked me. Seeing as how I kept forgetting who I was. I lost the time phone. My memory was just a mess. But I was glad to hear what Nadia truly thought of me.

"Wow," I looked at Nadia. "Thank you."

"Don't thank me," Nadia returned my gaze, then looked at Zyanya. "He deserves the credit after the amount of times he stabilized the timeline."

Zyanya looked at the time phone, and the device I had gotten from Sasha and Albert.

"So this is the device?" Zyanya asked.

I put the device on the counter. "Yes ma'am. And a lot of people were angry when we took it from that gala."

"You have, yet again, helped to save the timeline. Let me show you something."

There was a tablet in front of her. She swiveled it toward Nadia and I.

"Do you see this?"

On the screen, there was chaos, destruction, and buildings on fire.

"Oh my," I gasped. "Where is this happening?"

"Not where," Zyanya said with a serious look on her face. "When."

"When?"

"This is one of many possible futures," Zyanya continued. "But look at the people causing the destruction."

I took a close look at what was on the tablet screen. There were big mechanical suits stomping around, wreaking havoc, as civilians ran from them. In the suits, you could see a single human powering each one. And the lead machine was powered by Mircea Evander. The same guy I saved from getting botulism. The same guy that came on stage at the gala. But he looked older here.

"Wait, is that…"

Zyanya interrupted me. "Mircea Evander would never do this. He brings peace in the years ahead of us. Look closer."

I looked for some sort of sign that something was off. But I couldn't see anything.

"That's the problem," Zyanya admitted. She picked up the device from the gala. "Once this technology gets perfected, it becomes the size of an implant. And there is no physical evidence to suggest foul play. That isn't Mircea Evander. That's someone else, wearing this technology."

Studying it intently, Zyanya nodded, and looked at me.

"So, does that future already exist?" I asked.

"No," Zyanya started staring at the device while she continued. "Well, technically, kind of. But it doesn't have to. Thanks to you. With this technology out of the enemy's hands, we should be alright now."

"But can't Sasha and Albert just recreate it?" I asked.

"Not for a while," Zyanya said, as she pressed a couple buttons on the device. A small glowing gem popped out, and fell onto the desk. "Not without one of these."

I stared in awe at the small glowing jewel. Then I looked at Nadia. She, too, was in awe of it.

"Faer. Nadia. You two have proven to Shard how valuable you are. With your expertise, Faer, and your direction, Nadia, Shard has procured a vital piece of alien tech to help us thwart the enemy, stabilize the timeline, and save everyone."

"It was our pleasure," Nadia said as she blushed a little.

She was proud of herself. And of me. So was I, honestly. I'm not sure where that glowing rock was from. I had no idea aliens were even involved.

"Look," Nadia exclaimed.

Zyanya swiveled the tablet just a little so she could see what Nadia, and now I, saw. The man inside the big mechanical suit changed to look like someone I had never seen before. Looks like the enemy wouldn't be able to develop the technology that quickly after all. The robot that he was controlling faded away. The chaos of the city, the fires, all of it, faded into a glorious image of peace. The man himself disappeared.

"Wow," Zyanya smiled.

"Where did the man go?" I asked.

"Who knows," Zyanya shrugged. "He probably just wasn't there at that time, so he disappeared from there and appeared somewhere else, but without a big evil robot suit. So thank you."

"Oh, it is an honor to help out Shard."

"Faer, let me see your time phone." Zyanya reached her hand out.

I handed her my phone. She plugged it into the tablet.

"I'm promoting you two," Zyanya said.

"Both of us?" Nadia cried.

"Yes. I think you two work well together."

Nadia looked at me, then back at Zyanya. "You won't regret this."

"I don't have reason to." Zyanya looked at me. "I'm downloading new software onto your time phone. It's called a time phone for a reason. And pretty soon, you're going to find out why. The two of you are a team now. Out on the field. I am your director, so you can answer directly to me. I'm removing all those menus that everyone hates, so you can get straight to me if you need to. Nadia, you're going to need this."

Zyanya reached into a drawer behind her and took out a time phone that looked identical to mine, except for the clock on the back of it. A different design there would help us distinguish which phone was hers I'm guessing. Zyanya handed Nadia the phone.

Nadia screeched in excitement. I thought a director would be a higher position than an operative like me. But Nadia was excited to be out in the field so to speak. And I was glad to be able to work with someone.

"Your time phone, Nadia, is all up to date. Faer, yours will have all the new updates in three… two… one… there we go."

She unplugged my time phone from the tablet, and handed it to me.

I looked at Nadia, who in turn, looked back at me. We both looked at our new director.

"So, Nadia, Faer, are you ready for your first official mission together?"

Chapter Ten
Time Machine

Ever since my wife vanished in front of me, I've always wondered where she went. I never even thought I would have to worry about when she went. But since I've joined Shard, a lot of things I thought were impossible have become possible.

As I stood here with Nadia, and our new director, I had a feeling we were about to begin some amazing, elaborate mission.

"I need to send one of you to the past," Zyanya said.

Wait. I thought Nadia and I would be working side by side. And hold the phone. Shard actually has the capability to time travel?!

Zyanya continued, "And one of you needs to stay in the present. We have operatives throughout time already, but the less people that know of this mission, the better. Only you two, and I, will know of this."

"Zyanya," I said hesitantly. "Shard has time machines?"

"A time machine, yes," Zyanya admitted. "But we try our best not to use it, as it drains so much power."

Zyanya picked up the gem that fell out of the device we procured earlier.

"Does that power it?" I asked.

"Not this exact rock," Zyanya said. "We already have one of these in the machine. But it could run out of power at any moment. So it's a fail-safe, in case you get stuck in the past. We'll use it if the machine runs out of energy."

"Where did that come from?" I asked, curiously.

"Space," Zyanya said.

I could tell she wasn't going to give any more details on the mysterious gem, so I just nodded and looked at Nadia.

"You're okay with going to the past?" Nadia asked me.

Was I okay with it? I was terrified. But, maybe, just maybe, there was a small chance that I could find a clue about my wife.

"Yes," I said.

"Great," Zyanya smiled. "Follow me."

Zyanya stood up, still holding the alien rock. Nadia and I followed her. We walked past dozens of workers, some on computers, some on tablets, and some were on phones.

After about five minutes, we reached a door that was bolted shut. Zyanya took out a key card, and held it up, as she allowed the computers above to scan her face. The door unbolted, and opened, to reveal another door. She then entered a very long code, and yet another door opened.

As we continued on, she kept looking forward. Never missing a beat. We passed by five security officers on the way. This was clearly some highly guarded secret of Shard.

"Just beyond this archway," Zyanya said. "But stop here!"

It looked like we could just walk right through, but Zyanya stood right in front of this doorway with no door. She looked like she was trying to concentrate on something.

"What is that?" I whispered.

"Telepathic lock," Nadia said.

Wow. It must be scanning her head for some sort of code. That's wild.

As it seemed Zyanya got the telepathic code right, a bunch of lasers appeared where a door should be.

"Glad we didn't walk through that," I whispered.

Zyanya reached her hand out, only inches away from the lasers. Something scanned her hand, and the lasers flickered off, one by one.

Zyanya walked through, without giving us direction. So we followed.

"Here, in all its glory, is our time machine," Zyanya turned toward us.

It was underwhelming yet again. It was a large metal box with a sad looking chair. Worn out lights could be seen along with a control panel that looked like something from times gone by. I could see a gem similar to the other one that powered the whole thing. Clearly this technology was in beta form.

"It's pretty impressive, isn't it?" Zyanya winked.

"Well, I, um…"

"Faer," Zyanya interrupted me, "calm down. This technology is the most archaic we have. It's crude. Old.

But any updates we try would take more power than we could ever get our hands on."

"So what's the mission?" I blurted out, both excited and concerned.

"We are Shard," Zyanya began. "We save the timeline. We stabilize it. Usually, it involves another life. But this time, this specific mission, it doesn't. There was a war, years ago, that split open the skies. Multiple timelines were leaking into our own. Multiple universes. Realities. Dimensions. Whatever you can think of. All of time and space was at risk. Everything was taken care of thanks to some friends of ours, but some debris from alternate dimensions came through. That debris needs to be collected, all of it, so we can assure no one else gets their hands on it. It is powerful. It's what is powering this primitive time machine. It's what Albert and Sasha tried to use. We still aren't sure how they got it. Our friends found and collected what they could following the weeks after that event. But somehow, they missed some."

"But why do you need me specifically to collect it?" I asked.

"Nadia can go if you don't want to," Zyanya said coldly.

"No, that's not it, I just–"

"Faer," Nadia interrupted, "I believe in you."

Zyanya handed me a big, black, cloth bag that was hanging on the side of the time machine.

"I updated your time phone to scan for the anomalies. I tried to scan them from the present, but the readings will be more accurate once you're there. We

61

have to collect all of it, in the past, before our enemies have a chance to find and collect any of it. That's why we have to travel in time. Also, I've left out an important detail. Do not lose your time phone. This time machine is going to sync to your time phone. This kind of time travel is basically unheard of, but it's our last hope. We have to fully clean up that mess before it's too late."

"A connection through time?!" my eyes widened.

"Basically, yes, but powered by that gem," she pointed to the rock in the time machine. "And that connection back to the other stones will not only send you back to the days after that war, it'll also move you in space, as that war was many, many miles away from where we are now."

"Is the time machine moving with me?"

"No," Zyanya said. "The connection from the time machine is going to be held on your phone. That's why you can't lose it. Don't lose it, or you'll be stranded in the past. That would be a disaster. You would become one of the messes Shard would have to clean up. So just get back there, fill the bag with all the debris, and once it's all collected, open the menu on your phone and hit the 'return home' button on the screen. The connection should be open for as long as you're there. And once you're done with everything, it will ask for a code. Don't forget this code, Faer. Five nine five seven."

"Fifty-nine, fifty-seven. Got it. I think I'm ready now."

Zyanya guided me up to the chair. She input coordinates on the outdated console. She took my time phone for a second, and paired it with the machine.

"Don't. Lose. It."

She handed it back to me. She stepped back and told me to flip the switch that was next to me when I was ready. I looked at Nadia, who gave me a reassuring nod.

As I was about to throw the switch, Zyanya said something to me.

"It isn't on Earth, Faer. I'm sorry, I should have told you sooner. It's a distant planet. All the pieces of debris from the alternate realities landed on a planet that was closer to that war. It's on the other side of the galaxy. Don't worry, the planet they landed on has an atmosphere. You'll be fine. I've been studying it for months. Somehow, a few pieces of gem made it onto our planet a year ago. Whether someone brought them here, or they somehow traveled that far in such a short amount of time, is a mystery to me. But I promise you, Faer, this mission, this lone mission, if you complete this, and bring back all the anomalies, we will find your wife."

That was all I needed to hear. Yes, I was scared. Yes, I was angry that she held that information back until now. But this was a once in a lifetime opportunity.

I said nothing. I threw the switch and closed my eyes. I heard sparks fly. I could tell that I had moved. I felt the cold wind against me as I opened my eyes.

Chapter Eleven
Stranded

There wasn't much to see. I was on a desolate planet. I looked at my time phone. It immediately began to guide me to the first anomaly. I saw in the top left corner that it was still connected to the time machine in the present.

I could breathe the air. I was safe. I was alright. But I wasn't going to waste time. So I walked toward the first gem. I picked it up and put it in the bag Zyanya had given me. This seemed a bit too easy. I looked around, and saw nothing else. Was I sent across the galaxy for one piece?

All of a sudden, the time phone started beeping mysteriously. I looked at it, and saw another anomaly. I walked about five minutes before I actually found it. This one was slightly glowing. I picked it up and threw it in the bag.

This would be a pretty boring mission if I wasn't across space collecting magical alien rocks from alternate universes. As I somehow mindlessly continued wandering around this planet collecting this rubble, I began to zone out, thinking of Shard, my wife, and everything I had been through to get here.

I was awakened from this mindless daydreaming abruptly. The time phone rang. The caller ID said 'unknown'. But maybe that's because I was so far out in space? Against my better judgment, I answered it.

"You have gotten in too deep, Faer," the voice on the other end said. It was distorted.

"Who is this?" I demanded.

"It doesn't matter," the voice retorted. "It would be a shame if you lost your link, would it not?"

"Wait, what do you mean? Tell me who you are right now!"

"Oh Faer, Faer, Faer. You have no idea what you've gotten yourself into. Imagine being stranded on a desolate planet with no way to get back home? You are out of your own time, and millions and millions of miles from them. You will never make it back. Shard will be busy trying to rescue you, while I just take over everything. What an interesting game this is going to be. This is as it should be. Thank you, Faer. Thank you."

I was about to respond when I heard a click and the connection was lost. My bag had quite a few rocks in it. A dozen or so. That had to be enough. Whoever that was, they were cryptic, and threatening to somehow strand me here. So Zyanya would have to be okay with what I had. I looked at the top bar on my phone. To my horror, it said, 'no service.'

Oh no. No please no.

I frantically tried to press buttons on the time phone, to somehow restore service. The connection to the time machine had been severed. Any and all links to the present seemed to be gone.

I had nowhere to go. I had everywhere to go. But everywhere was nowhere on this planet. The time phone was not even helping me track the anomalies anymore. All service was gone. I was stranded.

I began to search for any signs of life, even though I knew that could be dangerous, and would prove to be moot. I honestly had no idea what I could even do.

Since I was still on the planet, and though it was a low priority, I still kept an eye out for any rocks. I found none. Why was there a planet all the way across the galaxy that was habitable but it was completely empty? No people. No animals. Not even a sign of bugs. This seemed like a wasted opportunity. But maybe it would be my new home forever?

But wait, I had no food. I wouldn't last that long. And no water. Surely there had to be some sort of water source or something. But I'm guessing it would be dangerous to drink.

I searched on. I felt alone. The deep feeling of being lost without rescue enveloped me. Why was I even out here, really? To maybe have a chance to possibly see my wife again? Yes, that was worth the risk, but, maybe the reality was, I'd never see her again? Maybe I am just a fool.

I sat down on the ground next to a jagged piece of land. I looked at its sharp edges and shook my head. I put the bag of collected rocks in front of me. I looked inside for the first time, and noticed something. The one that was glowing earlier was still glowing. And only that one. I picked it up without thinking, and heard a bizarre noise.

It was the time phone. It received a notification. I saw it regain service for a moment, then it went back to 'no service.' But in that moment, a text came through. It was from Nadia!

'Faer? Faer, where are you? I think you've been there long enough. Return home! Please!'

I'd certainly love to, Nadia. If I could.

Trying to understand why I had service for a second, I put the glowing rock directly on the back of the time phone. The gem started to heat up. But I did not care. A ton of notifications started to flood in. But I was more concerned about getting home.

My eye caught one notification that said 'No anomalies detected' so maybe that means I actually found all of them. Great. But can I please not be stranded here anymore? These hours felt like days. And they have only made me worry even more, if that's possible, about where my wife went when she vanished. I had to get home. So I looked at the top left corner, and I was finally reconnected to the time machine in the present.

I clicked on the menu, grabbed the bag of gems, and hit the 'return home' button. Still holding the glowing rock against the time phone, that piece of debris kept heating up to nearly a dangerous level.

The phone asked me for a code. And for the life of me, I couldn't remember it. It's like when you're put on the spot. You know the answer to whatever question you're being asked, but in the moment, you forget it.

I forgot the code.

What was it? Maybe nine something? Five something? Oh no. I couldn't be left on this desolate planet forever because I forgot a code! As the gem nearly burned my hand, I had a flash of memory. Fifty-seven? Wait. Five… nine… five… seven? Fifty-nine fifty-seven. That was it! I entered the number into the time phone.

What looked like lightning formed around me for a moment, and I heard some loud crashing noises. Slowly, but surely, I saw the present materialize around me. I was sitting in the time machine, waiting to see Nadia and Zyanya's faces. As everything came into view, I was confused as I saw no one.

The feeling of being stranded stayed with me as I was alone in that highly guarded secret room. I threw the now sizzling rock into the bag with the rest of them. The gem in the time machine was glowing too. Maybe those two pieces were from the same alternate universe? If there were ones from multiple universes, maybe two from the same could connect to each other like a beacon through time and space? I'm no scientist, but that was just my guess.

I looked around and saw no sign that anybody had been here recently. I finally looked at my time phone again, and started going through my notifications. I had a ton of texts from Nadia. Even some from Zyanya. Countless missed calls. Wait, how long was I gone? It couldn't have been more than five hours. It felt like forever, but that doesn't mean it was.

I frantically looked for Nadia's number in my phone, and called her.

"Come on, Nadia. Pick up!" I whispered.

It rang, and rang. Until finally, she answered.

"Faer?! Faer?! You're alive?!"

"Alive? Of course I am! I collected all the rocks for Zyanya and Shard! I think I cleaned all those anomalies up. There weren't more than a dozen."

"Faer, where have you been?" Nadia said, sounding like she was in tears.

"I've been on that planet! It was the longest five hours of my life!"

"Five hours?!" Nadia questioned me.

"Yes, maybe seven, maybe... but–"

"Faer, that trip you took in that time machine? That was not five hours ago."

"What do you mean?"

"That was five MONTHS ago!"

Chapter Twelve
Glitch

"What do you mean it has been five months?!" I said frantically.

"Faer, we were waiting for you for days. We sent you multiple notifications. Zyanya felt terrible. But that time machine's rock burnt out after a couple months. So Zyanya had to use that backup gem in the time machine. Even after us trying to recalibrate the coordinates and press buttons, and honestly, even after sending up a prayer or two, we had to move forward."

"So you just gave up on me?!"

"Never! Zyanya and I visit the time machine every day! You think we think so little of you, Faer?"

"No, it's all just so weird. I was only gone for a few hours. So how is it five months later?!"

"That's a mystery to us," Nadia admitted. "Did something happen while you were on that planet? We lost signal hours after you left. There was nothing we could do. Except try to check on you and the time machine every single day. Just in case."

"Where's Zyanya?" I asked.

"I'm sure she's in the Shard HQ like she always is."

"And where are you?"

"I've been going on missions for months now. With you missing, they were down one operative."

"So that's why she needed one of us in the past and one in the present. It was a fail-safe."

"I'm sorry, Faer. But you're back now! We should notify Zyanya immediately!"

I heard beeping as if Nadia was pressing buttons, and then I heard ringing.

"Hello?" Zyanya said as she joined the call.

"Faer is back!" Nadia said excitedly.

"Where is he?!" Zyanya asked.

"I'm in the room with the time machine," I interrupted.

"Faer!" I could hear Zyanya scrambling around. I think she was at her desk, and about to come find me.

"I'm on my way to HQ," Nadia said. "I just finished that mission, Zyanya. I'll be there shortly. Faer, it's really good to have you back. We have missed you so much."

Nadia hung the phone up.

"I am just about through the security measures to get to you, Faer!" Zyanya said. "How have you been? What happened in all those months? How did you survive? I have so many questions!"

"Zyanya," I said softly. "I am so tired. And confused. It may have been months for you guys, but for me?"

Zyanya came bursting into the time machine room, out of breath. She gave me a hug. I didn't expect that. They must really have missed me. I had no reason to doubt that. This was all just so weird.

Now in person, Zyanya looked at me, then at the bag of rocks, then back at me. "For you, what?" she asked.

"It's only been five hours for me."

"That is fascinating."

"I guess, but that is not all. Something really weird happened while I was out on that planet."

"What?"

"Someone called the time phone before it lost service... they said I had gotten in too deep. They threatened to leave me stranded while they took over Shard."

"Good thing we have the best security in the galaxy then," Zyanya smiled. Her face became serious. "But Faer, I am sorry about all of this."

"I am okay," I admitted. "I just don't understand any of this."

My time phone rang. I had a pit in my stomach as I checked to see who was calling. I was afraid it was the mysterious voice again. Luckily, it wasn't. It was Nadia.

"Nadia?" I said as I answered the phone. I put it on speaker so Zyanya could hear what was going on. "You are on speaker phone."

"Someone just called me. Are you still with Zyanya?"

"Yeah, why? What–"

"This distorted voice just called my time phone. The number said 'unknown' but after everything you just went through, and the time dilation, I felt as if I should answer it."

Nadia was holding back tears.

"Nadia," I said, "a distorted voice called me back when I was on the desolate planet. I think it severed my connection to the present and tried to strand me in the past."

"That is not what I did at all!" I heard someone say. "Well, technically… okay, I guess it is. Guilty!"

"Nadia, that is not funny! Why–"

"That was not me, Faer!" Nadia cried.

"Let me see the phone!" Zyanya demanded.

"Oh, I have all three of you?!"

It was the same distorted voice that called me earlier. I can only assume it was the same voice that called Nadia too.

"That's the voice!" Nadia admitted.

"This is delightful!" the voice continued. It laughed. "Say, I think I should introduce myself! Well, I'll give you a code name for me. Just call me Glitch. Hi Faer! Nice to hear you made it home! Sorry about the whole stranding you thing. No hard feelings, right?"

"Who are you?!" Zyanya demanded. "Why are you trying to infiltrate Shard? What do you want with us?"

"Oh Zyanya," Glitch laughed. "You do not listen! My name is Glitch!"

"That is not what she meant," Nadia interrupted.

"And Nadia! I apologize if that cryptic message scared you earlier. I am just learning how to communicate like this, you know? This is going to be so fun! I hope you're all ready for the future! Well, the present. Or is it, the past? What time is it, really?"

"Where are you even calling from?" I asked.

"Good question!" Glitch screeched. "But maybe the wrong one. Ask yourselves this: WHEN am I calling from?"

"That is enough!" Zyanya said, angrily. "You will not mess with me, Faer, or Nadia. You will leave right now. Do not pursue us, or Shard. I am giving you this one warning. This is the mercy we at Shard offer you. Go. Back to your planet or time or wherever you came from. If you choose to stay, and cause issues, we will not hesitate to destroy you. You get one warning. This is it."

Glitch thought that was hysterical. "Zyanya. You've changed! Oh wow. Okay, I'll go. But I promise you, this isn't over. Nadia, think about what we discussed earlier. Faer, nice to hear from you again. Until next time, Shard. Glitch out."

"Is he gone?" I asked.

"I think so," Zyanya said.

"What did he mean 'think about what we discussed'?" I asked Nadia.

"I was about to tell you when he interrupted. I'm here now."

Zyanya and I met Nadia at Zyanya's desk in Shard HQ. We started talking quietly among ourselves.

"Zyanya, what is going on?" Nadia asked. "It sounds like Glitch knows you. He said you've changed."

"I have no idea what that was about."

"Glitch asked me to join him," Nadia admitted.

"Join him how?" Zyanya asked.

"He said that Shard would be overtaken by the end of the day. But since we have no idea when he was calling from, that's a cryptic threat."

"Does he actually exist?" I asked. "Is he more than just a voice?"

"That is a question I simultaneously do, and do not, want the answer to," Nadia said.

Off in the distance, we heard a scream.

Zyanya rushed toward the noise.

"What is wrong?" she asked an employee.

The employee was sitting at a computer with a headset on. Sparks could be seen flying from both his computer, and his headset.

"Ouch!" someone else yelled. "What is going on?"

Zyanya turned to see another employee tear off her headset. It landed on the ground, electricity coursing through it.

I looked around. Lightning began to form around every inch of technology in HQ. And every inch of HQ, unfortunately, was technology.

"No, no, no," Zyanya said, in a slightly panicked voice.

"Is this him?!" I asked.

"EVERYBODY OUT!" Zyanya screamed. "GO OUT THE EMERGENCY EXIT. FOLLOW PROTOCOL. THE OFFICERS AROUND THE PERIMETER WILL GUIDE YOU ALL TO SAFETY!"

Everyone rushed toward the emergency exit.

"I will wait here to make sure everyone is evacuated," Zyanya said, trying to stay calm.

"I am staying too," Nadia said.

She looked at me. I nodded. I wasn't going anywhere. We both looked at Zyanya, who allowed a half smile, as she monitored the exit door.

Five minutes went by. The electricity became violent.

"Is that everyone?" I asked.

Officers came running from the direction of the time machine.

"Other than them, yes."

"Madam," an officer said, out of breath. "The time machine is about to blow up."

"Go!" Zyanya said hastily. "All of you! This isn't safe."

The officers obeyed. Only Nadia, Zyanya, and I were left in the entirety of HQ.

"We are not leaving you," Nadia said.

Hesitantly, Zyanya nodded. "This is dangerous. I do not know what we are dealing with. But I have to go check on the time machine. Wait, Faer, where are those rocks?"

In the chaos, I realized I had left them by the time machine. They should be safe, though. Right? That was a heavily guarded area. Was. Oh no.

"I left them by the time machine... I'm sorry."

Zyanya went running toward the room. The security measures were all but extinct at this point. With everything malfunctioning, the doors were all left open. The laser beams were flickering off and on. It wasn't that difficult to time it so we weren't hit by them. The only real danger was the fact that we were running deeper into

HQ. An HQ that had the chance to become a giant explosion.

Nadia and I kept up with Zyanya. We all entered the room with the time machine at the same time. The bag that held the rocks was still on the floor by the time machine. The time machine itself had an unsafe amount of electricity coursing through it.

Zyanya stared at the bag on the floor and wanted to pick it up.

"No, allow me," I said, running toward it, trying to avoid all of the sparks and electricity.

The moment I went to pick up the bag of gems, to my horror, I could tell something was wrong. If things weren't already bad enough, they were definitely about to get worse.

The bag was completely empty.

Chapter Thirteen
Silhouette

"What is wrong?" Zyanya asked.

"It's empty!" I admitted.

"How?!"

A spark of lightning from the time machine hit my shoulder.

"Faer!" Nadia screamed.

I felt the electricity through my entire body. It stung. And my automatic reaction was to jump away.

"Be careful, Faer!" Zyanya warned me.

"I am so sorry," I cried. "I didn't mean to–"

Zyanya hushed me. I looked at her, confused. She put her finger to her lip as if to tell me to be quiet. Nadia wasn't sure what was going on either, as she gave Zyanya a weird look. Zyanya silently gestured for me to walk over and stand with them.

I looked at Nadia, who shrugged. I walked toward the two of them, and turned to face the time machine.

In about five minutes, if that, this room could be completely gone. All of HQ would be. So why we were standing here in silence bewildered me. All that could be heard was the malfunctioning equipment.

Where could those rocks have gone? Did the officers steal them? I looked at the time machine closely, and realized there should still be one gem left powering it. The one we had before I went back in time. The one from Sasha and Albert's device, since the original one shorted out while I was stuck on that desolate planet.

I focused on where that rock should be, and noticed that it, too, was gone. I pointed, and Zyanya nodded.

Nadia noticed and whispered, "How is this time machine still running without the power source?"

Zyanya had a concerned look on her face. But for some reason, she wasn't evacuating. It's as if she knew something was going on.

"Residual, pent up energy. Something is wrong here. And I don't think we're alone like we thought. You two leave. Go out the emergency exit. I'll handle this. It's too dangerous."

I looked at Nadia. Without saying a word, both of us knew we weren't leaving Zyanya, even now.

Before we could decline her request, my time phone started ringing. I looked at the screen and shuddered. I turned it to show Nadia and Zyanya.

It was Glitch.

"He must want us to know it's him since it doesn't say 'Unknown' this time."

"Let me see that," Zyanya said, reaching for the phone.

She answered it. "Glitch. What have you done?"

"You blame me?!" Glitch squealed. "I don't even know what you could be talking about."

"Glitch, this is not funny. Somehow, you have infiltrated HQ. It's about to explode."

"Well, I suggest you get out of there, then!" Glitch snorted as he laughed.

"Why are you calling?!" Nadia demanded.

"What a valiant effort from the three foolish musketeers! You have no idea what is going on. And you have no idea why. This is fascinating. With the three of you, I thought one of you dodo birds would have figured it out. But hey, I don't want to rock the boat. I'm quite a gem!"

"Zyanya, I think he somehow has the rocks!" I whispered.

"Listen to Faer!" Glitch sneered. "He is, after all, the smartest one in the room! Well, other than... you know."

Nadia looked around, then back at Zyanya. "Does he mean you?"

"Nadia, do better! All of you, do better! It is not as fun to win when you are all so... uninformed. Fine. I'll tell you who the smartest one in that room is. Well, I'll give you a hint. It's not any of you three!"

Glitch hung up.

The electricity was about to overtake every inch of the room.

"We have to go," I sighed.

Just then, from behind the time machine, we heard a noise.

"Is someone back there?" Nadia asked.

"They couldn't be," Zyanya responded. "They would surely be dead with all that energy coursing through this machine, and this room."

We heard another noise from behind the time machine. Someone was, and must have been, hiding back there! Zyanya ran toward the most dangerous part of the room. Behind the time machine. She screamed, as she saw something.

She came running back out. "Someone is glowing back there! Hiding in plain sight. Becoming one with the electricity!"

"Wait," I said. "They're glowing? Or do they have the rock that was glowing?"

I ran to look. I saw a glowing silhouette of a body. It looked terrified. And it was hiding something.

"What do you have there?" I asked.

The silhouette pointed at me, and stood up. It began to walk toward me. I slowly backed out, and found myself next to Zyanya and Nadia again. The glowing figure continued to point at me, as it advanced toward us.

"What did you do?" Zyanya asked. "Did you anger it?"

Electricity formed around the glowing silhouette itself. It stopped right in front of us. It reached into what I assume would be where pockets would be, if it had pockets.

It pulled something out of its invisible pocket and showed us. It was the glowing rock! It reached into another invisible pocket, and showed us the other glowing gem. The one that powered the time machine.

It then gestured for us to follow it back behind the time machine. For some reason, I trusted it. So I went and looked. The pile of eleven other rocks were sitting back there behind where it once was hiding.

I think it was specifically looking for the two glowing gems. And it was telling us to take the other eleven back?

"Zyanya, hand me the bag!"

She tossed it to me, and I collected the rocks back in the bag. I walked back out from behind the time machine, and handed the bag to Zyanya.

"Can I have these back, please?" I asked, pointing at the two glowing gems the silhouette was holding.

A burst of electricity surged from the glowing figure, which in turn sent a shockwave through the entire area. Something electrical hit Nadia, who fell to the ground.

"Nadia!" I screamed as I ran to her. "Are you okay?"

"I think so," Nadia said, standing up.

We all looked at the mysterious silhouette, who shook in terror. It seemed sorry. I wasn't convinced that it was even bad. It looked lost. It fell to the ground.

"I need these," I reached out to take the glowing rocks.

It pulled them closer to itself.

"Hey," I said softly. "It's okay. We can help you, okay?"

Zyanya walked over, and got down to the silhouette's level. She studied it carefully. It was as if she figured out exactly what was going on.

"We have to get out of here," I whispered. "It's unsafe. I'm sorry, Zyanya. I don't think we can save the time machine, but we have the rocks back."

Zyanya slowly reached for one of the glowing rocks. The silhouette pulled away, but then let Zyanya take it. Zyanya immediately put it in the bag with the other eleven rocks.

The silhouette's glow became more dim, as Zyanya reached for the second glowing rock.

"It's alright," Zyanya said, reassuringly. "We'll find a way to get you home. I promise."

"Home?" Nadia asked.

All of a sudden, Nadia's eyes widened.

It was like everyone knew what was going on except me.

"Where is home?" I asked.

Zyanya took the second glowing rock, as the silhouette's glow slowly faded away even more. She put the final gem in the bag. We had all thirteen again.

I could hear crying. I looked at Nadia and Zyanya, but it was neither of them. The silhouette had their hands on their face, as the glow from around them completely faded away.

And what was left behind was no longer a silhouette. It was a human. She had long brown hair.

"Hey, it is going to be okay," Nadia said, as she stared at what once was a silhouette.

"I just want to get back to my home."

That voice sounds so familiar.

"Where is your home, honey?" Nadia asked.

"Wherever those rocks came from," she admitted.

Wait. Was she from an alternative universe? How? And why does her voice seem to echo through to my soul? Who was she?

"Hey, look at us," Zyanya said. "It is going to be fine, okay? We will help you. You have my word."

What once was a scared, glowing silhouette, finally began to trust us. As she removed her hands from her face, we all could finally see what she looked like, and who she was.

My heart fell into my stomach in shock, awe, horror, and amazement.

Both Nadia and Zyanya recognized her as well. They looked at me, as tears formed in my eyes.

She looked like my wife.

Everything around us was chaotic with electricity. The bag of rocks was now glowing from the two gems. Everything was moments away from exploding. With a faulty time machine, multiple time phones in the room, and all the rocks, this could punch a hole through time and space. But in that moment, I just had to know if this was somehow her.

I never mentioned her name. She does have a name. Tylin.

"Tylin?" I said, afraid of the answer I would get.

"How do you know my name? Who are you?"

Zyanya looked around. "We have no more time."

"What do we do?"

84

"We are never going to make it out of here alive. If we try to run, it would be deadly. We are safest here. And I have an idea."

She took the two glowing gems back out of the bag and put them both in the time machine where one usually sat.

"This might not work," Zyanya admitted as the sound of electricity grew deafening. "But it is our only hope. Everyone gather together by the time machine!"

"What are we doing?!" Tylin asked.

Zyanya put the rest of the rocks on the chair in the time machine.

"I have no idea where, or when, we'll end up. I don't know if it will even work. I don't even know if we will have our memories on the other side of this. I just know at this point, it is our only hope of survival."

Tylin looked at me. "I just want to get back to my universe."

We all stood as close to the time machine as we could.

"Take my hand," Zyanya said to Nadia. "Everyone, hold hands. Maybe we can at least make sure we all end up in the same place, wherever, whenever, that will be."

We all took hands and waited not even a minute, when the entire room exploded around us. The last thing to explode was the time machine itself. As everything became so unsure, and as we were hopefully about to survive this, Tylin looked at me.

"Faer?" she said.

Everything went dark.

Chapter Fourteen
Lost and Found

In order to understand my story, you first need to understand how I got here.

Hello. My name is Faer.

I was lost. I didn't have much to live for. After losing my best friend, I was so sad all the time. She was my everything. My wife.

Wait a minute. This isn't right. I've already said this. Hello? Where am I? I can't see anything.

Finally realizing what just happened, I shook my head. The explosion from the time machine must have disoriented me. And my friends. My friends!

"Hello? Is anybody here?"

I tried to open my eyes, but I still only saw darkness. Did I die? Was this the afterlife? Was I in limbo? Also, did Tylin just remember who I was a moment ago? Everything happened so fast.

After what felt like an eternity, but I am sure it was no more than a few moments, I started to be able to see. Only shapes and shadows at first. As a few more seconds went by, I started to actually be able to see again. I immediately looked for any of my friends.

Wait. Shouldn't I still have my time phone? I reached into my pocket. The time phone was still there. I took it out and tried to turn the screen on.

Nothing.

The power must have been completely drained from it. I put it back in my pocket and started to look around. I didn't recognize where I was. I was in a building. That's all I knew. I saw a desk. A tall plant in the corner. There was a gigantic window that overlooked the city. Or town. Or wherever I was.

I walked over to the window to see if I recognized anything. Everything looked normal enough. I turned back around. The ceiling was high. The floor was wood. The walls were painted a sort of eerie dark gray.

I walked over to the desk. There was an elaborate futuristic looking chair. But a lot of chairs from my time look like they are from the future. There were some papers on the desk. I walked over and noticed a drawer right by the chair. Without thinking, I sat down in the chair and opened the drawer. Before I could read or see anything of importance, I heard something in the distance.

I got off that chair faster than you could imagine.

"Hello?" someone said.

"Hello? Who's there?"

"I should be asking you that question," the voice replied. "How did you get in here? This is my private office. No one is allowed—"

I walked closer to him, I just had to know who it was. All fear left me, because I just wanted answers now.

As I got close enough to recognize him, I gasped. This couldn't be. How was this even possible?

"You, again?!" the man cried.

It was Mircea Evander.

"Mircea?!"

"I have not seen you since the gala! Since you stole that device right off of Albert's arm!"

"I... I can explain, sir."

"I hope you can!" Mircea said, excitedly. "You have not aged a single day! That is quite fascinating."

"I'm sorry?"

"You never technically introduced yourself to me. That is sort of rude."

"Okay, what is happening right now?" I asked.

"Faer," Mircea began.

"Wait, how do you know my name if I never introduced myself?"

"Do you think someone such as I would not have the resources to look into the man that had shown up in my life twice, once at a grocery store and again at a gala? Whoever you were was fascinating to me. I wanted to know why you met me at that grocery store. And I finally found that out about a year ago. I never thanked you for saving my life. Thank you, Faer."

"I, you are very welcome, sir. But I still do not understand—"

"Then, for you to show up at that gala, Albert and Sasha's precious little gala, and for you to steal that device, and get away with it? It takes a lot to impress me, but Faer, you can color me impressed."

"You said I have not even aged a day since you last saw me."

"You look the same as you did all those years ago."

"All those years… Mircea, how many years has it been since that gala?!"

"What a preposterous question! Why do you ask?"

"Mircea, please! It is important!"

"Seven years."

Seven years? I landed seven years in the future?! In that moment, I felt stranded yet again. This time, I was at least on my home planet, I think, but I had no idea where any of my friends and family were. I had no idea when they were. My time phone was dead. I had no idea where to go from here or even what to ask. My head started spinning with anxieties.

"Faer!" Mircea yelled, snapping me out of my thoughts. "She would want to see you."

She? Who? Who could this man possibly know that I would know? And why would they want to see me?

"Who, sir?"

"Just follow me."

We walked out of his office and down a hall. We came to a door. Mircea knocked.

"Hello? I have someone here that needs to speak with you."

"Hold on, Mircea, let me finish this call."

I recognized her.

After a minute, the voice said, "Okay, Mircea."

Mircea opened the door. I immediately took in my surroundings. The room looked identical to Mircea's. A different plant in the corner. A different view out the window.

"Faer," a woman said. "Faer?!"

I turned to see who this familiar voice was. And my heart became full of joy. Just to see any of my friends at all was a comfort to me.

"Zyanya!"

Chapter Fifteen
Zyanya's New Life

"Where have you been?!" Zyanya asked. "It has been a while!"

She got up out of her chair and gave me a hug.

I am guessing this is more time dilation. Just like five hours was five months for me. Except, I had a feeling she had been here a lot longer than five months.

"Seven years, right?" I asked. "Mircea told me."

"Yes, Faer. But where have you been all this time?"

"Nowhere! The time machine explosion was seven years ago for you, but not even an hour ago for me! How long have you been here? When did you end up?"

"Five months after," Zyanya admitted.

"And Nadia?"

"She landed the same day as me. The same place. We moved through time, but not space. So we landed in an abandoned, exploded building, in the aftermath of it all. We looked everywhere for you."

"And you never found me."

"I found you now! Well, Mircea found you."

"How is Mircea even connected to any of this?"

"Faer, after Nadia and I landed, we had to rebuild this branch of Shard from the ground up. We had little to no resources. No money. Nothing but what we had on us that day."

"So you found Mircea?"

"Mircea found us," Zyanya admitted. "After the explosion, Mircea's small business noticed smoke off in the distance."

"Mircea had a small business?"

"Of course I did!" Mircea interrupted. "You do not stay rich by doing nothing with your money."

"What was your business?" I asked.

"We monitored the area for weird phenomena."

"Wait, were you ghost hunters?" I held back a smile.

"What we were, and what we are now, are two very different entities."

Zyanya continued telling her story. "They are the ones that began to clean up our mess. Nearly everything was gone and destroyed, so they did not find much. But then they found us."

Mircea smiled. "And I am glad I did."

Zyanya smiled back.

Hold on. There was something more going on between the two of them. But before I could ask, Zyanya spoke to me.

"Nadia and I, with the help of Mircea and his small business, have rebuilt Shard HQ right here!"

"In the open like this? I thought that would be dangerous!"

"With a man like Mircea, hiding something in plain sight became possible. The outside world just views us as another one of his many office buildings. Mircea is a household name after all."

"Where is Nadia?"

"On a mission," Zyanya said. She sighed. "Do not misunderstand what I am about to say. Mircea and I never gave up on you, but I think Nadia feels guilty or something. She spends a lot of the time she is not on missions looking for clues to where you might be."

"Well then we better tell her I am here!"

"Mircea already has," Zyanya smiled. "He sent her a message while we were talking. Nadia has been worried about you for nearly seven years, Faer. Just as I have. But she processed everything differently."

"Is she okay?"

"Of course. She still had to focus on her missions. She still helped us stabilize the timeline countless times. She just did not understand why you were gone. And neither did I."

"Nadia should be finishing up that mission," Mircea said. "She will be here shortly."

"Did Nadia's time phone have power when she landed?"

"Very little," Zyanya said. "Everything that had power in that room was basically drained. We used what little power her phone had, and resources from other factions of Shard, to rebuild here."

I handed Zyanya my time phone. "It was completely dead upon arrival."

Zyanya took the phone. I had forgotten about the moving picture of the analog clock on the back.

"Wait, is that still moving?" I asked.

"Of course. That moving analog clock is Shard's design, so that even in such an event as this, even if all power is completely gone, you can still know what time it is. After all, time is what we are all about!"

"Poetic," I laughed softly.

"I can get you a new time phone, Faer. Or I can try to fix this one if you want."

"Where is she?" I asked. I wanted to ask this question the entire time but there was so much going on.

"Who, Nadia? We told you, she is—"

"Tylin."

"Oh," Zyanya's face became somber. "Faer."

"Zyanya, she recognized me."

"No, she asked who you were."

"After that. Right before everything went dark, she looked right at me and said my name."

"Are you sure?"

"Yes, I am. Where is she, Zyanya? Was she with you guys all those years ago?"

"No," Zyanya admitted. "There has been no sign of her."

"So twice now. My wife has disappeared in front of me twice now?!"

"I am so sorry, Faer," Zyanya cried. "I completely understand how you feel. I would be devastated if I lost my husband."

"You're married?! To who? You never told me."

"Last time you saw me, I was not married."

Mircea walked over to Zyanya and took her hand.

"You married Mircea?!" I said, shocked.

"Yes, so thank you for saving my husband's life all those years ago. Now, Mircea and I are co-directors."

I was shocked, but honestly, it somehow made sense.

"Well congratulations! Sorry I couldn't be at the wedding."

"I am so sorry about Tylin," Zyanya sighed. "But she might still be out there somewhere. And if she is, somehow, we will find her again. I promise."

"Thank you."

Zyanya had an office phone on her desk. It began to ring. She pressed a button, answering it on speaker so we could all hear.

"Nadia!"

"Mircea sent me a message that you found Faer?! I would have called sooner but I had to take care of business out here. Mission completed by the way."

"Great job, Nadia!" Zyanya said. "Yes, Faer is right here."

"Nadia?!"

"Faer," Nadia cried. I could hear her trying to hold back tears. "Nearly seven years. First five months, now seven years. I was worried sick about you. What happened to you? Where have you been? How long has it been for you this time?"

"No time passed for me," I admitted. "I landed here with Zyanya and Mircea."

"Funny how those two got married," Nadia laughed. "I am on my way back right now. We have to catch up. I have been through a lot in all of these years.

I can not wait to tell you everything. Zyanya. Mircea. Thank you for finding him."

"We will see you soon," Zyanya said, ending the call.

"What has she been up to?" I asked.

"That is her story to tell," Mircea said.

Zyanya nodded.

"I am glad you are back, Faer. Can you believe we all survived that crazy explosion?"

Not all of us. Tylin was still out there somewhere. All these years later, it was like I was back to square one. Yes, I had friends now. But my wife was still missing. And she had just vanished in front of me. Again. Was it actually her, or just a copy of her from an alternative universe? The answer to that bewilders me. But she remembered me in that moment just before we were all split up.

Maybe Nadia had the answers I was looking for. Maybe she found some clue while looking for me. I couldn't wait to find out.

"That was a crazy idea," I said to Zyanya. "But it mostly worked. So thank you for saving us."

"Like I said, she might be out there. She has to be somewhere."

I nodded. It seemed hopeless. Time and space are so vast. The odds were definitely against us. But impossible things were unfolding all around me. All around us.

"Nadia will be here soon," Zyanya said. "Are you hungry, Faer? Let's get something to eat while we wait."

After about an hour, Nadia finally showed up. She came into Zyanya's office where the rest of us were waiting.

She ran toward me and gave me a hug.

"Faer! I missed you! We have a lot to talk about."

Chapter Sixteen
Glitch's Game

"Well, we will leave you two to catch up," Zyanya gestured for Mircea to follow her.

She took my time phone with her. "We will have this fixed by the end of the day."

The two of them got up and left Zyanya's office, leaving Nadia and I alone.

"I am so sorry," Nadia said.

"For what? None of this is your fault."

"Yeah, but still."

"How have you been all these years? I can't believe how much time has passed. How much I missed."

"Well, like I said, a lot has happened these seven years. For starters, I have traveled the entire world going on all these missions. I met people you wouldn't believe. Famous people. Even some movie stars! This job definitely has its perks. But every second I had, I was trying to look for any sign of you. But you were nowhere."

"Why do you think I keep moving through time faster than all of you?"

"That is definitely a mystery. But I don't think we have to worry about that anytime soon. We almost never use time travel these days."

"Zyanya and Mircea?"

"That was a lovely ceremony. They even had a speech dedicated to you. It was lovely."

"Can I ask you something?"

"Anything!"

"Have you found any sign of Tylin?"

"Honestly? I think Tylin may have somehow been thrown back into her own universe."

"She recognized me right before the time machine blew up. I have no idea how or why she only recognized me then, but I really miss her."

"I am sorry," Nadia said.

"What about your time phone? Did they fix it and give it back to you? Zyanya said it had little power left."

"Yeah, it's right here!"

The time phone rang.

It was Glitch.

Nadia's hand began to shake. "Glitch? We haven't heard from him in seven years!"

Nadia composed herself and answered the phone.

"Hello Nadia!" Glitch screeched.

"What do you want?" Nadia demanded.

"Well that was quite rude," Glitch scoffed. "I was trying to call your boyfriend Faer but his phone seems to be offline! Do you have any idea where I might reach him? Could it be, he is with you?"

"Glitch, why are you bothering us?" I asked.

"Me?! Bothering you?! That is quite the accusation. Nadia. Am I bothering you? No, I think not."

"Why did you wait seven years to call us?!" I screamed.

"Is that how long it has been? Faer. Simple, close minded Faer. Time means nothing to me. Nothing! And I think you might be fibbing! Because for you, Faer, it has not been seven years, has it? For me, the last time we talked was not seven years ago either! It was, well, that's the point! I have no idea how long ago it was! Is that not cryptically spectacular?!"

"Then why are you even calling us?" Nadia said, gritting her teeth.

"Oh, the game!" Glitch laughed. "The game continues, and I want to give you a clue!"

"A clue about what?"

Glitch began to sing a little, in a mocking voice. "I know where Tylin is."

"Where?! Where is she?!" I cried.

"Faer, if I told you where she was, the game would be over! You have to look. Look inside your heart."

"My heart was broken the day she vanished in front of me!"

"Now which day would that be? The first time she vanished? Or the second time, in the room with the time machine?!" Glitch held back laughter. "Faer, I truly hope you find her. Honestly. Because you know what they say. The third time's the charm! The third time she vanishes in front of you will be so funny!"

"Enough!" Nadia yelled. "Glitch, I have no idea who you are, why you are, when you are, or even what you are. Do you even exist?!"

"Do I exist?" Glitch sounded puzzled. "Do I exist? Do I? I never thought of it like that. What a beautiful question. Tell you what. I will go figure out if I exist, and you two can figure out where Tylin is. Oh, the clue! What a rude host I have been. Your clue is this: Time can be phony. Get it? Like the time phone? Oh, that will make so much sense in five minutes."

"Glitch, why are you like this?"

"The answer to that would shock you. You are not ready to hear it. But I do love our little game! Goodbye you two!"

"Glitch, wait!"

He was gone.

"Time can be phony?" I looked out the window in Zyanya's office. "Where even are we?"

"Remember when Zyanya showed us those giant machines overtaking a city, but then the future changed and everything was peaceful? There. What was on that tablet, that place, is where we moved Shard HQ to."

"And in all those years, you never heard from Glitch?"

"No."

"Why is he following me then? Is he the reason I never end up in the right time?"

"I wish I knew," Nadia sighed. "We have been through so much. But then I think about it all and realize that, although you too have been through a lot, everything must feel so different for you."

"Considering what has been nearly seven and a half years for you has not even been a full day for me? Yeah. I am so tired. But there is no time to rest. We have to figure out what Glitch is up to, on top of constantly saving the timeline."

All of a sudden we heard a commotion. Zyanya and Mircea came running into the room.

"Faer! Nadia! We have a problem," Zyanya said, out of breath.

"What is it?" I asked.

"I think I found the reason why we could not locate Tylin," Zyanya cried. "And it is not because she went back to her universe."

"Wait, where is she?"

"Faer, I have no idea what we can do to help her. Even Mircea has never seen anything like this."

"What is it?!"

Zyanya handed me my time phone.

"I fixed it. We gave it power. But the moment the screen turned on, we saw this."

I looked at my time phone. I was horrified. Nadia looked over my shoulder and saw what I saw.

It was a message from Tylin.

The message said, "I have been stuck in here for years. I am not sure how to get out, but I am thinking now that there is no way out. After trying everything I could for months and months, I have decided to succumb to the darkness. Ever since that time machine exploded, and I recognized Faer, I have been stuck in here. Where is here? Where am I? Hello? No one answers. No one ever answers."

I looked back and saw countless messages that led to that one, of someone who was lost and slowly losing hope.

"Get her out!" I cried.

"We have no idea how!" Mircea admitted. "This is far beyond anything I can do!"

"All I can guess," Zyanya began, "is that when the time machine exploded, sending me and Nadia five months, and you seven years, it must have somehow saved Tylin? Maybe there was not enough energy to send us all so this was a fail-safe? Maybe it was the glowing gems in the time machine mixed with the time phone energy?"

"Or the fact that you feel so strongly about her?" Mircea added. "Your emotions, your need to find her, could have played a factor in the time phone saving her."

"What do my feelings have to do with the time phone?" I asked Mircea.

"When you are dealing with an exploding time machine, multiple time phones, a glowing human from an alternative universe, rocks from many multiple alternate universes, you just have to look at all angles and believe anything is possible."

"You were back on that desolate planet right after that great war in the sky," Nadia said. "You were so close to all that energy. Plus, that is the first time we encountered Glitch, right?"

"It is."

Nadia's time phone rang. Mircea looked at her, confused.

"Who is calling you?"

"I forgot to tell you," Nadia said as she took the phone out to look at it. "Glitch called us today."

Zyanya's eyes widened. "We have not heard from him in seven years! What did he want?"

"This is him again now," Nadia sighed. "He is playing games with us."

The time phone continued to ring.

"What kind of games?" Mircea asked.

"He said he knew where Tylin was," I said. "Maybe he has answers. None of us have answers."

Nadia answered the phone on speaker.

"Glitch," Nadia said, "this has gone far enough. Whatever your game is, stop. Stop it now."

Glitch snickered. He spoke in a singsong voice again. "Time can be phony. Time can be phony."

"What is he talking about?!" Zyanya demanded.

"Zyanya!" Glitch said, excitedly. "How is my favorite woman?"

Mircea stared at Zyanya, who looked just as confused.

"Is there anybody else with you three?" Glitch asked. "Come on, you can tell old Glitchy. Have you found her yet? Time can be phony. That is an easy one! I am sure you found her."

"How do I get her out of the time phone?!" I cried.

"Well," Glitch began, "rumor has it, if you throw the phone on the ground and stomp on it, that would force her out. But, that has about a fifty-seven percent chance. Forty-three percent chance that kills her. What an exciting game we are playing, Faer! What are you going to do?!"

"Who are you?!" Mircea interrupted. He reached for Nadia's phone. She handed it to him. "Who are you, really?"

"Mircea Evander?!" Glitch cried. "We have a celebrity in our midst, people! So, Mr. Evander, what would you do if you were Faer?"

"This is the Glitch you told me about?" Mircea laughed. "He is nothing but a voice hiding behind a phone. What a joke!"

"Mircea, what are you doing?" Zyanya whispered.

"You dare challenge me, Mircea?" Glitch laughed.

"In order to challenge you," Mircea said, "you would have to actually be a challenge. I can take you out in one move."

"Go ahead and try!" Glitch sneered.

Mircea hung up on Glitch.

"I am not so sure that was a good idea," Zyanya said, disapprovingly.

Just then, my time phone made a weird noise. I looked down and it was as if the screen was taken over by someone. A video opened up, and I found a little hope as I saw Tylin. She began to speak.

Chapter Seventeen
Tylin

"I really wish someone could hear me. Please help me. It has been so long. I have lost track of time. I have lost track of me."

"Tylin?! Can you hear me?"

"Hello? Is someone there?"

"Tylin! It's Faer!"

"This isn't fair," Tylin cried.

"Yes, it is! It's me, Faer!"

"Life is not fair," she continued. "Why am I forced to live such a meaningless life?"

"Is this a live feed or an old message?" Nadia asked.

"Give me the phone," Mircea said.

Hesitantly, I handed it over.

"This might actually be live right now?" Mircea wondered.

"Faer, if you ever see this message, I need you to know something."

Mircea handed the phone back to me.

"Tylin!" I cried.

"I am not quite sure how, but I have split memories. I remember multiple lifetimes. I do not understand this. But I remember vanishing in front of you twice."

"Nadia," I cried. "Nadia, it's her!"

"How?!"

"When she vanished in front of me, the first time, maybe this is where she went?"

Mircea's eyes widened. "The time machine explosion merged both versions of her!" he cried. "That actually makes sense!"

"What does that mean?!"

"Just before the time machine exploded," Mircea said, "and leading up to it, maybe Tylin never recognized you because that Tylin never knew you. That Tylin was from another universe!"

"The same universe as the glowing rocks, right?" Nadia asked.

"Presumably, yes!" Mircea said. "When that insane time machine explosion happened, I think the universe got confused and pulled your wife through time as well. Your Tylin."

"Wait, so when my wife vanished in front of me, the first time, months before I even joined Shard, she was taken to the moment when this other version of Tylin vanished in front of me, during the time machine explosion?"

"And she was now tethered to this other version," Mircea continued. "When the time phone tried to save her, it must have been confused. There is not supposed to be two of the same person in the same universe. That itself is an anomaly."

"But what was the version of Tylin from the other universe even doing here in our universe?" I asked.

Zyanya's jaw dropped. "Wait a minute," Zyanya furrowed her brow. "Our friends, the ones that closed all those rifts in the sky, they spoke of transferring memories via rock. I think that is how most of them survived."

"What do you mean?" I asked.

"I never got all the details, but one of the many beings that helped close off the other timelines and universes, Quo, once traveled to another timeline himself. He and his friends could not all survive the trip, so all of his friends' memories, their very being, one could say, were placed into a magical rock. On that other timeline, he went on a journey to help all of his friends remember who they were to him."

"That sounds fantastic," Nadia said.

"After they all remembered, they had duel memories. Just like Tylin does now."

"How did he save his friends?" I asked.

"Their bodies from this timeline were destroyed. The memories, who they were, were transferred back from the rock to the alternate versions of themselves."

"So he lost his friends, but he found his friends?" I wondered.

"I think most, if not all, of them decided to stay with Quo in this reality."

"So that could be what happened to Tylin!" I cried. "The other version of her! Maybe her universe, or timeline, was too destroyed, or she was on some sort of adventure and she was forced to do the same thing that Quo and his friends had to do!"

Deep in thought, Zyanya continued to speak. "Faer, that one rock you found on that desolate planet was glowing, right?"

"Yes," I said.

"That was her! You brought the alternate version of your wife back here!"

"What about the second rock that was glowing? The one you used after the time machine lost power? Tylin was holding two glowing rocks. Was that from her universe?"

"If I had to guess," Zyanya said, "Yes. However Sasha and Albert got their hands on it is beyond me. But that rock must have also been from Tylin's alternate universe."

"But there was nowhere for her to go," Nadia said. "There was no body for her to inhabit. If we assume her body from the alternate universe was destroyed, that still leaves one mystery. Faer's Tylin, from this universe, her body was missing somewhere in time. So how did we see a physical representation of her? After the glow faded."

Mircea was deep in thought. "You were in the eye of the storm. Everything was happening right then and there."

"Tylin's glow faded when we took the rocks from her," Zyanya said. "Maybe somehow, in all the confusion, when she vanished from Faer's sight the first time, the original time, she appeared in the eye of the storm. Her body was there, but she was confused, simultaneously having her memories, and the alternate memories from her glowing rock, so she did not recognize you at first. Then, she finally began to."

"That sounds about right to me," someone said.

Everyone looked down at the time phone. Tylin was looking right at us. The time phone itself began to glow. There was a pile of debris by her.

"Zyanya," I said, "where did all the rocks go when everything exploded?"

"Never found them," Zyanya admitted.

"I think they, too, might be in the time phone," I cried. "Look!"

The time phone heated up. It nearly burnt my hand. I accidentally threw it onto the ground. The screen cracked, and glowing wisps emanated from the phone.

We all watched on, as the glowing light danced around.

"Tylin?" I said, hopeful.

"No way," Nadia cried.

"Faer, I think your time phone is broken beyond repair now," Zyanya said, surveying the damage.

"I do not even care!" I said.

The entire phone turned into floating crystals of light and joined the wisps. As everything whirred around, it began to form a silhouette. That silhouette quickly turned into a body. It was Tylin.

After everything I went through, finally, my wife had returned to me.

"Faer!" she cried.

"Is it, is it you?"

"Of course it is!" Tylin laughed. "You will not believe the stories I have in my head right now. Stories of Elders, time travel, space exploration, strange creatures, aliens, I have multiple lifetimes in my head now!"

"All those rocks," Nadia wondered. "Were they other people's memories?"

Zyanya shook her head. "I don't think so. Tylin's rock had a different look and energy about it. But maybe the other rocks can hold faint memories of times gone by. Does every rock hold a memory? Probably not. But these gems, this debris, has been through so much. Deep space, time travel, alternate reality, and the fact that Tylin herself was in her rock for a while? Anything is possible. Now Tylin has these thoughts as well. That name she said. Elders. I have heard that name. They were friends of Quo. They saved us all."

"Tylin, I missed you so much!"

"I have one question," Tylin said, with a serious look on her face. "Who has been taking care of my garden all this time?"

Chapter Eighteen
Third Time's The Charm

"You have so many stories to tell now, don't you?" I said, smiling at my wife.

She gave me a hug.

"Yes!" she cried. "Something about a collision? Why do I care about the number fifty-seven so much? What is up with that?"

"I have no idea," I laughed. "It is just so good to see you!"

"What have you been up to, Faer?"

"Well, other than traveling through time, getting stranded on a desolate planet millions of miles away, and being harassed by this crazy character named Glitch, time has been different for me."

"What do you mean?" Tylin asked.

"Time has moved differently for me. Seven and a half years for my friends has barely been a day for me. When I got stranded on that planet and when the time machine exploded, I lost time."

"Maybe time moved differently for me too, then," Tylin said. "Although hours felt like an eternity."

"Even though I had the time phone with me when the time machine exploded, it lost all power, except for the clock animation on the back. Maybe that is why you experienced time differently too."

"I was also stuck in a time phone, so time could have been different there anyway."

Zyanya looked at Tylin, then at me. "The infinitesimal power used to keep that clock moving might have been the only thing keeping your wife alive. If that had stopped working, and all power was lost, we could have lost Tylin."

"Or," Mircea said, deep in thought, "the only reason the clock was still working at all was because all the debris, and Tylin herself, were powering it."

I shrugged. "She is alive. She is here. That is all I care about."

Nadia's time phone rang. Tylin jumped.

"What is that noise?" she asked.

"Someone is calling Nadia. Are you okay? Why did that scare you?"

"I, I am not sure," Tylin admitted. "I just fear something bad is about to happen."

"Ignore that call," Mircea advised.

"I do not think we should," Zyanya added.

Nadia handed the phone to me. "Do what you think is best."

I looked at Zyanya, Mircea, Nadia, then Tylin.

"What do you mean you fear something bad is about to happen?" I asked Tylin.

"So many stories in my head," she cried. "Villains. Heroes. Division. Ships. Ow."

"What's wrong?" I cried.

"Just a little headache," Tylin smiled. "I am alright."

The time phone continued to ring.

"I can not make him!" Tylin cried.

Everyone looked at her.

"You can not make who?" Nadia asked.

"Who are you talking to?" I said, worried.

"You can't hear that voice?" Tylin began to shake.

"What do I do?" I yelled.

Tylin raised her voice. "No! Leave me alone!"

Zyanya put a hand on Tylin's shoulder. "Honey, are you alright?"

Tylin had tears in her eyes. "He wants me to go back."

"Go back where?" Zyanya asked, somehow staying calm.

"To my reality. But this is my reality."

"Who?"

"I hear this voice in my head. I am so confused."

Tylin grabbed the time phone and answered it.

"Finally!" Glitch laughed.

"Him!" Tylin cried. "That voice was just in my head, even before we answered the phone!"

I snatched the time phone and screamed, "Glitch, if you do anything to my wife, I will personally destroy you. Do you hear me?!"

"Faer, I already told you," Glitch said, angrily, "you are in way too deep. This goes far beyond your little pathetic life. There is more out there than just you."

"Why did you say that to her?!" I demanded. "Why did you try to tell her she needed to go back to her reality?!"

"You are not ready for the truth, Faer," Glitch screeched. "So that is why I have decided to tell you. Third time's the charm!"

"Tylin," Glitch said, in a singsong voice. "Do you remember me?"

"Do not speak to my wife like that," I said.

"Alternate universes and alternate timelines can be messy," Glitch continued. "Tylin, do you remember?"

"Remember what?"

"Think. Think of your reality. That moment. The choices."

"Ow!" Tylin cried. "Ow! No! No, please!"

"What are you doing to her?!" Nadia yelled.

"Nothing," Glitch said. "She just needs to remember everything. From both realities."

"Who are you?!" Tylin demanded.

"In our universe, we were running out of time," Glitch laughed.

"Wait, you are from Tylin's reality?" I interrupted.

"When the skies opened up, all realities, timelines, even alternate universes were affected! Some were damaged to the point of destruction."

"What does all of this mean?" Tylin said softly.

"There is a difference between an alternate timeline, and an alternate universe," Glitch said.

"How so?" I said, gritting my teeth in anger.

"Let's just say, there are more issues with alternate universes. Things can be a lot different, than say, an alternate timeline. On an alternate timeline, maybe you change the course of history, and it causes changes. But they connect back to a single point. The point of divergence."

"How is this relevant?" I demanded.

Zyanya's eyes widened. "Oh no."

"What?!" I cried.

Glitch sighed. "In an alternate universe, there can be completely different, unrelated things going on. Does this make sense yet?"

Tylin began to shake.

"Two timelines in one's mind, well, that's a lot more acceptable than two universes. Two completely different, unrelated lives. Maybe timelines can share. But universes? They are a bit more selfish."

"Faer," Tylin said, tears streaming down her face. "I am so sorry."

"For what? Do not listen to him! He makes no sense!"

"But that is the problem," Tylin cried. "He makes perfect sense! Hearing his voice, even as a glitch, I am reminded of my other universe. But I have your Tylin's memories as well. This is bad."

"Tylin!" Glitch's smile could be heard through the phone. "Do you finally remember who I am?"

"Faer," Tylin frowned. She gave me a hug. "I am sorry. I am so sorry."

This was bad. Extremely bad. Whatever it was, it was going to kill my soul.

"What is it, Tylin?" I asked, both wanting and not wanting the answer.

"Back in my universe, I worked on scientific research. We were studying time travel, alternate universes, alternate timelines, all of it. So when the skies opened up, I was instructed to send myself and my partner through. Our mission was to land in another dimension, whether that be a new timeline, or universe. Our commander gave us the idea of putting our very being in the rocks. Using them to travel through realities."

"You made it safe, but I was not so lucky," Glitch sneered.

"Wait," I was trying to understand everything. "So Glitch is your partner?!"

"We were both supposed to make it over," Tylin admitted. "Your universe merged my two consciousnesses into this one body."

"Why is Glitch just a voice stuck in the phone with no body then?!" Nadia asked.

Mircea was just listening to everything, but he stayed completely silent.

"My rock was severely damaged!" Glitch snorted. "Plus, I do not think the host of my body in your universe would be receptive to me. So I am stuck like this."

"Who are you to my wife?" I said, trying to calm myself down. "Just a partner? Or more?"

"You do not want the answer to that," Glitch warned.

"Tell me right now!" I demanded.

Tylin looked at me. Fully crying, silently.

"Life. Isn't. Fair," Glitch said coldly. "Tylin makes it alive, and I am forced to be a glitchy voice forever. Oh Faer! Remember what I said earlier?"

"What, Glitch, what do you want from me?"

"I told you, third time's the charm. Do you get it yet?"

"She is not vanishing in front of me a third time, Glitch. So do not even try to mess with me."

"Not physically," Glitch said quietly. He spoke in a singsong voice, "Mentally."

"Faer, I am so confused. My head hurts so much."

"I've got you, Tylin," I said, holding her. "It is going to be okay. You are my wife. We will get through this."

"I'm scared. My memories. They are so great. Glitch unlocked more."

Nadia looked like she wanted to ask a question.

"What is it, Nadia?" I asked.

"He never answered," Nadia cried. "Glitch, who are you to Tylin?"

"Nadia, I will tell you. That way, at your request, I get to damage Faer's heart. Oh Faer! Remember when I said you were in too deep? This game is so fun!"

"Enough of this!" Nadia said. "Why do you want to hurt Faer?"

"Do you think I am heartless?!" Glitch hissed. "Oh wait, I am! I am nothing but a glitch in the cosmos now. A voice. No body. So, you tell me, why would I be angry?! Faer, are you sitting down? Oh, who cares. Guess what, Faer? In my universe, Tylin is my wife."

"What?!"

"Different universes cause completely different lives," Zyanya said. "Even more so than an alternate timeline."

Glitch cleared his throat. "Third. Time's. The. Charm." He laughed hysterically. "You all have a lot to talk about. But remember, even now, the game is not over quite yet! Soon, though, very soon, when you finally feel you have won, that is when out of nowhere, game over." He ended the call.

Chapter Nineteen
The Machine

I wanted to ask her who. I wanted to ask who, in the other universe, was her husband. But the answer might not even be relevant.

"So what is Glitch's game?" Nadia asked. "Does he want you to go back to your universe like you thought? Or does he just want to hurt everyone?"

"I think their universe is destroyed," Zyanya guessed. "Everything Glitch said was double sided, though. He wants Tylin to go back to their universe, and their universe was nearly to the point of destruction? I don't even know if Glitch knows what he wants."

Tylin wiped tears from her eyes. "It might not be gone. Him and I traveling here was something our commander wanted regardless."

"Is there anything we can do?" Nadia asked. "Maybe we can try to open the skies back up and send Glitch back?"

"I think he is too damaged," Mircea spoke.

Zyanya looked at him. "Plus I don't even know if there is a way to punch a hole through to another universe on command like that, let alone to find his exact universe."

"Who was it?" I asked. I felt selfish, but somehow I just had this nagging feeling that we all needed to know who her husband was in the other universe. Glitch said whoever it was wouldn't be receptive to his consciousness. Although, I would agree since Glitch has no morals. At all.

"Faer," Tylin said.

"I can take it," I said.

Tylin looked over at Mircea.

"Yes?" Mircea said.

"Him," Tylin cried. "My husband, in the other universe, is Mircea."

Nadia looked shocked. I was shocked. The differences in these two universes were wild just in that thought. And remember, in my universe I saved our Mircea from botulism at a grocery store. Even though that had no ramifications on the other universe, even that small connection was a bit wild.

Mircea looked around. Zyanya looked at him.

"You don't have to look guilty," Zyanya said with a small grin. "That's a whole different universe."

Tylin looked back at me. "This is so weird," she said. "I don't like having two sets of memories. I think it–"

She grabbed the side of her head and fell to the ground.

"Tylin!" I screamed. "Are you alright?"

"No!" she said. "Ow! I need help! Someone help me!"

Zyanya looked at Mircea. "Would it work?"

Mircea looked disturbed. "It has not even been tested yet!"

"What is it?!" I cried.

"Ever since Quo and his friends came back from saving everyone, some of them have had to deal with dual memories from alternate timelines. There hasn't been any issues with their bodies maintaining both timelines."

"How does that help us?" I questioned.

"Shard likes to be ready for anything," Zyanya said. "Once I told Mircea the story of Quo and his friends years ago, he had the idea to make a sort of antidote just in case. Something that could cure any sort of chaos that was caused by multiple consciousnesses. A machine."

"It isn't ready yet!" Mircea warned.

"This wrenching pain!" Tylin screamed, falling to the floor. "My head hurts so badly. I can't take this."

"How long until it's ready?" I said softly, trying not to sound upset.

"Months," Mircea admitted. "Years."

"I don't think we have that much time," Nadia said.

"Use it," Tylin advised. "I don't care if it's ready or not. I am not going to last through the end of the day if these waves of pain keep hitting me."

I looked at Tylin, then at Mircea. "Is it safe?"

"Of course not," Mircea said. "It isn't ready!"

The more Mircea talked, the more it seemed to agitate Tylin. Maybe hearing his voice was awakening more memories from the other universe.

Writhing in pain, holding her head, Tylin stood up. "Take me there. Now."

Mircea looked at Zyanya, who nodded. "It's on a different floor. We have a whole floor dedicated to figuring out the mystery of dual consciousnesses. And we have a machine that, in theory, can separate them. We'll take you there."

As everyone got up to leave, Tylin and I stayed behind for one moment.

"Are you sure?" I asked her. "I want what is best for you, so I support whatever you choose to do. I am just scared because the tech isn't ready."

"Faer," she said, holding onto my arm to keep her balance, "I have to. My brain is holding way too much information. And even if it could handle multiple universes, I can't handle the thought of being married to two different people. I can't handle the thought of Glitch being my husband. He used to be such a kind man. He would never harm a soul. But whatever that Glitch is, that shell of the Mircea in my universe, I somehow want to forget about him."

We began to follow everyone, but we stayed far enough behind to continue the conversation.

"Do you think that's what the machine can do?" I asked Tylin.

"If it actually separates the consciousnesses, yes."

"But where does the other one go?" I asked.

Tylin nearly fell, wincing in pain, but I caught her.

"I have no idea," Tylin sighed. "Maybe it's because this body is from your universe, but I want to eradicate every memory from that other universe. There are some scientific advancements that I have learned on the other universe, and maybe they can be put to use here somehow, but I just want to go home and tend to my garden. Maybe my other consciousness can be contained and they can figure out a way to take the information. But Faer, I am so tired. My head is killing me. Literally. I never asked for any of this. I just want everything to reset. I need everything to go back to the way it was when it was just you, me, and my garden. No time travel. No alternate universes. No tales of Elders. I am so tired."

A few moments went by as we continued to walk the same floor. I wanted to help my wife. All I ever wanted was to help her. I just wanted her back in my life. All of the time travel, alternate universes and alien talk made me miss the simple old days too.

"There is an elevator just down this corner," Mircea yelled back to us.

We quickly caught up to everyone. The elevator's interior was chrome, with lightning painted on it.

"That lightning looks an awful lot like what we saw when the time machine exploded."

Zyanya nodded. "It was meant to pay homage to everything we lost that day. To you. Everytime Nadia and I saw it, we thought of you."

The elevator door closed. A logo could be seen.

"Shard has a logo?" I asked. "I thought this was a secret organization!"

"It is!" Zyanya laughed. "That doesn't mean we can't have our own special logo, even if it is just for us to look at!"

Nadia smiled. "I designed that!"

"It looks awesome," Tylin said softly. "You are very talented."

The elevator came to a stop.

"This is it," Mircea said. "This is the floor."

The elevator doors began to open. Hopefully, my wife would have a clearer mind after we detached her other consciousness. Hopefully this would all work.

Chapter Twenty
Detachment

There was a lot to see when we first got off the elevator. From fancy paintings on the wall, to the weird ceiling tiles that somehow looked like broken shards. Oh, I see. Shards. Like Shard. I guess that is clever. The floor was the same as it was in Zyanya's office. This was all just the hall that would eventually bring us to the machine. We continued to follow Mircea and Zyanya.

Finally nearing the end of the hall, we began to walk by a Shard employee who was on a computer. She smiled at us, and pressed a few buttons. A door off to the side appeared on what was just a plain wall.

"Afternoon, Mircea," she said. "Zyanya. Everyone."

"Hello," Mircea nodded.

Zyanya smiled back at the employee.

"That door is cool," I said.

"A chameleon door," Nadia said. "Looks like a wall until it is told otherwise."

"The machine is beyond here," Mircea said. "After the research room."

As we entered the chameleon door, it disappeared behind us.

"So it does that on both sides," I said.

"Of course," Tylin jokingly scolded me, smiling. "Why would anybody install a one sided chameleon door?"

To see my wife joking and laughing warmed my heart. I missed her so much.

We walked by a dozen Shard employees all doing different tasks. Some on computers, some were using whiteboards, calculating complex problems, and others were simply drinking coffee and talking about their research.

We walked past everyone and came to a locked door. Mircea took out a key card and placed it by the lock. Zyanya did the same.

"This is our project," Mircea said. "So we both have to be present in order to modify the machine." He laughed. "We can't be trusted to work alone. Not when it involves detaching."

"Is that the official name of it?" I asked. "Detaching?"

"Yes," Zyanya said. "In theory, it will detach the multiple consciousnesses."

Mircea opened the door and we immediately saw an entire room filled with machinery.

"Where will the other consciousness go?" I wondered out loud.

"We built, a sort of, container," Mircea said, pointing to something in the middle of the room next to a chair. "In theory, the detached consciousness will be contained there. Both consciousnesses will travel from the host in the chair to the container. There, they will be detached from each other. One will stay behind in the container, the other will return to the host."

"Then what would happen to the contained consciousness?"

"We can study it, if the host allows us to," Mircea said. "But we must have their permission before the procedure."

"Study it," Tylin said. "Just get this other life out of my head. As a scientist, I do not want to lose any possible advancements in science that this other life may have. But as a human, I can not handle two universes in my mind. Please."

Mircea nodded. He pointed to the seat in the center of the room right next to the container. Tylin was eyeing the chair. She didn't want to wait a single second more.

There were wires connected from each side of the chair to the machine on either side of the room, then back to the container where the detached consciousness should, in theory, be kept for study.

"I love you," Tylin said to me. She took my hand.

"Love you," I responded. "Always have, always will."

Tylin smiled. She held on to my hand as she walked to the chair. She sat down.

"What are the odds of failure?" Tylin asked Mircea.

"Honestly," Mircea said, "I am not going to make up statistics. I have no idea since we have never tried this on an actual being. We have only theorized."

Nadia looked worried. "Then maybe it isn't a good idea."

"It's the only idea," Tylin said, looking at Nadia. "These headaches will only get worse. Eventually, a great battle will ensue internally, and that will tear this body apart. I will die."

"But what if this kills you?" Nadia asked.

"This has a greater chance of working than doing nothing," Tylin said softly. "Come here, Nadia."

Nadia walked over and stood on the other side of Tylin. Now holding both my hand and Nadia's hand, Tylin smiled, and looked at Mircea and Zyanya.

"I'm ready," she said.

Mircea and Zyanya each went to opposite ends of the room. It looked like there were control panels on both sides.

Tylin whispered something to Nadia, who was taken aback. I wanted to ask what she said, but Mircea and Zyanya began to fire up the machine. Tylin let go of our hands, and motioned for us to back away, just in case it became too dangerous. Nadia went and stood with Zyanya, but I refused to go.

"Faer," my wife whispered to me. "It will all be okay. I promise. I will never leave you again if I can help it. After this, we can both go back home. I have a garden to tend to. I love you. Always."

"Always and forever," I whispered back.

I hesitantly walked toward Mircea, slowly.

"Faer, you must get out of the line of fire," Mircea warned me. "The last thing any of us want is for this to go wrong."

I looked at my wife and quickly moved to the side of the room with Mircea.

"It's time," Tylin said. "Go!"

Mircea and Zyanya pressed buttons and threw switches like there was no tomorrow. The chair where Tylin sat began to light up. Two different shades of what looked like electricity could be seen forming around the chair.

I guess the physical form of consciousness looked like electricity.

It honestly looked so cool. I had never seen electricity, or consciousnesses, dance so elegantly. Whatever Mircea and Zyanya had done to invent this machine, it was actually going to work. I was going to get my wife back. Just my wife. With her memories.

I watched, as both consciousnesses, still intertwined together, simultaneously traveled up the left wire and the right wires toward the container.

This was it. We did it. After everything we had been through, we finally beat Glitch. In mere moments, everything would be back to normal for my wife and I. As normal as it could be, anyway. We would be in the garden in no time.

The electric consciousnesses danced through the wires and formed in the container. They began to detach. One shade on the left, and one on the right.

This was all so amazing to watch. And the best part of it all was that we won.

Nadia's time phone rang.

"No, not now!" I cried.

Nadia took out the time phone and shook her head. She went to place it back in her pocket when a spark flew from it. She accidentally threw the phone.

"Hello?!" someone said. "Can you hear me?!"

It was Glitch. Somehow, the phone had been answered.

"Oh, don't be shocked, everyone!" Glitch said. "You don't think I have the power to answer the phone when you choose not to?"

"You have lost, Glitch!" I cried. "Whatever you thought you were going to do, it's too late! My wife is going to be free."

"Are you detaching consciousnesses without me?!" Glitch gasped.

"How do you know—"

"Oh just quit playing dumb, Faer," Glitch demanded. "You know full well what is about to happen here. Go ahead. Try and stop me. Just remember what I said! Once you think you have won..."

"Game over," Mircea whispered.

"Mircea?" Zyanya cried. "What is happening?"

Glitch laughed, and the consciousnesses in the container began to merge together again.

"No!" I screamed. "What have you done?!"

The time phone began to spark and flicker.

"I'm done being locked up in time phones," Glitch said. "I'm done being just a voice. I want a body. And the best compatible match would be my doppelganger. I am sure you all had that awkward conversation with Tylin. Oh no! Mircea is her husband in the other universe. So

131

that makes me Mircea. And that makes Mircea the perfect host."

Before anybody could react, energy shot out of the time phone and straight into Mircea. He began to shake and fell to the ground. He stood back up quickly.

I was standing right next to him. I looked him directly in the eyes, and I could see hate. I could see pain.

"Well that was much easier than I thought," Mircea said.

Zyanya screamed, "Mircea! Are you alright?"

I shook my head to signal to Zyanya that he was not okay. Glitch had taken over his body, and voice.

"Without so much as a fight," Mircea said, shaking his head. "What an amazing, world renowned man. Can't even fight off a little glitch."

"Let him go!" Zyanya cried.

"No," Mircea hissed. "He is mine. And I have something to say. Never underestimate me. Never underestimate my wife. We may be from another universe, but we are more powerful."

Glitch, in the body of Mircea, started pressing buttons on the console.

"What are you doing?!" I demanded.

"What we intended to do the entire time," Mircea laughed. "Survive."

"Stop! Please!" Nadia said from across the room.

Tylin's consciousnesses began to detach inside the container again. Mircea continued flipping switches and pressing buttons on his side. I could do nothing. I had no idea how the machine worked. I felt powerless.

132

Zyanya tried to counter whatever Mircea was doing by flipping switches and pressing buttons on her side of the machine, but to no avail.

One consciousness stayed in the container, the other went back through the wires to Tylin.

"Faer?" Tylin said. "Faer, I need to tell you something."

I walked over to her. Mircea said nothing. Zyanya and Nadia watched on, as I stood by my wife.

"Tylin," I cried. "Is it actually you?"

Tylin smiled. She stood up. She gave me a hug, and looked at Mircea over my shoulder.

"Of course, Faer," Tylin said, reassuringly. "Of course it's me."

Mircea ran over to the container with the other consciousness. He looked at it, then ran back to his side of the machine. He lifted a panel and pressed a few hidden buttons. I watched as the consciousness inside faded away.

"I thought we were going to study that!" Nadia cried.

"Foolish girl," Mircea said. "So all of you think you have won? Faer. I finally made good on my word."

"It's over, Glitch. You just destroyed your wife."

Mircea laughed. "No, no. You see, a while ago, I said the third time your wife disappeared in front of you would be so funny. I also said the game wasn't over."

Nadia ran toward me. "Let go," she said. "Let go of her hand."

Tylin squeezed my hand tighter. "No! Faer, I don't understand! Please don't let me go!"

133

Zyanya walked up behind Nadia. "It's not her."

Mircea began to laugh. He looked at Zyanya. "How is my favorite woman?"

Zyanya must have remembered Glitch saying that over the phone a while ago. That sentence was hauntingly chilling.

"My Mircea will prevail," Zyanya said. "He is strong!"

"No," Mircea shook his head. "He won't. He is only as strong as the woman he married. So go ahead. Try and stop me."

Zyanya stared directly at Mircea.

"You know what the best part of being just a voice for such a long time is?" Mircea said, trying to instigate Zyanya. "I learned how to do this."

Mircea placed his hand on the console. Electricity began to course through him. He looked like he was in pain, but he continued to allow the electricity to course through his body. Something shot through the machine and landed in the consciousness container. Mircea tried to pull his hand off the container.

"Help me!" he cried. "Glitch is killing me!"

Confused, and not knowing who to trust, Zyanya rushed to the aid of her husband.

"Nadia!" she cried. "Help!"

Nadia rushed over, but no one could touch Mircea without getting shocked.

Zyanya rushed back over to the other side of the machine to hit buttons to counter whatever Glitch had just done. Anything she tried to do seemed to make things worse.

"I am so sorry," Mircea cried.

Zyanya rushed back over to him. "No," she said. "Don't be sorry. You will be okay. You have to be okay!"

Mircea pointed to the container. He tried to say something, but it was becoming nearly impossible to talk for him.

"Does he want us to put his consciousness in that container?" Tylin asked.

"Wait a minute!" I said. "If that's Mircea, then that must be Glitch in the container!"

"Maybe we should destroy him where he is!" Nadia said.

Zyanya thought about it.

Mircea managed to muster up enough energy to whisper, "Destroy it."

Zyanya was hesitant, but she wanted to save her husband. And as long as Glitch was around, no one was safe. She pressed the same hidden buttons that Mircea had pressed earlier to destroy Tylin's other consciousness. The consciousness that was currently in the machine faded away.

Mircea removed his hand from the console. "Thank you," he said.

"We did it!" Zyanya said.

Tylin smiled at Faer. Mircea smiled at Zyanya.

Then Mircea smiled at Tylin. And Tylin smiled back.

Nadia was the first to realize the truth. Her eyes widened.

Mircea looked at everyone. "So, who's lost in a fantasy world still?" he chuckled.

Tylin let go of my hand. "Faer!"

I was terrified at what I was seeing.

Mircea shook his head. "Tylin, do they really think they just destroyed Glitch? Do they really think that is who was in that container?"

Tylin looked at me and slowly walked to Mircea. "I really think so," she said. "Otherwise, Zyanya would have to admit that she just killed her own husband."

"What?!" Zyanya cried. "No, that's impossible!"

"Impossible?!" Mircea cried. "As impossible as me loving you?!"

"Oh no," Zyanya began to cry, hysterically.

"I think they need us to explain it a little more," Tylin smirked.

"Tylin?!" I cried. "But that means—"

"Yes, Faer!" Mircea hissed. "You just saw your wife vanish in front of you for the third and final time! I may be evil, but I am a man of my word! Usually."

Tylin looked at Zyanya. "Don't worry, honey, I'll take good care of your husband. Well, technically you killed your husband so why would you care? This is my husband."

Nadia was trying to console Zyanya. I walked over to them. I lost my wife. Again. This time forever. There were two maniacs from another universe standing in front of us.

"We just wanted to survive," Tylin said. "Sorry it was at the expense of our doppelgangers."

"No you're not, dear!" Mircea said, laughing.

"Oh yeah, that's right," Tylin said somberly. "I'm not! At all."

My Tylin was gone. Zyanya's Mircea was gone.

Glitch, now forever in control of Mircea's body, said in his singsong voice, "When you finally feel you have won, that is when out of nowhere…"

Tylin smiled at Mircea.

In unison, they both said, "Game over."

<u>Chapter Twenty-One</u>
Weeding Out the Truth

After everything we all went through, we had truly lost. It's as if Glitch was in control the entire time. My wife vanished in front of me, again, for good. And this imposter from another universe gets to live. This other Tylin. This other Mircea who was now permanently controlled by Glitch. Zyanya also lost the love of her life because of Glitch. So the villains get a happy ending, while the heroes all lose? What sort of story is this?

"What will you do now?!" Zyanya said, angrily. "After what you've done today, just to survive? What is your endgame? Why do this?"

Mircea had a big smile on his face. He looked at Tylin, then at Zyanya.

"It would appear that this is my building," he laughed. "Oh Tylin, how would you like to be my partner here at this division of Shard?"

"Oh, I would love that!" Tylin said, taking Mircea's hand.

Nadia looked at Zyanya. "They'll never allow it."

"Who?!" Mircea hissed. "I am number one. Anybody else in this building will believe me over anyone. And anybody that works at the other divisions has no reason to suspect any foul play."

"Not unless we tell them the whole story!" Nadia retorted.

Mircea gasped. "Snitch! Tylin, what do we do with snitches?"

"Leave her alone!" I cried. "Please."

"Faer," Mircea said. "From the moment I contacted you through the time phone on that planet way out in space, I told you. You are in too deep. Did you not even realize that I said your name before you told me? I knew a version of you in my universe too, you know."

"And who was I to you?!" I screamed. "Clearly not a friend if you can take away my wife from me without blinking!"

"She is my wife!" Mircea screeched. "And the only reason I knew of you was because you tried to stop Tylin and I from leaving our universe!"

"So I was your friend?!"

"No!" Mircea growled. "The reason you wanted to stop us was selfish!"

"And what would that be?!"

"Tylin and I were tasked with this mission instead of you and your precious wife."

"Wait," I said, pausing. "Who was my wife if it wasn't Tylin?!" I had this weird curiosity in the midst of loss, anger, and grief. There were so many emotions surrounding me.

Tylin looked over at Nadia. "I whispered something to you earlier. How long were you going to keep that secret?"

Nadia looked embarrassed and confused. She said nothing.

"Oh please," Mircea rolled his eyes. "Nadia. You were married to Nadia in my universe. And when Tylin and I were chosen to travel to this universe instead of you two, you were obsessed with sabotaging me! It is pretty poetic. The fact that in my universe, you were like the villain while we were the heroes. And now in your universe, well, I don't think I'm quite the villain you think I am. But after being stuck as a glitch for such a long time, I may have lost my way. But I found it. I found her."

Mircea held Tylin close.

"That's it!" I yelled. "So now what? Do you plan on taking over Shard? Just this division, or all of it? If you were such a hero in your universe, what does that make you here? What is the point of traveling here to get information or even just to visit if you can't even get back to your universe to tell the tale?! Your entire plan is full of plot holes. So, you control Shard. A hero to your universe for making the trip, but still somehow a failure since no one will ever know you made it alive. Those rifts are never going to open again. You can't go back. I lost my wife. You lost everything else. So what now, Glitch? What are you going to do? The game is over. You have your wife."

"They still believe we came here just to travel," Tylin smirked. "They have believed every single lie I have thrown at them since I've entered this universe."

"Well," Mircea shrugged, "I haven't been that truthful either. Even just now. My lies have been so great, I began to believe them. We were not chosen to travel. In fact, you and Nadia were."

"Why should we believe anything you say?" Nadia interrupted. "It's all just another lie."

"Believe what you want," Tylin said. "This is the truth. Maybe you will understand why we did what we did."

"In my universe, I was in a horrible accident," Mircea sighed. "Tylin and I were partners and yes, married, before this. I lost my body, but my consciousness was saved in a container similar to what your Mircea built here. In fact, Tylin and I built our version, which works much better I must say." Mircea looked at me, and smirked. "My wife, Tylin, spent years trying to find a way to fix the situation of me having no body. Since my body was completely destroyed. Once an opportunity to travel to another universe arose, Tylin asked to be chosen to travel. But you, Faer, you and Nadia were selfish. You were insistent that it had to be you two."

"Why would I, or that version of me, want to travel to another universe?"

"Exploration," Tylin said. "Fascination. Curiously."

Mircea shook his head. "Not even thinking of anybody but yourself. So Tylin took care of you two. She hijacked the mission, and put her consciousness in one of the gems. That rock. She tried to get my consciousness into a rock, which should have been easier since I was already without a body. However, me being the firecracker I am, I tried to travel through the rift without the rock. I guess you could say I sort of just, glitched over here. I landed in your time phone, Faer. I was able to then travel to Nadia's time phone. You know

141

the rest. Oh, thanks for the lift again, Faer. If you weren't put on damage control on that distant planet, well, I may not have survived. I guess, that means it's almost your fault that your wife died. That's unfortunate."

I nearly lost my mind when he said that. The nerve of these two doppelgangers. Imposters.

"Did you kill Nadia and I in your universe too?!" I asked. "Clearly killing means nothing to you."

Tylin walked over to me. "I did what I had to do to save my husband. The only reason we came to this universe, to whichever universe we could get to, was so he could have a body. And we have achieved our goal. Are we going to have a little fun taking over your universe now? Maybe. But we can't get back to ours."

"Unless," Mircea said, wondering. "We could. If we find the right tools, we could punch a hole through the cosmos and find our way back."

"Mircea, no," Tylin cried. "Don't any of you see?! The cost to get over here was too great. Mircea, if we go back, we'll be detained immediately. We sabotaged a mission on our universe to get here. We can't go back even if there was a way."

Mircea nodded. "Then I guess we'll just settle for this new life here then. This is my building, and I want these intruders out. Immediately."

Zyanya had been silent the entire time. I could tell she was trying to stay strong and not cry.

"Zyanya," I whispered, "I feel the same way. It's okay to cry."

Mircea walked out of the detachment room and yelled, "Guards! We have intruders! Get them out of here!"

Three guards came into the room. Mircea pointed to Zyanya, Nadia, and me.

"But sir," a guard said, "I thought these were your people."

"Not anymore," Mircea sighed. "They betrayed us. They all betrayed Shard. Get them out of my building."

The three of us were escorted out, as Tylin took Mircea's hand, and they watched us get taken away.

I overheard Tylin say, "Why did you let them go?"

Mircea replied, "They have nothing. They can go live their miserable lives out in the world. We have work to do. Shard needs to be rebuilt from the ground up. In our image. I am so glad you found me a body. I love you."

"I love you too, Mircea," Tylin said.

I could no longer hear them. I didn't want to hear them. My original mission was to find my wife. Now that I had done that, and she was taken away from me, I felt lost again. But my universe was in danger. Nadia, Zyanya and I had to somehow come up with a plan to stop Mircea and Tylin before it was too late.

But I was starting to fear that it already was.

We were escorted completely out of the building. Zyanya sighed. Nadia gave her a hug. I looked around. This building was smack dab in the middle of the city.

"Wow," I said. "Mircea really hid Shard HQ in plain sight."

Zyanya nodded. "We have to figure out what our next move is."

I heard a car unlock. Zyanya was holding keys. She walked over to her car and got into the driver's seat. Nadia sat shotgun, while I took the backseat.

Zyanya took a deep breath and started the car. "This has gone further than we can handle alone. We are going to need help. But anybody deeply involved with Shard can be manipulated by Mircea's twisted mind games."

"What are we going to do, then?" I asked.

Zyanya began to drive. "In order to fight these villains, I think we might need a villain or two. I think it's time we pay Sasha Kiyla and Albert Heron a visit."

Chapter Twenty-Two
Abandoned

"Sasha and Albert?!" I cried. "I don't think they want to see us. They definitely won't want to see me!"

"Years can change a person," Zyanya said.

"But last I saw Albert, I stole his device! And last I saw Sasha, she tried to shoot at me! Besides, how do you even know where they live?"

"Shard can keep tabs on anybody they want. Until they can't."

"What does that mean?" I asked.

"Until about a year ago, I knew where both of them were. They lived in different neighborhoods, but the same city. However, they both went off the grid. Even Shard couldn't keep tabs on them."

"So where are we going?"

"Their last known address," Zyanya said. "Maybe they're still hiding there. Probably not, but it's the only lead we have."

"Nadia," I said, "you have been quiet for quite a while. Are you alright?"

"Yeah," she said softly. "I'm just sorry to see so much loss. It hurts my heart."

We drove on for thirty minutes. In silence. We had all been through so much. Taken so much loss. Tylin. Mircea. Shard. And our only hope was to join forces with a couple of people that hated our guts. And that was if we could even find them.

My purpose in life used to be clear. Now I had no direction. Where would I go even if we defeat Mircea and Tylin? We thwart their evil plan, send them back to their universe, then what? My Tylin, Zyanya's Mircea, both completely gone forever. Destroyed.

My thoughts were interrupted by a break in the silence.

"Just beyond here," Zyanya said.

We rounded a corner and drove straight. Off in the distance, we could see an old warehouse.

"They lived in a warehouse?"

"Not both of them," Zyanya said. "Albert. This is Albert's last known address."

"But no one could ever find this unless they were looking," Nadia said.

"Exactly."

After about five minutes, we finally reached the warehouse. It did not look like it was in good shape.

"What happened here?" I asked.

"I'm going to guess Albert isn't here anymore," Zyanya sighed. "But let's take a look."

We all got out of the car. Zyanya walked over to a window and tried to look in. Nadia went a different way.

"Yeah, there is nothing here," she said. "I think Albert has moved on. I see an empty box, some abandoned, but possibly damaged, tech. He clearly isn't here anymore. Maybe we could use that abandoned tech."

Nadia was inspecting something off in the distance. "Faer! Zyanya! I found something!"

"What is it?" Zyanya asked as we both walked over.

"I found this suitcase just sitting on the ground underneath this window."

"Why would there be a suitcase just left outside like that?" I asked.

"Maybe he had to leave in a hurry," Nadia said.

"Maybe it isn't even his?" Zyanya guessed. "Can you open it?"

"No. It's locked."

"Maybe the key is inside the warehouse," I shrugged.

"We could check," Zyanya said, trying to force a little smile.

"No, I don't think we should!" I cried.

"What if the door is unlocked?" Zyanya said. "If they left a suitcase out here, I don't think they took time to lock the door. Clearly Albert was either in a rush, or he wanted someone to find this."

Zyanya walked over to the front door of this gigantic warehouse. Sure enough, it was unlocked.

"Looks like we have some exploring to do."

The three of us walked in, Nadia was holding the suitcase. Zyanya immediately saw the box she had previously seen from the window. She walked over to it.

I noticed all the abandoned tech she mentioned. It was fried beyond belief. No wonder Albert left it all behind.

"Eureka!" Zyanya exclaimed.

"Did you find the key?" Nadia said, excitedly.

"No," Zyanya said. "I found blueprints."

"For what?" I asked.

"I am not quite sure," she said.

"Okay, I have tried to stay optimistic," I sighed. "This is clearly some sort of trap."

"So let them trap us," Zyanya said. "If this is all Albert and his love for showmanship, then let's embrace it. We want to talk to him. This could be the only way. So now, knowing it's a trap, we have the upper hand! Or, it's all abandoned."

"I guess you're right," I conceded.

I walked over to look inside the box. Other than the blueprints Zyanya was holding, it was empty. I picked it up. The floor looked a little different, but I dismissed the thought quickly.

Zyanya looked at where the box once was, then up at the shelves of damaged technology.

She held the blueprints up, then moved them away.

"What is it?" Nadia asked.

"Look!" Zyanya said, handing Nadia the blueprints. Nadia placed the suitcase on the floor.

"No way!"

Nadia handed them to me.

"The tech!" Zyanya said. "I think we have to use that damaged technology left behind to build this thing!"

"That tech is completely destroyed," I said.

"Mr. Showmanship might want us to think that," Zyanya shook her head.

Zyanya took the blueprints and closely surveyed the charred tech on the shelves.

"Okay, you two. I think we can do this."

Zyanya began to direct us, as she read the blueprints, trying to decipher exactly which pieces of tech we might need.

"That piece over there," Zyanya pointed to the far left. "That is a decoy piece. There is nothing that looks like that on here. And there is another piece to the right of that one. It is on here, but the blueprints show a skull on it. I would think that one means death or destruction."

Nadia and I gave each other a slight look. We found comfort in this familiar chain of command.

Zyanya pointed out piece after piece, which Nadia and I gladly retrieved. She instructed us on how to build whatever we were now tasked to build. All three of us worked as a team to get to the finished product. And after nearly an hour of labor, we were finally almost done.

"There are only three pieces of tech left," Zyanya said. "The decoy piece, the one with the skull, and that." She pointed to the last piece.

"But that doesn't look like the right piece either," she sighed. "Are we missing something?"

Zyanya handed Nadia the blueprints. "What we built looks exactly the same, it's just missing whatever that is."

"Can I see that?" I asked. I glanced at the sheet of blueprints without taking it and walked over to the last three pieces. I picked up the decoy piece and the other piece, leaving the one the blueprints warned us against.

Zyanya was staring at me, but she started to realize what I was doing.

"Maybe we have to take pieces of tech from these two, and build that final piece ourselves," I smiled, feeling proud.

"Well done, Faer," Zyanya said.

Nadia reached for one of the pieces. "I see it now!"

We jury-rigged the final piece as best we could to match the image on the blueprints. We then quickly placed it on the main project. Whatever we were tasked to build, was now complete.

"Now what?" I asked.

"Maybe it was all a waste of time," Nadia admitted.

Zyanya looked at the blueprints one final time, then at the machine.

"I wish I knew what we built," Nadia said.

"And why," I added.

"Maybe the tech is too far gone to work," Nadia said. "Unless we are missing something."

I looked around, and glanced at the floor where the box was again.

"Look," I said. "I noticed earlier, but forgot. That looks interesting."

Zyanya walked over to the spot, then looked at the machine. "I think we have to place it here!"

"That machine is too heavy for one of us to lift," I said.

"Everyone take a corner," Zyanya instructed, as she walked over to the machine.

We all picked it up, and carefully placed it down on the floor, in the exact spot.

"Still nothing," Zyanya sighed.

"Is there a codeword or button or something?" Nadia asked.

I reached for the blueprints. "Do you think that last piece is required after all?"

"The blueprints show a skull on it," Zyanya said.

I looked closer. "Is that actually a skull?"

Nadia looked over my shoulder. "Why does it almost look like a flower?"

"Oh yeah, I see that," I agreed. "Wait, if I remember correctly, there was one flower that looked like a skull when it died."

"Is it an orchid?" Zyanya asked.

"No," I sighed. All of this flower talk made me think of Tylin. But I had to stay focused. I walked over to the piece on the shelf and picked it up. I looked closely at it. "Snapdragon!" I yelled.

Suddenly, the machine started to move.

"It was never a skull!" Zyanya said. "It was a clue!"

"But we still weren't supposed to use that piece, right?" Nadia said, worriedly.

The machine began to twist, turn, and light up. Steam started to emanate. A slow, low, hum could be heard.

"Is this thing going to explode?!" I cried.

"We might need to take cover," Nadia said, looking to Zyanya for direction.

Zyanya looked at Nadia, then at me, and at the machine. She was about to speak, when we heard a noise. Something had clicked.

The machine slowly wound down. The lights went off as it sputtered black smoke. It immediately fell apart. Completely.

"The suitcase!" Nadia exclaimed, running over to it.

Zyanya and I looked over where the suitcase sat. Somehow, it had opened. And we could finally see what was inside.

Chapter Twenty-Three
The Suitcase

"What is it?" Zyanya asked.

Nadia had reached inside the suitcase and found a notebook.

"What does it say?" I asked.

"The cover is blank," Nadia said.

She opened the notebook, and had a surprised look on her face.

"Faer?" she said, handing me the notebook.

"What is it?!" Zyanya asked.

"That notebook," Nadia cried, "has Faer's name in it!"

"Well what does it say?!" Zyanya said, excitedly.

I read it out loud.

"'Faer. You may be confused. I bet you have a ton of questions. I will answer them. In time. But first, let me get this out of the way. Sasha and I should be mad at you and your team, yes. You left me on my own stage, in pain, after stealing our technology. And from what Sasha told me, you're the reason she went flying back from your car when she shot at you? That is quite a wild story. But, as you know, I love showmanship.'" I stopped reading for a moment and looked up at Nadia and Zyanya. "Wait, did I tell them my name?"

"I have no idea," Nadia said.

I continued reading out loud from the notebook. "'Oh, stop being confused, Faer! If you wonder how I could know your name and everything about you since the last time we met, just know that the glass can be looked through both ways. I am aware of Shard, and everything they tried to do now.'"

"He knows about Shard," Zyanya said, nodding.

"How?!" I cried.

"A glass can be looked through both ways," Zyanya said. "I think what Albert means by that is, just as we looked him up and found everything out about him, including the tech he was working on, he can, with the right knowledge and resources, look us up."

"But I thought Shard was a secret organization," I said.

"It is," Zyanya sighed. "But still. He found a way to learn all about us."

"What else does it say?" Nadia asked.

"'Snapdragon. Yes, Faer, I chose a flower, because I know how much you love your wife, Tylin. And I had to make sure it was you that took on this mission. The reason we forgave you so quickly, is quite simple. Because of you and Shard, we had to start over. From scratch. That was frustrating at first. Until we found something even stronger than those magical rocks. Oh, don't you worry about what that could be. I'm sure you're standing there, scratching your head, maybe with a friend or two, trying to figure out what power source we could have used. Don't. You won't.'"

"Okay, I can't be the only one that needs to know what they used," Nadia interrupted.

154

"He's Albert," Zyanya sighed. "We might as well not even bother. Maybe he is telling the truth, maybe he is lying. Maybe he had more of the debris on hand somehow."

"So what is this mission he mentions?" Nadia asked.

"There isn't much more in the entire book. It's mostly blank, except for this final entry."

"How cryptic is it?" Zyanya said.

"'Even in death, you can sometimes find life. Bring death to life.'"

"That's it?" Zyanya shook her head.

She took the notebook from me and shook it. Maybe she thought there was something hiding in it? She checked cover to cover, to look for some sort of clue.

Meanwhile, Nadia was looking at the suitcase again. I was just shocked that Albert knew about not only me, not only Shard, but Tylin. And the flower connection. My wife loved her flowers. And everything. She was such a kind spirit. The fact that she was taken away from me, for good, was a pain I would never lose. I could only try to suppress it enough to stay focused on whatever this mission was.

I guess I was lost in my thoughts, because I heard both Zyanya and Nadia calling my name.

"Yeah?" I said, confused.

"You collapsed, Faer!" Nadia cried.

"What?" I had no memory of such an event. I was still standing in the exact spot I had been, before I got lost in my thoughts. "Are you sure?"

155

"Definitely!" Zyanya said, worriedly. "You fell to the ground. We helped you stand back up. Somehow, you managed to stay standing on your own. You were out for five minutes."

"Oh, maybe it was the time dilation," I said, groggily. "I've been traveling through time so maybe it's a side effect."

"Faer!" Nadia said. "Faer, what's wrong?"

I didn't understand what was going on. This time, I saw flashes of the ceiling, as I fell to the floor.

I thought I saw a shadow of a man over by the last piece of technology. Then, somehow, shadows of the already used technology were back on the shelves. I heard a voice.

"This will be just fine," the voice said. "Faer will be able to find it."

Another voice spoke. "Why do you trust him?! He stole what was rightfully ours. And for what? Some shadow organization that thinks they can control time and space?!"

Sasha and Albert. Somehow, these shadows were them. But how? I continued listening.

"We have built something so much better than Shard could dream of. Honestly, Sasha, how could a time phone even compare to what we have done?"

"Why are we leaving all of this behind?"

"Some time in the future, I'm sure Faer will be found again. And when he is, he and his team will be able to find this setup."

He walked over to a certain piece of tech. He whispered, "Snapdragon."

"Why the flower obsession again?" Sasha asked.

"Faer's wife Tylin loves flowers. It will get his attention. Now, once we can confirm it is Faer, not someone else, we can offer him the mission. I am sure he would love to help save the timeline, for real, from Shard."

"But Albert. I don't trust him."

"Do you trust me?" Albert asked.

"Of course," she nodded.

"Then trust him."

"But why would Faer or his friends believe us?" Sasha asked.

"By the time Faer sees this message, Shard will have gone rogue."

I shook my head and blinked. The shadows were gone. I blinked again. Zyanya and Nadia were both staring at me.

"What happened?! You were completely out of it again!"

"I saw their shadows. Shadows of when they were here. Albert and Sasha. They left everything here on purpose!"

"Why?!" Zyanya asked.

"I am not sure. But they somehow knew."

"Knew what?!"

"That Shard would go rogue."

"I wish we had more answers," Zyanya said.

"I want to go back," I cried. "Let me see that last piece. The one we were afraid to use earlier."

Nadia walked over, picked it up, and handed it to me.

I whispered, "Snapdragon."

Nothing.

I tried whispering again.

Nothing.

"I noticed something in the suitcase that might help," Nadia said. "There was nothing else besides the notebook, but a peculiar image on the bottom of the inside."

We all looked inside.

"Another flower," I sighed. "He really wants to make sure this is me."

"What kind of flower is that?"

"It's a perennial flower called Phlox. Every year, even though it dies, it always returns the next year."

"Even though it dies!" Nadia exclaimed.

Zyanya smiled.

We all said, in unison, "Even in death, you can sometimes find life! Bring death to life!"

I took the piece of tech that we once thought was attached to the skull symbol of death, and I placed it inside the suitcase that had the image of a flower that symbolized hope of new life.

"I think it's like a key," I smiled, looking at my friends. My smile quickly faded as they vanished in front of me.

I saw Albert and Sasha's shadows again. This was it. I found a way to communicate with them. Somehow.

Albert's shadow walked toward me. The shadows slowly came into focus. I saw Albert and Sasha, and all the tech. It was as if I had traveled back in time. I stared on, as Sasha pointed at me. Albert smiled as he saw me standing there, confused.

"Hello, Faer. Glad you can finally see us. Can we have a chat?"

<u>Chapter Twenty-Four</u>
Time Copy

"How can you see me?!" I said, taking a step back. "Have I traveled in time?"

"No, Faer," Albert said, laughing. "Remember that technology I wrote about in the notebook that you read? Or will read, from my point of view. In a weird way you traveled through time. But your body is still in your present. Your friends are probably confused. But they'll figure it out when you return to your present. That technology is a fraction of what we've been working on."

"I have so many questions!"

Albert sighed. "You're seeing a time copy. Basically, Sasha and I are technically already gone from this location in your present. A version of you has traveled here to talk to these versions of us. We are kind of outside the laws of time and space here."

"Isn't that dangerous?" I asked.

"Indubitably," Albert beamed. "And doesn't that just make this all the more fun? We made disposable copies of ourselves and hid them in that device. That piece of technology that was unused when building that other machine. Once our conversation is over, this entire conversation will be uploaded to us, the real us, in the present. We will have immediate knowledge of everything said here. Isn't this all exciting, Faer?"

"Yes, but I still need answers."

"That piece of technology had the information needed to create this illusion. Like I said. We aren't actually here, and neither are you. But here we are!"

"So this is all a fake reality?"

"In the simplest terms, I suppose so. But you're wasting time! We have but two minutes left before you wake up!"

"So what is all of this for?" I asked.

"The mission," Albert said, looking at Sasha. "Well aren't you even going to say a word? No need to be rude to our guest!"

Sasha rolled her eyes and stared at me. It was clear she wanted nothing to do with this collaboration.

"Albert," I said frantically, "focus! What is this mission you need help with?"

"Faer, you aren't here for the mission! You're here for the next clue! I have to make sure that you are ready!"

"Please, sir," I said, tired of all of the games, "can you just tell me about this mission?"

"Not yet," Albert said, sternly. "Go back to your friends. Tell your wife we said hello."

"My wife is gone!" I said, angrily.

"She's what?" Albert looked shocked.

"Just tell me why I am here," I demanded.

"All of this, the warehouse, the box, technology, the suitcase, the flower references, that was all to bring you to me here and now. Well, I don't think this realm is technically here. And it definitely isn't now. Not really. But I digress. All of that so I could tell you where to find us in the real world. But one final thing before I tell you."

I was just about done with all the games. I was infuriated.

"What?!" I said, gritting my teeth in anger.

"What would you give to save the ones you love?"

Taken aback by this question, yet without skipping a beat, I thought of my wife and simply said, "Everything."

Albert looked at Sasha, then back at me.

"Good. Because that is what this mission will cost you. You may be confused. Who can you trust? Is it us? Shard? You decide. Find us in your present, at the place where this all began."

I blinked, and I was back in the present with Nadia and Zyanya.

"I saw them," I said. "Talked to them. Everything we went through seems so empty."

"Why?" Nadia asked. "What did they tell you?"

"Whatever I just experienced was something called a time copy. They took a copy of themselves, and a copy of me, and had a conversation that both them and I are currently aware of."

"So what do we have to do now?" Zyanya asked.

"Mr. Showmanship did all of that just to ask us to meet them where it all began."

"Where it all began for who?" Nadia asked.

"I think, because he was talking to me, that he wants us to meet them where the gala was years ago."

"The gala!" Zyanya said. "Of course! I remember exactly where they held that event!"

162

"Are Sasha and Albert actually going to be there?" Nadia asked.

"Only one way to find out," Zyanya said, as she headed out the door of the warehouse.

Nadia and I followed Zyanya to the car. Hopefully, we would find Sasha and Albert there, where that gala was once held, so we could figure out what this mission was and why they wanted our help. I was a bit skeptical.

Zyanya started the car, and we drove away from the warehouse, leaving everything behind. Nothing from the past was needed to move forward, except the knowledge of where it all began.

It was silent for a few moments, as we all continued to wonder what Albert and Sasha's endgame could be.

"It is all going to be okay," Zyanya said, breaking the tension. "No matter what. Everything always finds a way to just be okay."

Nadia and I stayed silent. Zyanya's words, though meant to comfort, weren't enough to quell my thoughts of the neverending scenarios of what might be awaiting us.

As time went by, whether it was minutes, or hours, I honestly couldn't tell, I began to recognize the surroundings.

We had arrived. There was only one car in the lot, which was weird, but expected. I wondered if that was their car, or if this was just another test to make sure it was me.

Zyanya parked the car. We all walked toward the doorway of the building. I couldn't believe I was back here for yet another time. I had been here two times before. So this was number three.

Without thinking, I whispered, "Third time's the charm."

I immediately had flashbacks of Glitch saying that phrase, and I regretted whispering it. It was as if he were somehow here. It was unsettling.

Nadia and Zyanya didn't notice me stumble, but that was alright. We finally reached the building. Zyanya peered in. She heard something, and motioned for us to follow her.

We walked through to the main hall, where it sounded like someone was giving a speech. As we got closer, we could hear them talking clearly. They mentioned a mission. They said my name. And they were staring directly at us as we were walking into view.

"Finally!" Albert said. "Sasha! Faer found us! And he brought company! I told you this would all work out!"

Sasha walked into view and rolled her eyes. "Hello, Faer."

"Everyone," Albert said, "thank you, thank you for joining us tonight. It's finally time we told you about this mission! Remember the cost, Faer."

"What does that mean?" Nadia asked.

Albert interrupted before I could say anything. "We brought some friends too!"

He motioned for someone out of our view to walk forward.

Who we saw completely shook us all to our cores. The confusion. The betrayal. So many emotions.

Albert laughed. Sasha smiled.

Tylin and Mircea, the evil imposters themselves, both stood with Sasha and Albert opposite the three of us.

"Had to make sure it was actually you, Faer," Albert said. "You know Glitch, I mean, Mircea. Oh, and Tylin. Have you met Tylin, Faer?"

"Is this a sick game to you, Albert?!" I screamed.

"Quite the opposite!" Sasha hissed.

"Faer," Albert looked at my friends, my enemies, then at me. "Time for that mission."

<u>Chapter Twenty-Five</u>
Life Isn't Faer

"You lied to us, for what?" I asked, staring at Albert.

Sasha shook her head. "You really think we care one iota about any of you? You derailed years of research and work. And for what? Shard?"

"For the greater good," Zyanya said, sternly. "Not for us. For the timelines. The universes."

"Well," Mircea, still also known as Glitch, said, "since I've taken over this faction of Shard, even in that short time, I have done so much."

"And everything with the time copy?" I asked Albert. "All those puzzles you had us solve? Everything was a lie."

Albert smirked. "Oh, Faer. Have you not realized yet?"

"Realized what?"

Albert looked at Sasha, then at Mircea and Tylin.

Tylin walked over to me. Even though she wasn't my wife anymore, I cautiously watched her every move, confused.

"Faer," Tylin said, "the reason the four of us joined forces is quite simple. Maybe you will understand it some day." She leaned in close, and whispered, "Your Tylin fought against me during the detachment. But she was weak, so she lost. She missed you so much. But because I am stronger, I am here, and she is not."

I stood there, frozen, as Tylin walked back over to Mircea.

Mircea laughed. "Faer, remember when you saved this body all those years ago? I need to thank you. I often still wonder if you let this Mircea die if, maybe, your wife would still be alive. Funny how things work out."

Nadia and Zyanya looked at me, as I tried to keep all the anger I was feeling inside.

"This is all your fault," Sasha said to me. "Because you stole our technology, for your version of Shard. So for years we have been planning revenge."

"Years?!" Zyanya cried. "Mircea and Tylin's evil reign just began today!"

"Zyanya," Mircea said. "As Glitch, I have been here for far more time."

"Stuck in a time phone!" I cried.

"Do you really think anything can restrain me?!" Mircea laughed. "I found a way to subliminally influence all of you throughout these years!"

Albert and Sasha smiled. "Glitch was very persuasive," Albert said.

"How?!" Nadia asked.

"I glitched through every electronic my heart desired," Mircea said, cryptically.

"And we are so glad you did," Sasha said.

"As Sasha and I continued to rebuild our technology, that you stole, Faer, something interesting found us. Someone interesting. It seemed we had a common enemy. So we planned all of this to get you here and now."

"And all of the theatrics were for nothing," Faer said.

"On the contrary," Albert said. "The time copy technology is very real. It gave us progress as to where you were, and let us know that you were on your way to this moment. Oh, and it did one more thing for us."

Albert reached into his coat pocket and pulled out a remote control. He pressed a button. Lights across the main hall turned on. We all heard a noise from above. Looking up at the unnaturally high ceiling, we all saw a giant device slowly descending.

"The time copy," Albert said, "gave us your imprint. The imprint of not only your DNA, but your molecular structure itself. Every little atom of whatever you have become."

I was nervous, and confused. "What do you mean, whatever I have become?"

Mircea looked at Albert, who nodded, as if to allow him to explain.

"Ever since I saw you on that planet all those years ago," Mircea began, "I could tell there was something special about you. Maybe it's because I was nothing but energy. Or call it a hunch. Maybe I was just obsessed with you because you saved me by bringing your time phone to that exact moment at that exact time. That doesn't matter. Faer. There is something wrong with you."

Nadia put her hand on my shoulder. "No there isn't," she whispered.

"Nadia, no one asked you," Mircea said. "Have you not noticed all the time dilation, Faer? Your body is a mess. I'm surprised you're still here. I'm surprised you're all in one piece. The universe should have torn you apart by now."

As the machine lowered to our eye level, Albert walked over to it with confidence.

"Behold!" he said. "This machine is going to right all the wrongs in all the universes and timelines."

"Your fight is with Shard," Zyanya said. "We are the ones that took your technology. But now you're working with the new head of Shard itself, corrupt as it will now be. Why would you even care about other timelines and universes? This doesn't even add up!"

Albert shook his head. "I don't have to explain myself to you. But did it ever occur to you that sometimes, utter chaos is the answer? You took years of work away. And although I am grateful for that setback, and although it changed the course of my life and allowed me to create something even better, sometimes, revenge is a good enough reason. That's it, Zyanya. Revenge."

"These other timelines and other universes did nothing to you, Albert!" Nadia cried. "I don't buy your response. I think there is something you're not telling us."

Albert looked at Sasha, then sighed. "No," he said. "None of you people in this pathetic universe understand! I may be from this universe too, but that doesn't matter! This is all your fault! When that great war in the sky split open the universes and timelines all those years ago, you thought it was all okay once everything stabilized. It wasn't. Universes were brought to the brink of destruction! Someone from this universe needs to pay for the damage that was wrought throughout all of time and space!"

"But none of that was in our control!" Zyanya cried. "There was a villain. His name was Smedge. He caused the chaos that split open the skies."

"And if you can't keep the villains in our universe, or timeline, or wherever, in check, then maybe you don't deserve to make such decisions for the greater good." Albert began to pace. He looked at Sasha again.

"Sasha," Zyanya said. "Where are you from?"

"You leave her alone!" Albert said.

Mircea began to laugh.

"I'll tell them," Sasha said, softly. "My universe was torn to shreds because of you people."

"It wasn't Shard," Zyanya whispered.

"I don't care!" Sasha yelled. "I don't even know quite how I got here. In my universe, everything was dying. Our technology was not as advanced as anything I have seen here. Just before everything exploded and ended in my universe, I saw a man." She looked at Albert. "This man saved me."

"What can I say? I make innovative technology. I wasn't even looking for her. I was trying to make interdimensional travel possible. I wanted to meet people from other universes. The moment I turned it on, it somehow picked up Sasha. Maybe it was her desperation to survive, or just random luck. But the technology was not ready. Since her universe was already about to end, she wanted to take the chance. Because a one percent chance of survival is better than a zero percent chance. So she walked through and survived. Since then, it has been my mission to make sure someone pays for the damage."

"But you were a man of science!" Zyanya cried. "Your technology was supposed to advance time travel in your lifetime alone!"

"Oh, enough!" Sasha hissed. "Destroy them, Albert!"

Albert pressed another button on the remote, and the big chrome machine began to beep.

"Why do you listen to Sasha?" Zyanya said, looking at Albert.

"I saved Sasha," Albert said. "Sasha needs me to destroy you all! Revenge!"

Zyanya walked over to Albert. She smacked him. "Albert! You are a man of science! Why would you destroy the universe you are from? You're destroying your technology! You're destroying everything!"

Albert blinked and shook his head, as if he wasn't in control of himself up until now.

"Sasha?" Albert looked over at her. "What have you made me do?!"

"What's going on?" I whispered to Nadia.

Sasha shook her head. "You couldn't just leave things alone, could you?"

"Were you mind controlling him this entire time?!" I asked.

Zyanya looked at Sasha, then back at Albert.

"What are you?" Nadia asked Sasha.

"YOU ALL NEED TO JUST DIE ALREADY," Sasha screeched.

Mircea's eyes widened. "Well that's crazy even by my standards! I love this chaos so much! Now is as good of a time as any to interject even more! The confusion has always been from me, Faer." Mircea laughed. "Once I entered your time phone, I had free reign to go back in time, forward in time, just to mess with you. You're welcome. The confusion was my favorite part of all of this. I made you question the mission. I made you question your sanity. This has all been so fun. But Sasha, Tylin and I really need to get going. I hear this event will be more devastating than the last one. Except, this time, it is more controlled."

Tylin took Mircea's hand.

Sasha walked over to Albert and snatched the remote. "Your universe is exploding for a good cause. And this time, it is only your universe that will die. All the timelines on it, all the people. All of this was needed to open a rift for the three of us to get out of this selfish universe. The one that caused so much damage and destruction will pay the ultimate price."

"And how will you three survive such an event?" Zyanya asked.

Sasha held the remote up. "I am from another universe. Mind controlling is second nature to my people. Thank you Albert, for your service. I may not be able to get back to my universe, but anywhere is better than here. Tylin, Mircea, you don't want to go back to your universe, and I can't get back to my universe. So let's go exploring other universes. I quite enjoyed destroying this one. Maybe we should destroy others. For fun."

Mircea squealed in excitement.

Tylin smiled. "I love to see you so happy!" she said. "Okay, Sasha. Hit it."

Sasha pressed a series of buttons on the remote. A shield formed around Mircea, Tylin, and herself.

"This great explosion will propel us to other universes," Sasha said. "Thank you for the time copy of your molecular structure, Faer. Ever since that time dilation, and Glitch, I mean, Mircea, messed with your mind, whatever has been changing you ever so slowly was able to be integrated, and the process immensely sped up, so we could create this great machine. Again, all of this is thanks to you."

Zyanya and Albert walked over toward Nadia and I.

"Look at them trying to plan something!" Sasha laughed. "Your molecular structure, Faer, mixed with Albert's know-how, created this very machine. Every rock we could get our hands on from the great war in the sky was procured over the last few years. Albert is a genius. He tracked down a ton of debris from that event. Cosmic gems plus the instability of your DNA, that DNA that is now mixed with all that time dilation, time travel, confusion, sadness, loss, those things together created this doomsday weapon. I can't stress this enough. Your molecular structure was the last piece this machine needed. Your universe is about to be destroyed, and there are no Elders in sight to save you like last time an event like this happened. You are helpless. You are nothing."

Albert had tears in his eyes. "I am sorry everyone."

The great machine over our heads showed a number. Fifty-seven.

"That was my idea," Mircea laughed. "Start the countdown to the end of the world at fifty-seven!"

We watched the number move backwards, as time was officially running out.

Tylin looked at me. She laughed, and talked in a mocking voice. "Bye, Faer! I'll miss you! I love you forever!"

Mircea laughed. "Zyanya," he began. "I, too, love you. Thank you for this body. Shard really did come through in the end. They sure saved us!"

Sasha looked at Nadia. "Wow. You had no one. That's sad."

Zyanya and I looked at Nadia. "Don't listen to her," I said. "You had us. We love you, for real. Unlike these imposters."

Albert looked at Sasha. "I should never have brought you into this universe. This is all my fault. Think, Albert. There has to be a way to stop this!"

"Oh no!" Mircea shook his head. "Does the king of showmanship not like the show we put on for him?"

"You think he would be grateful," Tylin added.

The timer was now at thirty seconds.

"You gave it your best shot," Sasha said. "No one is here to save you. No savior. No magical beings. No one. The rest of the world, no, the rest of the universe has no idea. This abrupt end will hit everything all at once. All those people. Gone. Goodbye, Albert, Zyanya,

Nadia, and Faer. You gave it your all. Everything is over for you, now. Everything."

"Everything?" Albert said out loud. The word must have echoed through his mind. He looked at me, and I remembered what he said to me earlier, during the time copy.

"Faer!" Albert said to me. "What would you give to save the ones you love?"

I looked at Zyanya and Nadia. I looked around the entire room. There was no other choice. I wasn't sure what was about to happen, but I knew what I had to do.

"I love you guys," I said to Nadia and Zyanya. "Thank you for everything. But I have to go now."

Sasha furrowed her brow. "What are you doing?!"

I hugged Zyanya. "Take care of Nadia, okay? You promise me?"

"Faer, what are you doing?"

"Promise me," I said.

"I promise!" she replied.

Ten.

"Nadia, it was a pleasure working with you."

Nine.

"Faer, what are you planning?!"

Eight.

Nadia hugged me tightly. "What I have to do."

Seven.

"Whatever you think you're doing, it isn't going to work," Sasha said.

Six.

"Tylin," I said. "You're not my Tylin, but if she were here, my wife, I would say, this is all for you. I don't know what the repercussions of this could be. But I'm taking a chance." I looked over at Sasha. "Like Albert said. A one percent chance of survival is better than a zero percent chance."

Five.

I looked over at Mircea, who had given me so much trouble. "I forgive you, Glitch. In fact, I forgive all of you. It's time for me to let go. I lost my wife, multiple times, and I'll never see her again. I will carry the love and memories for all of time. Now, and wherever I end up.

Four.

"This is madness! You'll be dead in seconds," Sasha growled.

"She's right," Tylin added. "We are superior. We destroyed your wife, Zyanya's husband, and now, your entire universe."

Three.

Mircea locked his eyes on me. "What an amazing game it was, Faer. Game over."

Two.

I looked at Zyanya and Nadia one final time, then at Albert.

"I am so sorry," he said. "This is all my fault."

"No," I said, placing my hand on his shoulder. This is not your fault. This is not my fault. This is their fault. But I can make it right. Thank you for everything."

I walked toward the machine, and placed my hand on it.

One.

"So you used my DNA, my molecular structure, to build this doomsday device, huh?"

Sasha stared. "Don't you dare!"

"Well maybe this device would like to listen to me, then. Maybe, because you thought creating such destruction using a mere copy of what I have gone through, just maybe, this machine will attune to my thoughts. My voice. My feelings."

Zero.

"TOO LATE!" Sasha screeched. "You're all going to be destroyed now!"

Nothing happened.

"I once read that a glass can be looked through both ways," I said, looking at my friends. "Remember that. But once the glass breaks, we are left with nothing but shards."

I glanced one final time at my friends, and closed my eyes. Then, there was an explosion that engulfed everyone and everything.

Since that moment, I am not quite sure where I am, or if anybody can even hear me. All I know is, I see them. I can see them moving forward with their lives.

I realized that the only way to stop mass destruction was to try and take over the machine. It was based on a copy of me, and my instability. So when the real thing, me, came in contact with it, the machine was easily responsive to my commands. I infiltrated the very workings of it. And just like Albert predicted in that notebook, I believe it cost me everything.

I used what they had built, and the explosion, to send Mircea, Tylin, and Sasha back to Mircea and Tylin's universe. Since Sasha's was destroyed, I figured the authorities on their universe would put two and two together, and take care of the situation.

I tried to take on the rest of the energy from the explosion. I thought about trying to bring back those we had lost, but was unsure of the ramifications. So I left that alone. I managed to contain the explosion to simply the building we were all at, and I got my friends safely away. I'm sure they were confused when they teleported miles away, but they figured it out.

I closed any and all rifts that could lead to future issues. Traveling to and from other universes was better off being impossible. Our universe, with our timelines, has more than enough of its own issues without inviting all the problems and people from other universes. And I finally managed to locate and destroy all traces of debris from alternate universes. Zyanya would be proud. I finally finished that mission from long ago.

Clearly, Mircea was right. There has been something wrong with me for quite some time. Whether that originated from the faulty time and space travel I endured working for Shard, or the fact that I had carried a time phone with me as I traveled, or something else unknown about me, even now, I have no idea. But whatever is wrong with me, whatever reason I was given such a gift, it was enough to save my friends. That is enough for me.

Zyanya and Albert took back Shard fairly quickly. The disappearance of Mircea brought fear to that local faction. Everyone listened to Albert and Zyanya as they picked up all the pieces.

Nadia is still with Shard. She's amazing. She helps stabilize the timelines daily.

I often think about that time Shard had me save Mircea from botulism. I thought he was an important man of the future. That is what Shard thought. But I guess that was just one of the many possible futures. It looks like Albert will be the man Shard thought Mircea to be.

Everything worked out for my friends. I don't regret my decision. It was either everyone dies, or I try this. I had to.

Even though she is forever gone, I did all of this for Tylin. She is the reason I found the strength and courage to do what had to be done. I thought of all the times in our marriage that she showed such selfless love. And chose this fate.

Where am I now? I'm looking through the glass. I can see them. I can't help them much, as I used all the power from that explosion to keep everyone safe, and to send the villains away. But what little energy I have saved up, I use for emergencies. I'll help them in the most dire of situations if they need me.

The glass is broken now. But if I can still see them, I wonder if they can find a way to see me? No matter. What's done is done. Time moves forward here, and I can only see through the shards of broken glass now.

From working for Shard, to seeing through the shards, my fate is locked in now. I will protect my friends. No matter the cost.

In order to understand my story, you needed to understand how I got here. And now you do.

Hello. My name is Faer.

I am currently lost, but content. I have much to live for. After losing my wife, finding her, then losing her again, I somehow managed to find friends that became like family, even in the face of such heartbreaking death. They care about me immensely.

I have had many questions answered throughout this journey, but I do have more questions now. If anybody receives this message, please, if I can't go back, I understand. I just want to understand where I am. I want to understand why I am here. But maybe no one can hear me. Maybe this entire message is nothing but a thought or idea endlessly floating through the universe.

For now, I understand what I need to do. Watch from afar. Send out this message. And hope. Even if you can't save me, just know that I'm out here trying to help where I can.

Life, sometimes, doesn't go the way we plan. Life is love. Life is loss. Life is many things, but right now, where I am, how I feel, I end this message with one final thought.

Life isn't Faer.

The Elders' Universe:

Agnor's Book

Agnor's Book
By: Keith Imbody

Table of Contents

Prologue

The majority of the following story takes place in deep space. It is unknown quite when, in time, it occurred. The exact location is farther out than any galaxy you have heard of. It all started when a band of three explorers got on a spaceship to locate a missing item for their newly appointed boss, Agnor. I'll spare you the boring part of the story. Agnor, on his home planet of L-VII, pronounced El-Vee, hired three freelance travelers to locate an important item that he thinks was stolen from him.

The planet of L-VII is inhabited by many different creatures, and humanoids. Travel through space and time became a lot easier once the humans and the Elders started working together. Oh, who are the Elders? Well, to save time, I will just say they are as powerful as superheroes. Strong beings that each have different powers. Where are they from, you ask? They have had horrible luck keeping a home planet for too long, but that is a story for another day.

There are humans, Elders, Hybrids, Zovvlers, Cragglers… basically any species you have, or have not, heard of, has at least visited the planet of L-VII by this point in time. And many have started families there.

The planet is beautiful, by the way. I highly doubt you will ever get the chance in your lifetime, as it is so far away, but if you do, definitely visit. The mountains sparkle every time the suns set. I am sure you have heard of the aurora borealis, right? Well the skies on L-VII offer a show arguably greater than that once every month or so. The natural elements are superior to Earth's, according to some creatures. But, I better get back to the story. Unfortunately, we are not here to talk about L-VII.

Agnor had a magical book. Well, he always told everyone it was magical. It was definitely important to him. Our three wannabe heroes just believed that it was magic, because why would they want to risk their lives for a boring old book?

Money. The answer is always money. And Agnor was the richest on the planet. But he was advanced in years, so his days of traveling were over.

According to Agnor, two crafty shadows made their way into his castle one night, and took his magical book. He declared that if the book was missing for too long, everyone would notice. No one knew what that cryptic message meant. And no one really wanted to find out.

The day after the book went missing, Agnor called an emergency meeting of the highest council. No one on the council dared to risk their lives for such a mission, but they knew of pretty much everyone on the planet. So they put together this team of three. They were convinced that this exact combination of people would get the job done. So let me quickly introduce you to them so we can get to the good part of the story.

First, they appointed Kaimi. She was just a human. Do not take offense to that. Humans are amazing. Powerful. Some of the strongest minds in the galaxy.

Secondly, they called on an Elder named Omar. His power was teleportation, quite similar to his distant relative Clory.

And finally, to everyone's surprise, they called on a Zovvler named Bruto. Not much to this day is known about the Zovvlers. They are humanoid...ish. They have pointy ears like an elf. They have only one eye. No nose. A mouth. Two arms, two legs, a tail, and, this is really cool, they have wings. Yes, they can fly. Oh, and I forgot to mention. They are green.

Bruto was adopted by Cragglers and brought to L-VII. But that's enough backstory for now.

Kaimi, Omar, and Bruto were chosen for this mission. And they all immediately accepted. Traveling was what everyone dreamed of doing. Although space travel was easily accessible, one needs money to travel. So a lot of time on L-VII was spent working just to save enough to go on a trip. Can you imagine that? Working for months just to be able to afford a week off? I guess some things never change.

Agnor was not only paying for this trip, he was also offering a generous reward for the three of them. Enough money to spend the rest of their lives traveling, at no cost to them. Anybody would jump at the chance to collect such a bounty. But this mission was dangerous, and Agnor made sure they knew that. The risk was so great, they might not even make it back alive.

Kaimi, Omar, and Bruto had never met each other, until the exact moment they were all called upon.

Now that you know about Agnor, L-VII, the magical book, Zovvlers, Elders, and the mission itself, I think I can throw the story over to Kaimi, Omar, and Bruto, as they are leaving L-VII to chase after the criminals that stole Agnor's book.

<u>Chapter One</u>
Ready, Set, Go

"Can you believe they chose us?" Kaimi smiled. She had dark brown hair with blonde highlights. "I have never been chosen for anything this special!"

Omar nodded. "I have heard tales of my distant relative Clory and his friends saving everyone from some sort of war that threatened reality itself. That is a lot to live up to."

Kaimi wheeled supplies onto a spaceship. Today was the day they would embark on their mission to save old Agnor's book. Omar carried a backpack, and the two of them sat down, awaiting departure.

Omar had black hair, tinted with blue and white highlights. He loved the color blue, which was evident in his choice of clothing. He also wore blue gloves. Kaimi wanted to ask him about them, but she held back, as they had just recently met, and she did not want to upset him.

Kaimi and Omar looked over at their new Zovvler friend, Bruto, who looked scared, standing at the door of the ship.

"Bruto," Kaimi said softly, "is everything okay?"

Bruto looked back outside, then toward Kaimi. He knew their language. He could understand it. But he was not that good at talking. "Home. Family."

"I know, buddy," Kaimi said, "I am going to miss my family and friends too. But this adventure, this is going to be so glorious."

Kaimi stood up and walked over to Bruto, who was hugging the entrance in terror.

"If you don't want to go," Kaimi whispered, "I will call it off. I can go talk to—"

Bruto let go of the wall and straightened himself into a soldier stance. He put his tiny green hand up to his forehead, saluting Kaimi.

"Captain Kaimi," Bruto said, in his deep, yet somehow shrill, voice.

Kaimi looked around. "Wait, I never agreed to that!"

Omar laughed. "Someone has to lead us, Kaimi. And it ain't going to be me."

Bruto smiled. "Chair."

He walked over to his chair and sat down. Kaimi shrugged.

"I don't know much about being a captain," Kaimi admitted. "How about we are all just equals on this ship. We all have strengths and weaknesses, and if we play our cards right, I think we might just compliment each other."

"Can we still call you captain?" Omar smirked.

Kaimi laughed. "Fine."

Bruto clapped his hands, and flapped his wings in agreement.

"Do you have everything you need, Bruto?" Kaimi asked.

"Me carry nothing. Own nothing. Free spirit."

"Well alright then!" Omar exclaimed. "Captain, shall we?"

Kaimi sat back down in her chair. They had everything they would need for this mission. Agnor had stocked this small spaceship with food for months, possibly years. Everything was ready. Everybody was set. And it was just about time to go.

Bruto looked at Kaimi and Omar as they buckled into their seats. They were all facing a window that was basically a viewscreen. Cameras facing the outside of the ship offered different angles of view. State of the art shields would protect them from attacks, and they had the best weapons the planet could offer.

Kaimi signaled for takeoff. The engines began to roar. Bruto closed his eye in fear.

"It's okay, Bruto," Omar said. "Look!"

Omar teleported from his chair, to the doorway. Then he stood by Bruto and smiled.

"No matter what happens, we got you. I promise."

Bruto smiled. Kaimi gave Omar a disapproving look.

"What?" Omar cried.

"We are about to take off!" Kaimi said sternly. "Teleport back into your seat. Stay buckled. Don't sabotage the mission before we even leave the ground! Wait. Don't sabotage the mission at all! Just please sit down!"

Omar smiled at Bruto as he teleported back into his seat. "Yes, captain!" he snickered.

Bruto laughed.

"Oh, be quiet," Kaimi said, forcing back laughter.

Bruto looked out the window, as they began their flight.

"Me brave?" he said, excitedly.

"Yes, very brave, Bruto," Omar agreed.

Bruto smiled, and watched on. The ground beneath them was getting farther and farther away. The three of them watched, with their eyes glued, as if they were watching the best movie ever.

Before they realized it, they were merely seconds away from being in space.

"Make Agnor proud!" Bruto yelled.

As they continued their journey into the sky, they saw so much space. And it was beautiful.

Bruto gasped. "Shiny hat!"

"What is he talking about?" Omar said, worriedly.

Bruto hit buttons on the console by his chair. He changed what they saw on the viewscreen. A camera on the back of the ship showed the entire planet from a distance.

"Wow, we are that far away already?" Omar asked.

"As a teleporter yourself, this should not shock you," Kaimi laughed.

"Shiny hat on L-VII!" Bruto exclaimed.

"Wait," Kaimi looked closer at the live view of their planet on the viewscreen. "No way! Omar, look!"

Omar could not see what they were talking about. He teleported from his chair to the viewscreen. And he finally saw what they saw.

"The lights!" Omar cried.

194

"Legend speaks of something called the aurora borealis back on planet Earth," Kaimi said. "But it is definitely not as beautiful as this."

The lights danced atop the planet of L-VII. Every color in the visible spectrum could be seen.

"Bruto, how did you see that before we switched the camera on the viewscreen?" Kaimi questioned. "Can you see through the ship?"

Bruto shrugged. "I special."

"Yes you are," Kaimi nodded. "Omar, are you ever going to stay seated? Or should I get used to this now?"

"We're free to roam now!" Omar said. "Aren't we?"

Bruto unbuckled, and hovered just off the ground over to Omar.

Kaimi shook her head. "Just be careful, boys."

"So, uh, captain," Omar said, quietly.

"Yes, Omar?"

"What is the game plan again?"

"Well, Agnor knows this space very well. So he uploaded a ton of maps and directions on where he thinks the criminal shadows went."

"And what if we end up going the wrong way?" Omar said.

Bruto flew up high, then back down to Kaimi. "Adventure!"

"Bruto gets it!" Kaimi said.

"I get that," Omar said, "truly, I do. And adventure is what I live for. But how do we stay on track? I would much rather aimlessly travel after we return Agnor's book. Not so much at stake, you know?"

"Agreed," Kaimi sighed. "Well, I guess we hope for the best, and make sure the course is set to the coordinates Agnor gave us."

"What is the ETA?" Omar asked.

"Seven days," Kaimi answered. "So we have a lot of time to waste. Let's make sure we see the sights, all the beautiful planets as we pass by, the stars, suns, even any space debris. But if you brought anything to read or play—"

"Me tell a story?" Bruto interrupted.

"Sure, buddy," Kaimi said.

<u>Chapter Two</u>
Bruto's Secret

"Zovvlers great species," Bruto said. "Need to be protected from evil."

"Buddy," Kaimi said, "what do you mean by that?"

"Me safe. Cragglers save me. But ancestors not so lucky."

"What happened?" Omar asked.

"Zovvlers home planet taken. Way before Bruto born. Evil creatures stole. Zovvlers forced to run."

"That's horrible! Who would do such an atrocious thing?"

Bruto frowned, and looked away.

"We relocate, spread across stars. History of Zovvlers fade. Me bring us all home. But if impossible, just want to meet Zovvler. Talk to Zovvler. Cragglers protect. Cragglers family. But somehow, Bruto sad."

Kaimi unbuckled her seatbelt and stood up. She walked over to Bruto, offering a hug. Bruto accepted.

"We will find a Zovvler on this mission," Kaimi said, reassuringly. "And if not on this mission, it will be our pleasure to continue this journey into the next mission."

"I agree," Omar said.

Bruto smiled. "Kaimi, Omar, family."

"What else do you know about the ancestry of Zovvlers?" Omar asked.

"Before planet overtaken, Zovvlers offer sanctuary to everyone. All welcome on home planet. Way back, hundred years, Zovvlers at prime. We host Space Olympics, have special events every third moon cycle. Home planet sound beautiful, but me never see it with own eye. Only in pictures."

"That sounds amazing," Kaimi smiled softly.

"They want me," Bruto frowned.

"Who wants you?" Omar asked.

"I special!" Bruto started to get tears in his eye. "They want me! Save Bruto! Please help Bruto!"

Just then, the ship shook.

"Someone is firing at us!" Omar exclaimed.

Kaimi looked out the viewscreen to see a ship half the size of theirs fly by.

"Everyone to your stations!" Kaimi yelled.

Omar teleported to his seat, while Bruto hovered to his, shaking in fear. Kaimi sat down, and tried to hail the other ship.

No answer.

Shots were fired again, and the other ship stopped directly by the viewscreen. Kaimi tried to hail them again.

Nothing.

They flew away, heading in the opposite direction.

"Well that was terrifying," Omar cried. "We should have fired back!"

Kaimi shook her head. "If it came down to it, I agree. However, we had no information. Who they were, what they wanted."

"Bruto," Bruto cried. "They want Bruto."

"It's okay, buddy," Kaimi sighed. "They are gone, and they were traveling the other way. Whether it was a warning because they were scared of us, or just a random bunch of mercenaries, we may never find that out."

Bruto nodded, still shaking.

"It will be okay," Kaimi said. "I promise."

"Family protect Bruto," Bruto sighed.

Kaimi nodded. "Omar, how are the shields looking?"

Omar pressed a couple buttons. "Barely damaged. All other diagnostics look good. I'm glad Agnor gave us such a good ship."

"We have to be ready," Kaimi said. "The weapons are a last resort, but if it comes down to it, we can't hesitate at the risk of our own lives. At the risk of the mission. We will always try to understand first. Maybe that ship was sent back by the shadow creatures as a warning. And if that is the case, we have a lot of enemies ahead of us. We will not surrender to them. We will find Agnor's book. We will earn the right to freely travel all the remaining days of our lives. And Bruto, we will find another Zovvler."

Bruto smiled. "Zovvlers have one more secret."

"What is it?" Omar asked.

"You promise, tell no one."

"I promise," Omar and Kaimi said in unison.

Bruto sighed. "Trust."

Bruto closed his eye. "Bruto can see with eye closed. Test."

Omar walked over to the viewscreen. "What is currently outside, Bruto?"

"Space," Bruto chuckled. "But, no, watch out! Kaimi, navigate ship! Big obstacle incoming!"

Omar stared out the window and saw nothing.

"Kaimi," Omar said, "do you see anything?"

Kaimi walked over to stand next to Omar. She squinted, trying to see anything in their way. They both turned from the viewscreen to look at Bruto, who still had his eye closed.

"Buddy, are you sure—"

The ship hit something. Omar turned around to look back at the viewscreen. Something was directly in front of them as Bruto predicted.

"Is it invisible?!" Kaimi cried. She ran to her seat. "I'm turning off the engines until we figure this out. We can't move forward if there is something blocking us."

Ripples from the shockwave of impact began to reveal the object in front of them.

"It's like it was intended to be invisible," Omar said. "Whatever shields it had left, I think we just broke them."

"Bruto," Kaimi said, "how can you possibly have seen that?"

Bruto opened his eye. He had a tear. "You mad at Bruto? Bruto bad?"

"No!" Kaimi exclaimed. "You were trying to show us, and help us. This is not your fault, Bruto. Okay?"

Bruto hovered over to the viewscreen. "Ship?"

"Is it a ship?" Omar asked.

Kaimi walked back over to join her friends. As the object was now fully visible.

"If that is a ship," Kaimi said somberly, "then the crew abandoned it a long time ago."

Chapter Three
Derelict

"Should we just fly around it?" Omar asked.

"That would be the smart thing to do," Kaimi said. "And we have to stay on course for the mission."

"Then why do I want to stay and explore the ship?" Omar sighed. "I just said earlier how we should stay on track."

"Well," Kaimi said, "we could try to safely analyze from our ship."

"Or," Omar smiled.

He teleported away.

"Omar, no!" Kaimi cried.

Bruto looked at Kaimi. "Omar went to explore."

Kaimi stared at Bruto, then back toward the ship. "Is he crazy? Why would he do that? I want to be on that ship!"

"Kaimi?" Bruto said. "Kaimi acting funny. Omar too."

"Bruto," Kaimi said. "Use the ship's teleport to send me over there with Omar. You stay here as a fail-safe. Bring us back in five minutes if you don't hear from us, okay? The first switch teleports us out and the second switch retrieves us."

"Bruto want to join!"

"Bruto, please!" Kaimi cried.

"Me understand," Bruto sighed.

Kaimi walked over to the teleportation pad. Bruto threw the switch that sent Kaimi to the other ship with Omar. Bruto began to cry.

"Why Bruto always get left behind? Me want to explore. Me want to be with friends."

Just then, Bruto heard a weird noise. He looked out the viewscreen, and he saw the other ship start to light up.

"Ship works?" Bruto whispered.

The back of the ship went dark, and what looked like a small explosion could be seen.

"Friends!"

What first looked like an explosion, was revealed to be the thrusters, turning on after all the time this ship had been abandoned. The ship began to slowly fly out of view.

"Wait, do not leave Bruto!"

As the ship slowly flew to the left, beginning to leave his view, Bruto quickly hovered over to the viewscreen to try and see what was going on, then he quickly hovered back to the teleportation controls.

Bruto closed his eye, and gasped. "Explosion!"

He threw the other switch, teleporting his friends back to their own ship, safely. He flew to Kaimi's chair, and turned the engines back on. Now that the other ship was out of the way, Bruto knew he could just fly straight. He was no pilot, but he knew he had to get out of there. The ship began to move swiftly forward, as Bruto pressed buttons.

Disoriented, Kaimi and Omar stood up.

"Bruto!" Omar cried. "We were so close to the treasure!"

"Yeah, Bruto, we were going to find all the gold! It was just about ours! Why did you bring us back here?!"

Just then, a huge explosion rocked the entire ship. The impact sent the ship flying faster.

"Out of control!" Bruto cried. "Captain, help!"

Without thinking, Kaimi ran over to her seat. Bruto got up and tried to get to his own seat, but that was a bit difficult as the ship was starting to spiral faster.

"Bruto! I am so sorry!" Kaimi cried. "I don't know what any of that was!"

Omar got to his seat and sat down. He said nothing.

"Me understand why," Bruto said sadly.

Pressing buttons, and trying to keep her cool, Kaimi looked over at Omar, then Bruto.

"Omar, hit the second button on your panel. Bruto, you as well. We have to stabilize the ship. It's still spinning uncontrollably."

Everyone obeyed, and the turning slowed. Still a bit out of control, Kaimi pressed a sequence of buttons and managed to regain control. She took a deep breath. She checked the coordinates and frowned.

"This is impossible," Kaimi cried. "How is this even possible?!"

"What's wrong?" Omar asked.

"The coordinates!" Kaimi exclaimed.

"What about them?!"

"They say we are thirty days away now."

"But weren't we only seven days away before?!" Omar said, panicking.

Kaimi shook her head. "What happened? Can someone explain any of this to me? Omar, why were we even on that ship? Were we trying to fly it?!"

"I think so," Omar admitted.

"Bruto was forsaken," Bruto cried. "Me watch as family try to abandon. Bruto left alone on ship."

"But Bruto, we would never," Kaimi said, tears in her eyes.

"But somehow, we did," Omar sighed. "Thinking back, the moment I knew that ship was there, I felt... greedy. I just wanted nothing more than to explore it. At any cost. Without having all the information. That's reckless, even for me."

"Now that you mention it, that is exactly how I felt," Kaimi admitted. "Why did I feel so strongly about getting on that ship?"

"Kaimi," Omar said, scared, "after we were both on that ship, we had the sudden need to find some sort of golden treasure. We were about to abandon our mission, our friend, everything. And for what? A fraction of the treasure that Agnor promised us? That is not even logical."

"Bruto, that wasn't us," Kaimi said. "I don't understand how or why, but something must have overtaken our minds."

"But it tried to destroy us," Omar added. "It wanted us out of the picture."

"It was a trap!" Kaimi exclaimed. "On the heels of that other attack, we just happen to bump into that

205

invisible ship? Someone is doing this to stop us. To deter us. I fear they left an entire string of obstacles to stop us from finding Agnor's book."

"Well we should be safe now since we are so off course!" Omar said sarcastically.

"Bruto, I am sorry," Kaimi said.

"I am sorry too," Omar added.

"Bruto understand. Me forgive. Not your fault."

"How can we protect ourselves from something like that in the future?" Omar asked.

"Bruto, you weren't affected, when we were," Kaimi said. "If that happens again, will you protect us?"

Bruto saluted. "Me protect family."

Omar smiled. "Let's hope that doesn't happen again. Blindly chasing an unattainable treasure, that is doomed to fail."

Kaimi hesitantly laughed, and started to question the validity of the current mission. But she kept those thoughts to herself.

"I still don't understand how we were knocked over three weeks off course," Omar said.

"Me pressed all the buttons," Bruto said. "Right after me teleport you back."

Kaimi looked over at the teleport switches. "Bruto, did you remember to change those back after using the teleport?"

"Me did not," Bruto admitted.

"Oh, Bruto," Kaimi sighed. "With all the chaos, the ship spinning out of control, and the explosion, that must be how we got so far away. The ship accidentally teleported itself. I didn't think that was possible."

"Bruto sorry," Bruto said. "Me want to be helpful."

"You are helpful, Bruto," Kaimi said. She got out of her seat and walked over to the teleportation panel. "Let me just switch these back."

"Kaimi, wait!" Bruto yelled.

Kaimi tried to hit the switches. Electricity coursed through them, knocking her back. She stood up.

"Guys," Omar cried. "Something is happening!"

Outside, they could see what looked like a vortex of objects whirling around them. Stars. Planets. Debris. Kaimi walked over to her seat, a bit disoriented. She sat down to look at the coordinates.

"No!" she exclaimed.

In horror, she watched, as the distance between where they were now going, and where they were supposed to go, became greater. And greater.

"How do we stop this?!" Kaimi cried.

"What is it?!" Omar asked.

"We are now months, years, decades?! Decades from our original coordinates!"

Bruto quickly hovered over to the teleportation panel and managed to change both switches back. "Me save us."

As everything outside came to a stop, Kaimi hesitantly looked down at the coordinates of the ship.

"I have no idea where we are," Kaimi admitted.

Bruto and Omar walked over to see what she saw. Where it once showed a map of their position, leading to Agnor's book, it now said one single word.

Error.

Chapter Four
Lost

"Nothing but stars outside," Omar sighed. "What do we do, captain?"

Kaimi said nothing. She just stared at the screen where the coordinates once were.

Bruto saw how sad his friends were, so he just closed his eye, and mumbled, "Bruto fix."

The error screen began to glitch. Coordinates could be seen for just a split second, and then they were gone again.

"What was that?" Kaimi wondered. She sat forward and pressed a button. Omar walked over to her. Bruto still had his eye closed.

Again, the screen glitched to show numbers.

"Fifty-seven billion light-years?!" Omar cried.

Just then, someone tried to hail their ship. Kaimi looked at Omar, and they answered the call. A humanoid figure could be seen, sitting in a chair, covered in shadow.

"You dare trespass?!" it bellowed.

"No sir," Kaimi said, holding back fear. "We are lost. We mean no disrespect to you or your people. We just want to get back on track. We have been thrown off our mission."

"What mission?" boomed the voice. "Mission to destroy us?"

"No!" Kaimi exclaimed. "We mean no harm! What is your name?"

"I am the protector of the farthest corners of space. I am what some would call The Final Guardian. What lies beyond is so dangerous, I make sure no one stumbles into the void. For once one enters, one can never return. How far away from home are you?"

Kaimi frowned. "I am not sure, sir. My coordinates simply gave me an error message. Now they are saying we are fifty-seven billion light-years away."

The Final Guardian flinched. He looked at a screen, and shook his head.

"Human. Elder. Zovvler."

Kaimi looked at her friends, then back at the viewscreen. "What about us?"

"The three of you have traveled way off course. Your lifespans are far too short to complete your mission now. Even the Elder's lifespan is too short. How could you get so lost so quickly?"

Kaimi explained what happened. She was nervous. Unsure if this creature was trustworthy. But what other choice did she have?

The Final Guardian put a hand to his chin. "We could offer you a deal."

"What could we possibly have to offer you?"

Omar frowned. "We have nothing much of value."

The Final Guardian sat back, still covered in shadow. Kaimi wondered who, or what, he was. But she didn't dare ask him such a question.

"Your ship," The Final Guardian began, "is powerful. That would be quite the payment. However, that would be impossible as you need it to travel back. I have something else in mind."

Bruto's eye opened. It was bloodshot. But no one noticed.

"The Final Guardian needs some amusement. So, here is my offer for you. I will reverse the process that brought you here. I will send you directly back to where you came from. You will be just as close as you were. And I only ask one thing in return. Give me the Zovvler."

"What?!" Kaimi exclaimed. "No way!"

"Why are you so quick to deny me?" The Final Guardian bellowed. "Don't you want to complete your mission?"

"Yes!" Kaimi said, angrily, "but our mission includes all three of us. I am sorry, sir. We can not accept this arrangement."

"Suit yourself," The Final Guardian said. "I am more powerful than you could imagine. But I am also just. I will not help you, but I will not harm you. Turn around, and begin your fifty-seven billion light-year journey."

"Is there nothing else we can offer you, sir?" Omar chimed in.

The Final Guardian sat back. "No, I don't believe so. Perhaps your friend over there has something to say. His eye doesn't look so good."

"Bruto!" Kaimi ran over to him. "What's wrong?"

"Bruto scared you abandon him again. Bruto see life stuck out here. Fear so bad, strain eye. Eye hurt. I hurt."

"What do we do?!" Kaimi asked, nervously.

"There is one thing you could do," The Final Guardian interrupted.

"No!" Omar yelled. "Respectfully, sir, leave us alone. You can not have our friend. What do you want with him anyway?!"

"What do I want with a Zovvler? One of the most interesting and powerful creatures ever?"

"Who are you, really?" Kaimi inquired.

The Final Guardian sighed. "I will tell you, but then I think you might lose your friend."

"Bruto scared," Bruto cried. "Eye need help."

"You said there is one thing we can do. What is it?" Kaimi asked.

The Final Guardian sighed. "Bruto, close your eye."

"Bruto scared to close eye. Pain hurt."

"Bruto, trust me. I understand your pain. Close your eye."

Bruto obeyed.

"Think of your home planet. Think of your friends. Think of what makes you calm."

Bruto sighed. "Bruto want peace. Bruto see home planet. Looks just like pictures. Bruto think of Cragglers that adopt him. Bruto think of happy life. Bruto think of future, travel forever with friends. Bruto think of friends. Kaimi. Omar. Bruto feel better now. The Final Guardian is friend?"

211

"How do you know so much about Zovvlers?" Kaimi asked, skeptically.

The Final Guardian cleared his throat. He began to step out of the shadow that had covered him this entire time.

Bruto opened his eye. "Bruto feel better now. Thank you, Guardian."

"I never reveal who I truly am," The Final Guardian admitted. "And my intentions were not true. I don't want the Zovvler because I need amusement. I want Bruto to stay with me, because..."

Now finally in the light, the crew saw The Final Guardian as he truly was.

He was a Zovvler.

<u>Chapter Five</u>
Guardian

"My name is actually Guardian," the newly revealed Zovvler said.

"Zovvler!" Bruto exclaimed. "You talk well for Zovvler! Kaimi! Omar! Found Zovvler! Me so happy!"

"I don't understand," Kaimi cried. "Why is there a Zovvler billions and billions of light-years out here in space?"

"Banishment," Guardian sighed.

"By Zovvlers?!" Omar cried.

"No," Guardian said. "By the ones that overtook our home world. A lot of us got away, but unfortunately, they caught me. They were experimenting with technology. With us. Some of my friends died. And some, like me, were lucky enough to survive, albeit fifty-seven billion light-years away."

"But how do you have a ship?" Kaimi asked.

"They put me on a ship. They gave me provisions. And cloning technology. They wanted to see how far they could send me, and they wanted to see if I could survive the journey back. Or maybe they just wanted to banish me. Using teleportation technology that I'm pretty sure they stole, they sent this ship away, with me in it."

"How long have you been out here?!" Kaimi asked.

"How long ago was the planet overtaken?" Guardian inquired, looking at Bruto.

"Me think nearly hundred years?" Bruto guessed.

"You lose time after the first ten," Guardian said. "I have no idea why I am still alive. This ship is on the brink of destruction. But I have called myself The Final Guardian, as I do believe there is a void beyond this space."

"Have you met a lot of different creatures out here?" Omar asked.

"Some, yes," Guardian said. "But I have met some treacherous beings as well. Some terrifyingly evil Elders. Some nasty humans. But Bruto, you're the first Zovvler I have seen in all these years."

"But how is anybody traveling out this far?" Kaimi asked. "That is what I don't understand."

"The way I see it," Guardian said, "given enough time, anybody is eventually able to travel anywhere out into this vast greatness of space. Alternatively, I have met some amazing heroes. Maybe you have heard of them. Elders named Trolk, Gleck, and Clory."

"Clory is my distant relative!" Omar said excitedly.

"They wandered too far," Guardian said. "They were just as lost as you three. I like to think I saved their lives because I sent them back in the other direction, away from the void."

"What were they doing out here?" Omar asked.

"They were trying to find a missing book. They never knew I was abandoned or stranded. I just played the part of The Final Guardian. Because that was all I had."

"Wait, a missing book?" Kaimi said, shocked. "Agnor's book?"

"I never got the name of it," Guardian admitted.

Omar stared at Kaimi. "Maybe it is just a coincidence. There are many books in the universe. There must be more than one significantly important one."

Kaimi nodded. "I guess that's a question for another time anyway. Guardian, how did they get back fifty-seven billion light-years? Did you have anything to do with it?"

Guardian shook his head. "No. I have no idea. I just hope they found the book and actually got back home. That book sounded crucial to their mission."

"You said you could reverse the process that brought us here," Omar said. "That you could send us back. Can you actually?"

Guardian sighed. "No," he said somberly.

"Why did you lie?" Kaimi asked.

"I am sorry," Guardian said. "I was hoping you would agree to leave Bruto with me. I miss my people. I just wanted someone to talk to that would understand. Once Bruto knew I was a Zovvler, I thought he might choose me over you. And once that plan fell through, I had a change of heart. I showed you all who I am. But lying to you was not the answer. I am sorry."

"So you are not as powerful as you say you are," Omar said.

"Other than my Zovvler abilities, unfortunately, I can't do much of anything."

"Guardian join us?" Bruto interrupted.

Kaimi looked at Bruto, then at Guardian, who was still displayed on the viewscreen.

"Guardian, do you want to get out of here?" Kaimi asked.

"There isn't much left for an old Zovvler like me," Guardian said.

"What is the lifespan of a Zovvler?" Omar asked.

"Hundreds of years, in the best of conditions," Guardian said. "I am afraid my life has been cut short being out here for nearly a hundred years now. Time is not kind when it is all you have and you are alone."

"You could travel with us," Kaimi said. "For adventure. Help us find Agnor's book." She leaned into the viewscreen and whispered, "I think Bruto needs you."

Guardian sighed. "In all my years out here, I have done soul searching. I have met both beautiful and hideous creatures. I'm talking about their souls and who they are, not how they look outwardly. And in all this time I have been so alone. I have never had a chance to be reunited with my people. It has also been forever since I had a friend. So, yes. I would love to join you."

"Bruto meet Zovvler! Bruto travel with species!"

"What about your ship?" Kaimi asked.

"Like I said, there isn't much left. You can strip it for parts or power, but I don't think it is worth it."

"Can we just take the cloning technology?" Kaimi asked. "That should help the food rations to last longer.

Especially since there are four of us now instead of three."

Guardian nodded. "Again, I do apologize for trying to deceive you."

Bruto looked at Kaimi, Omar, then Guardian. "Family forgive you."

Taken aback, Guardian nodded again. "I hope I can be a positive addition to your crew."

"I have no doubt about that," Kaimi said.

Omar teleported to Guardian's ship. The two of them disconnected the cloning technology and they were both teleported back.

"Fifty-seven billion light-years," Kaimi said. "Every journey has to begin somewhere. Let's set a course toward home."

Chapter Six
Scrounger

"Which way is home?" Omar sighed.

"Not that way," Guardian said, looking toward his ship, and the possible void beyond.

"So we go the other way," Kaimi said.

She turned the ship around, and they began their long journey. Not much happened the first couple of days. The crew saw some space debris, but that was basically all they saw, other than the vastness of space outside.

By the third day, everyone on the ship was tired of seeing nothing but distant stars.

"Is there any chance at all there is a planet out here?" Omar asked.

"This far?" Guardian said. "I guess, it's possible. But I don't think so."

"Can we just mess with the teleport systems again, Kaimi?" Omar wondered.

"That's too dangerous," Kaimi said. "We might get thrown even farther away from home."

Omar shook his head. "Permission to speak freely, captain?"

"Of course," Kaimi said.

"What is the point of not trying? Can we even get any worse off than we are now? We aren't going to make this journey back alive without taking shortcuts. No one here has such a lifespan."

Kaimi sighed. She wanted to agree with him, because she, too, felt defeated. But she had the weight of acting captain on her shoulders.

"Being lost is definitely not ideal," she began, "and the mission is clearly second priority now, at least until we are back in the same quadrant of space. But, isn't this kind of what we wanted? Adventure? To travel the stars?"

"I love the sentiment, and I agree with it, but we are flying aimlessly. I want to find actual adventure."

Kaimi sighed. She nodded. She looked at Bruto and Guardian.

"Adventure," Bruto said. He closed his eye.

Just then, something shot at the ship.

"What was that?!" Kaimi cried, looking around at the viewscreen and the controls. She saw nothing.

"Look!" Omar exclaimed.

A ship about the same size as theirs zipped by.

"How is it moving like that?!" Kaimi said. "That is one evasive ship. We aren't even firing at them, so why are they acting like that?!"

"Hail incoming," Omar said. "Captain?"

"Let them through."

"It seems to be sound only," Omar said.

Kaimi nodded.

"State your intentions," a voice said.

"Hello?" Kaimi answered. "We are not your foes."

"Not my foes?" the voice laughed. "The only people out this far into space are either looking for trouble, or they are very lost. So which one is it?"

"We are not looking for trouble, I can tell you that," Kaimi said. "What is your name?"

"There is no need for me to have a name," it answered. "For I was born alone. I live alone. I travel alone. And I will one day die alone. But not today. For I think today, you will be doing the dying."

"Wait!" Kaimi said, frantically. "State your intentions!"

"This is my space," the voice growled. "I do not have to answer to you. I need your ship. Your food. Everything."

It fired more shots.

"Scavenger," Omar said quietly.

"No," Guardian said softly. "It's a scrounger."

"Please!" Omar said. "We are trying to reason with you!"

"I don't reason with outsiders," it said. "And everyone is an outsider to me."

It cut the communication.

Guardian had a concerned look on his face.

"What's wrong?" Kaimi asked.

"I think I saw this being many years ago."

Bruto opened his eye.

"Me see," Bruto said. "Scrounger lonely. Scrounger need family!"

"No, buddy," Guardian said. "I had an encounter with it, yes, I remember now, five years ago! It had traveled out of this space, and toward the void. It wanted to take my ship. Other travelers had warned me of it. They told me about the Scrounger. How it enters life alone. It just exists. It lives an entire life of solitude. Feeding off others. Anything and everything. That's where it got its current ship. From someone else."

"Bruto understand," Bruto said. "Evil Scrounger."

"I never realized that the creature that wanted my ship was actually the Scrounger itself," Guardian admitted. "We better become evasive ourselves, fairly quickly, because I have a bad feeling it can, and will, overtake this entire ship."

The ship was continuously attacked from all different sides.

"Scrounger is pure evil, with no intention of change. It will tear us all apart. It has no morality. It shows no mercy."

"Are we firing back?" Omar asked.

Kaimi tried to hail the other ship.

There was no answer. Shots continued to fire at them.

"It won't listen to reason," Guardian said.

"How did you ward this monster off last time?!" Kaimi asked, trying to navigate the ship out of the clutches of the Scrounger.

Shots continued.

Guardian shook his head. "I was afraid to do this a second time. But it seems we have no choice."

Guardian closed his eye, and the firing ceased. The ship slowly came into view, now directly facing the viewscreen. It flew closer, until the crew could see the Scrounger inside the window of the other ship.

Omar walked up to the viewscreen.

"Be careful, Omar!" Kaimi warned her friend.

"Why isn't it moving?" Omar wondered.

"Guardian send thoughts," Bruto said. "That how Guardian face Scrounger last time by void and live."

"Sending thoughts?" Kaimi said.

"Zovvlers very powerful," Bruto said. "Always have more secrets."

"Is it working then?" Kaimi asked, staring at the ship directly in front of them.

Guardian fell to the ground and screamed.

"Guardian!" Kaimi cried.

Omar teleported over to him, and the Scrounger's head tilted at the sight.

"Omar, no," Guardian whispered.

"What is wrong?! What happened?!" Omar cried.

"Last time I saw this creature, I sent it thoughts of treasure far away from the void. So it disengaged to try and find it. I had no idea what it was capable of. And I had no idea how lucky I was to survive that encounter."

"What do you mean?"

"It can mimic what it sees. The thoughts of a greater bounty somewhere else were powerful enough to send it away last time. By the time Scrounger realized of my trickery, it had moved on to another victim, forgetting about me for the moment. But it has now learned how to imitate my power of sending thoughts. It remembers me. And it is angry at me. That is why it revealed its secret to me right now. It wants us to know what it can do. Just to taunt us. To mock us. You shouldn't have teleported over to me."

The Scrounger disappeared from its ship.

"Where did it go?!" Omar cried.

"Right here," Scrounger said, standing right next to Omar.

Chapter Seven
Teleport

Scrounger looked around. "Nicer than I thought! I'll definitely be taking this ship."

"Bruto stop you!" Bruto cried.

Scrounger laughed. "You're just a Zovvler. I know the lies your species have uttered throughout the galaxies. I know all your secrets now. Guardian over here was kind enough to share everything, and I mean, everything, with me."

"You are one ugly beast," Omar blurted out, staring at Scrounger. "What are you, like, a dog?"

Scrounger growled at Omar.

Guardian whispered, "Scrounger, please."

"Please what? Offer mercy? No. Enough chatter. It's time you all evacuated my ship. If you don't leave, I'll force you all out."

"And go where?!" Omar demanded. "Why don't you just leave us alone?"

"Elder," Scrounger sighed. "I have a bit of history with your kind too. Does the name Clory mean anything to you?"

Omar said nothing.

Unbeknownst to Scrounger, Kaimi had been covertly pressing buttons the entire time.

"Clory, and his little friends, had an encounter with me some time ago. I nearly captured their ship. I was moments away from destroying those vile creatures, when they bested me."

"And how did they do that?" Omar asked.

"I would never tell you that," Scrounger said, laughing. "Taunting is so fun. Besides, tricks only work on me once. So even if I were to tell you, it would be worthless information."

Kaimi had her hand hovering above a newly revealed big red button. "Go back to your ship, or I'll destroy it."

Scrounger laughed. "Fool! Why would I care? Actually, why don't you all go on that ship?" A giant smile began to cover his wolf-like face, showing all his layers of teeth. "I promise not to destroy you. Much."

"Leave," Kaimi said. "I will not ask again."

Scrounger huffed, and looked over at Guardian. He picked him up with his left hand. "You listen to me. Leave my ship. Go somewhere else. Or I will destroy your friend Guardian."

"No!" Bruto cried. "Bruto finally meet Zovvler. Leave friend alone!"

Bruto rushed toward Scrounger, who backhanded him across the ship.

"Bruto!" Kaimi cried.

Bruto crashed onto the teleport pad. He immediately disappeared.

Guardian was so weak, he couldn't react to anything.

"I have grown impatient and tired of your pathetic games. You will all be destroyed by my hand."

225

He began to crush Guardian. He threw him at the wall. He trained his eyes on Omar.

"Clory should have surrendered to me. The Elders never should have become as powerful as they are. My revenge for Clory will be had today. Omar, you are nothing. Your people are nothing. After I destroy you and all your friends, I will take this ship, and search the entire cosmos until I have found Clory, and I have ended his miserable existence. I will then begin the decimation of all Elders, followed by every other species that has wronged me. Zovvlers. Humans. Cragglers. No one will survive."

"All of this for what? For revenge? What do you get out of such destruction?"

"Peace," Scrounger laughed.

He rushed toward Omar, who teleported to the other side of the ship. Scrounger, being able to mimic his ability now, followed suit. As the two of them were teleporting around the ship, Kaimi checked for life signs on the other ship. There were none.

"Where could Bruto be?" she mumbled.

As Omar and Scrounger continued to chase each other, Guardian slowly found the strength to crawl over to Kaimi.

"He is safe," Guardian said.

"Where?" Kaimi cried.

"He is safe," Guardian reiterated. He whispered something to Kaimi, and she pressed buttons on the console.

Omar accidentally teleported right next to Kaimi, scaring her, knocking her out of her chair.

Scrounger teleported into the chair, and cried, "Fire!"

He pressed the big red button, sending out a missile that blew up his own ship.

"Oh no," Scrounger laughed. "I hope Bruto wasn't on that ship. Bruto be so dead!"

"Do not mock my friend!" Kaimi yelled, standing up.

Scrounger got out of Kaimi's chair. "My dear," he hissed, "mocking is what I do."

He looked over toward Guardian. "So, buddy. Are you going to tell them the truth about Zovvlers, or should I?"

"You have done enough," Guardian whispered. "It is time you go."

"Where?!" Scrounger growled. "Someone destroyed my ship! I was never leaving, Guardian. This is my home now. Why don't you just do us a favor, and shut it?"

Guardian smiled. "As you wish. I just needed time."

He closed his eye, and began to float off the ground. Still weak from everything, Guardian began to form a shield around himself, Omar, and Kaimi.

"Oh no you don't!" Scrounger bellowed.

He rushed at Kaimi, knocking her out of the range of the shield.

"I'm done," Scrounger said. "Nuisance after nuisance!" He raised his hand in the air, and the edge of his fingers became sharp as claws. "Human. The easiest one to destroy. Feeble. Worthless. Die at my

227

hand, Kaimi. And do not fret. Your crew will all suffer immensely."

As Scrounger's hand moved toward Kaimi's heart, Omar teleported himself between the two of them. He managed to knock Scrounger back, but only for a moment. Scrounger looked around, and ran over to the teleportation pad.

"You have not seen the last of me," he growled.

Omar went to run toward him, but Kaimi pulled him back. "Let him go."

"But what if he lands where Bruto landed?" Omar cried.

Kaimi smiled. "Space is large. And Bruto is safe."

Scrounger punched the teleportation pad in anger. He immediately disappeared.

Chapter Eight
Displaced

"Where did you send him?" Omar asked.

"As close to the void as I could, thanks to Guardian's direction."

Guardian landed on the ground and turned his protective shield off.

"That was new," Kaimi said.

"Zovvlers have many secrets," Guardian smiled.

"But where is Bruto?" Omar asked.

"The teleportation pad was pretty messed up," Kaimi said. "That's why we haven't been using it much. But when Bruto fell onto it, before I could reconfigure it for Scrounger, I believe he didn't go far at all. Bruto is safe. Guardian?"

"That is quite true," Guardian said. "In fact, I don't think he went anywhere."

"Then where is he?"

Guardian closed his eye. "Bruto? Can you hear me?"

"Bruto hear," a voice said. Everyone could hear him talking. "Bruto scared. Confused. Where is Bruto?"

"You are here," Guardian said.

"It dark," Bruto cried. "Me see nothing. Bruto die?"

"No, buddy! You are a very lucky Zovvler."

"Please bring Bruto back. Me hate this dark. Remind Bruto of lonely feelings."

"I am not quite sure where you are," Guardian admitted. "But I am glad you can hear me."

"Bruto's friends all okay?"

"We are!" Omar exclaimed.

"It's gonna be alright," Kaimi added.

While Guardian's eye remained closed, Omar and Kaimi looked at each other, then back at Guardian.

"What me do?" Bruto asked. "If Bruto fall on teleport pad, me have to land somewhere."

Guardian was concentrating. "I am trying to pinpoint your location. Kaimi, can you please go to the diagnostics and tell me how many life forms are currently on this ship?"

Kaimi obeyed. She sat down, and looked at the numbers. "That's impossible," she said.

"What is it?" Guardian asked.

"It's fluctuating. Three. Four. Three. Four."

"I was afraid of this," Guardian sighed. "We have to move quickly."

"Bruto scared!"

"We have time, buddy," Guardian said. "We will save you."

"Save him from what?" Kaimi asked.

"Bruto, being such a special creature himself, a Zovvler, may have accidentally displaced himself from our reality. He is in limbo right now, between this reality and the next."

"But Bruto no see another reality. Bruto only see dark."

"You had a rough landing," Guardian said. "Maybe you're completely displaced between both realities. You're not in either, but have access to both."

"Bruto not scared of your words," Bruto said.

"Buddy, what was that?" Guardian asked.

"Bruto not scared of the lies you whisper and scream."

"What lies?" Kaimi whispered.

"Bruto smart!"

"Who is he talking to?!" Kaimi asked.

"I have no idea," Guardian said. "I can't hear anybody else. But clearly, he can."

"Me found true family, twice," Bruto continued. "Zovvlers abandon Bruto! Cragglers save! Me secretly angry with Zovvlers. Abandon family. Me left at orphanage alone. Months of sadness. Until Cragglers finally save. No tell Bruto Cragglers evil! Bruto refuse lies!"

"Bruto, can you hear me?" Guardian asked.

"Cragglers not problem!" Bruto continued. "Zovvlers leave Bruto to suffer. Cragglers save, just like friends. Why Kaimi try to hurt Bruto with insults?"

Kaimi's eyes widened. "Bruto, that isn't me!"

A frown appeared on Guardian's face. "Oh no."

"What is it?!" Kaimi cried.

"The other reality is becoming stronger to Bruto. There must be a Kaimi in the other reality saying these things to him. Where he is hearing from keeps changing. He hears this reality and the next."

"Bruto, please! I don't know enough about Cragglers to be saying such things."

"Kaimi," Bruto cried. "Kaimi end friendship over miscommunication? Bruto misunderstand. Kaimi want Bruto to leave forever?"

Kaimi began to tear up. "Buddy, no!"

"Bruto lose family again. Guardian. Omar. Where you go? Bruto feel lonely. Bruto only see dark. Me feel weak. Bruto ready to let go. Darkness overtake Bruto."

"We are here!" Omar yelled.

"Bruto, close your eye, concentrate, you belong to this reality," Guardian stated.

"Bruto eternally sad. Cragglers? Do Cragglers hear and save Bruto? No. Bruto too lost. Me sorry, Cragglers. Me sorry, Agnor. Kaimi, me forgive mean words. Omar. You funny. Bruto call you his brother. Guardian. Help lead friends to Agnor's book. Bruto fail. Bruto submit to defeat. Kaimi. Me confused why you hate Cragglers. Why you hate Bruto. But Bruto still believe in you. Captain. Bruto be dismissed?"

"Bruto, please!" Kaimi cried. "Guardian. What's happening to him?"

"He is surrendering," Guardian sighed. "He is surrendering to the space between realities. If we can't convince him to choose one, he will be lost forever."

"He thinks we abandoned him!" Kaimi cried. "He thinks I am talking bad about the very species that adopted him! Why would I even do that?"

"Perhaps Cragglers are bad in this other reality," Guardian said. "Or maybe Bruto has his own fears about them, and he is listening to his own thoughts, magnified by the Kaimi from the other side."

"Kaimi?" Bruto said softly. "Is Bruto dismissed?"

"No!" Kaimi screamed. "Bruto is most definitely not dismissed! We love you. This reality needs you. Please hear me!"

Kaimi walked over to Guardian. She reached out her hand. Guardian took it. Omar followed suit, taking Guardian's other hand.

"Bruto," Kaimi said sternly. "As captain, I demand that you return to this ship immediately. Your duty is to this crew. Not to surrender. You are part of this family. Of this reality. And of this mission. Hear your family calling out to you, Bruto. Family will always protect Bruto."

"Kaimi?" Bruto cried. "No hate Bruto?"

"Never!" Kaimi answered. "Bruto, you are family. We all love you."

"Where is Bruto?" Bruto cried.

"Close your eye, Bruto," Guardian said. "You are stronger than you know."

"Bruto close eye, but me see nothing with eye open, so make no difference."

"Yes, it does," Guardian said. "Choose this reality. Feel this reality. Follow our voices. We are family, Bruto."

"Bruto try," Bruto said softly.

"Think of the shiny hat back on L-VII!" Omar said. "The beautiful, magnificence of the dancing lights!"

"Bruto love shiny hat!"

"And remember when you were so brave, even though Omar and I had lost our way," Kaimi said. "You saved us from that derelict ship just before it exploded. You were our hero, Bruto!"

"Bruto like memories. Bruto concentrate."

233

"Okay," Guardian said. "Since you landed between realities, this might be difficult. But it's our only hope. Kaimi. Set the teleportation pad to the previous configurations, when Bruto left us."

Kaimi let go of Guardian's hand, and walked over to her chair. She hit a couple buttons. The ship remembered the previous configurations, which was a lifesaver, because Kaimi could not remember them herself.

"Are you sure the configurations are accurate?" Guardian asked. "We don't want to bring back the wrong being."

"Yeah, like Scrounger," Omar added.

Kaimi nodded. "The ship remembered."

"Omar, carefully go flip the second switch on the teleportation panel," Guardian said. "That brings things back, right?"

"Yes," Kaimi answered.

"Is it safe?" Omar asked Kaimi, letting go of Guardian's hand and walking to the teleportation panel. "Last time, these switches caused issues. And with everyone misusing this device, I'm afraid to cause harm."

"It has to be fine," Kaimi said. "This has to work."

Omar took a deep breath.

"This is it," Guardian said. "Bruto, are you ready to be home again? Focus on our voices. The memories."

"Bruto remember Omar teleporting everywhere. That make me laugh."

Omar hit the second switch.

A flicker of energy sparked from the console. Everyone turned to look at the teleportation pad.

"Bruto?" Guardian said.

No answer.

"Where are you, buddy?" Omar said, worriedly.

Nothing.

"Oh no," Kaimi cried.

More sparks of energy began to form around the teleportation pad. They seemed to be getting a bit dangerous. Everyone watched on, helpless.

After mere moments that felt like eternities, someone began to appear on the teleportation pad.

"That is Bruto, right?" Omar said softly.

Guardian hovered over to check. As the body fully materialized, he let out a sigh of relief.

"It's okay, everyone!" Guardian said. "It's Bruto!"

Kaimi and Omar ran over to see.

"Bruto home," Bruto said. "Family protect Bruto."

Chapter Nine
Invisible Friend

"We missed you!" Kaimi cried, hugging Bruto.

Omar smiled. "Glad to have you back, buddy."

Bruto hugged Omar. "Brother," he said.

Guardian saluted Bruto, who saluted him back.

"Guardian help save Bruto. Bruto never forget."

Guardian nodded, tears in his eye. "I'm so glad you're okay."

"What Bruto miss? Where Scrounger go?"

"He is gone," Guardian said. "We sent him toward the void. He won't be bothering us anytime soon."

"Bruto find new friend!" Bruto said, unexpectedly.

"What?" Kaimi asked. "Who is your new friend?"

"Invisible being make Bruto laugh! He dance on teleport pad!"

Guardian's eye widened, as he turned to look at the teleportation pad. He looked at Kaimi and Omar, concernedly. They both shook their heads, as to say they saw nothing at all.

"Bruto buddy?" Kaimi said, hesitantly. "What do you see?"

"Me see nothing! But Bruto feel presence. Silly friend walk funny!"

Omar leaned toward Guardian. "Is he okay?" Omar whispered. "This is very strange."

236

"Can your invisible friend talk?" Kaimi asked.

"Bruto ask! Invisible friend? You hear Bruto?"

Kaimi, Omar, and Guardian heard nothing. But Bruto smiled, as if he heard something.

"Friend glad to be on ship!" Bruto exclaimed. "Friend say he lonely for centuries, until he see Bruto. Me save friend!"

"Ask him what his name is," Kaimi said.

"Friend, what is name?" Bruto asked.

"And where is he from?" Omar added.

"I'm afraid to find out," Guardian said. "I may have a guess."

"Friend have no name," Bruto said, sadly. "He let Bruto pick? Bruto call him Sight."

"Bruto, can he see us?" Guardian asked.

Bruto nodded. "Sight glad to be free!"

"Glad to be free?" Guardian mumbled.

"Sight locked away between realities by evil being," Bruto said. "Until Bruto save!"

"What species is he?" Omar asked.

"No species," Bruto said. "He say he only one. But he been waiting to explore reality!"

"This is sounding more and more dangerous," Kaimi whispered.

The ship began to shake.

"What is that?" Kaimi demanded.

"Friend navigate ship!" Bruto said. "He silly!"

The ship took a sharp turn. Kaimi glanced over at the viewscreen.

"What is Sight doing?!" Kaimi yelled.

"He turn ship around?" Bruto said with a question. "Why Sight do this?"

Bruto began to shake. "Sight let ship go!" he cried. "Friends travel home! Not wrong way!"

"What is he telling you, Bruto?" Guardian said.

"He tell Bruto lies! He bad! He say evil being trap him from this reality. He say he take revenge on us?! He bring ship to void, make us suffer!"

Kaimi went to take the controls at her seat, but she flew backwards.

"Sight!" Bruto cried. "No harm friend!"

Bruto began to cry.

"Sight say no one understand him. He exist only to cause chaos. He say everything Bruto's fault."

"This isn't your fault!" Kaimi said, getting up. "Sight, as captain of this ship, I demand you let go of the controls."

"Sight laughing," Bruto said, frowning. "Sight say Kaimi not captain anymore. Sight claim ship."

"How do we fight something we can't see?" Omar said quietly.

The ship gained speed.

"How is he flying this fast?" Kaimi asked Guardian.

"He spent a lot of time between realities. I worry he learned a few tricks while he was stuck."

"Could he help us get home quicker?" Omar questioned.

"Maybe. If he wasn't evil," Guardian sighed.

"Maybe we can reason with him?" Kaimi added.

"No," someone said.

"Sight say no," Bruto reiterated.

"We heard him," Kaimi said, confused.

"I have been locked away for more time than you could imagine," the voice continued.

"Sight?" Kaimi asked.

"Do not call me that," Sight said. "This pathetic creature can not name something as ancient as me."

"What are you? What do you want with my crew?"

"The green alien told you," Sight said. "I am chaos. But I am revenge."

"How can we hear you now?" Omar asked.

"You hear when I allow," Sight said. "I traveled back with that thing. Once I saw an opportunity, I took it."

"And you would fly back into another void similar to the one you just escaped from?" Guardian questioned him.

"Chaos. To eternally strand the same bugs that banished me all those years ago, I would spend a thousand eternities in any void."

"Why were you banished? Who banished you?"

"That is not of your concern. I only wish to cause you pain," Sight said, as the ship flew even faster somehow.

"All that progress, gone," Kaimi sighed.

Feeling defeated, Omar shook his head. "What progress? We traveled days in a bucket of billions of light-years. Who are we kidding? This is not going to end well for us."

"Omar!" Kaimi shouted.

"I am sorry, captain," Omar cried. "We have faced obstacle after obstacle."

"Face the void," Sight laughed. "This void is connected to where I was stuck. Only, the void goes on for eternities of space. I was so far gone, never to return from the void. I was happy to hitch a ride back with Brutus over here."

"My name Bruto!" Bruto huffed.

"Whatever," Sight said. "Names don't matter. Your kind, all of you, whatever you may be, sent me away. I was wrongfully imprisoned, and now I want nothing but revenge. I have been thinking about ways to cause mischief if I ever escaped that abyss. But I find content propelling you all, with me, back into this never-ending space."

"But doesn't it eventually let you out on the other side?" Omar said quietly to himself.

"No," Sight said, hearing him. "This void never lets you out. I searched. Forever. Once we cross the threshold, we are immediately and permanently lost. Me finding a way out is impossible. And it already happened once. And one more thing. Once we are in there, communication will be gone. Forever in your own mind. Cut off from everyone here. Unable to die. You won't age. You won't be able to do anything. Except think. And when you have thought of every way you might be able to get out, when you have thought about those you used to care about, when you have thought about all the ways you might be able to change anything, and when you have tortured yourself with every possible thought, every fear, every single piece of your new reality, you will be forced to start those thoughts over. Again and again. And you will be forced to beg any being or deity you believe in to end your existence. And nothing does. Nothing hears you. Except the void. The void is all. The void is nothing. It is everything. The void is my home."

As the ship flew relentlessly toward the way of the void, Guardian looked at Kaimi, then toward Kaimi's chair, where Sight was sitting.

"Sight," Guardian said. "Look at me."

"No," Sight bellowed.

"I can give you peace," Guardian said.

"Peace is impossible for me to attain," Sight screamed. "I am chaos! I am every thought all at once. I hear myself screaming even when I am quiet. You can not give me peace."

"Do you want to go back into that void, really, just to get revenge? None of us had anything to do with your banishment. Listen to me, Sight. You won't have to think anymore. We can set you free."

"Is he suggesting what I think he's suggesting?" Omar whispered to Kaimi.

"Only moments away from entering the void," Sight cried. "You have ten seconds to convince me otherwise."

Chapter Ten
Ten Seconds

"Bruto, time stop!" Guardian cried.

Bruto and Guardian both closed their eye. They put their hands on their head, and slowly hovered off the ground.

"What trickery is this?!" Sight hissed.

"This is not trickery," Guardian said softly. "This is your salvation."

Kaimi and Omar were not moving. It was clear that everything was frozen in time, except Guardian, Bruto, and Sight.

"Way to prolong your inevitable eternal nothingness," Sight said.

"Bruto ask Sight question," Bruto said. "Does Sight want to experience peace?"

"You can not offer me peace!" Sight yelled. "I am too old, too tortured by my own voice. I don't even know my age. I don't even care."

Sight let out a burst of energy.

"I am stronger than you," Sight said. "Time will resume now."

As Sight's energy coursed through the ship, time began to move forward.

"Time stop?" Omar said, now able to move again.

"Eight seconds," Sight laughed.

"Bruto," Guardian said. "Now!"

Bruto flew over to Guardian, and they tried to stop time again, succeeding.

"I can do this all day," Sight said.

He started time again.

"Would you please just hear us out?!" Guardian cried.

Bruto and Guardian stopped time.

"Listen to this!" Guardian said.

Bruto and Guardian put their hands toward where Sight was sitting. And he gasped.

"What is that?" Sight cried. "I haven't heard such silence in ages."

"That is peace," Guardian said. "We can help you achieve peace."

"No," Sight said, "I want to make you suffer. I want…"

He became quiet, as he began to understand the serenity of silence.

"Why would you help me?" Sight said. "How can I keep this peace? I hear nothing. It is so beautiful."

"We can not control this peace for you. But you now know you can achieve it. You must seek it out. Find it. It will not be attained in that void. If you take us to the void, if you become like the very beings that put you in there against your will, you will never achieve peace. You will forever be living in a misery of your own choosing. You have the power, Sight. See. See!"

Sight started time again.

"What is happening?" Kaimi demanded.

"Bruto and Guardian try to show Sight peace," Bruto said. "He like peace, but has to search. No find in void."

"Fine," Sight said. "You managed to buy yourself some time. I'll bring the ship to a full stop, but I'm not turning this around until you help me achieve this peace. Five seconds away from the void."

"Sight, we can not give you constant peace," Guardian said. "You must search for that on your own."

The ship came to a stop. Engines turned off, they began to drift aimlessly, with no direction.

"So maybe we just go into the void then," Sight said, coldly.

"Sight," Kaimi said. "Do you have a physical form? Can you make yourself visible? Maybe finding peace would be easier if you were attached to your physical body."

"My physical body was lost in the void a long time ago."

"You said you don't age in the void," Omar said.

"And I did not age. I am still here. With no body. Unless someone wants to volunteer."

Guardian shook his head. "That might not even work," he said.

"I am aware," Sight sighed. "I am aware of all of this. Every scenario. Every possible reality has been echoing in my head forever. If I could get this peace you promised me, I would let you all go. But with no way of getting my body back, and no actual peace in my near future, I am afraid I will surrender to my thoughts. To the void."

He started the ship back up. It resumed full speed within moments.

"Four seconds until the void," Sight said, somberly. "Three, actually. Look closely, I think you can see the void in the distance. So much nothing."

"Bruto give Sight gift," Bruto said. "Bruto unsure if possible, but out of time."

He walked over to Kaimi's seat, and put his hands right next to where Sight was sitting. The ship halted immediately.

"What did you just do, Bruto?" Guardian asked. "I don't even know that trick!"

A figure began to take shape in Kaimi's chair.

"How?" Omar marveled.

"Bruto experience void too," Bruto said. "Me see nothing, but me try something. Sight lose body in void. Me powerful Zovvler. Me want to help. Maybe Bruto see something in void without realizing. All Bruto want is to give Sight peace and save Kaimi's crew."

As the figure fully appeared, everyone's eyes widened. A new creature that no one recognized sat before them.

"What species are you?" Guardian asked.

Bruto looked closely. "Sight look like Bruto! But Blue! And Sight have two eyes!"

"I am an ancient species," Sight said. "Yes. I think some of my good memories must have been lost with this body. I remember more. I hear more. But it is not all bad like I imagined."

"The void drove you crazy," Guardian said. "You lost who you were."

245

Sight just sat there, as more memories came flooding back.

"I must find my people," he said. "My thoughts were clouded. Missing. I am sorry. I do not want to enter back into that void. Being separated from my body, and being alone with my own thoughts for eternities, I think I began to believe any lie I could think of."

"Sight let us go?" Bruto asked.

Sight looked around at everyone, and nodded. "Can I travel with you? To find more of my people?"

Kaimi looked at Guardian.

"I understand the hesitation," Sight said, "but I have nowhere else to go."

Kaimi, unsure if she could actually trust Sight, had to admit that he was right.

"We must turn this ship around immediately," Kaimi said. "Sight. Could you use your powers to get us back on track? Fifty-seven billion light-years is going to be an impossible journey."

"I will do my best," Sight said. "But ever since I reconnected with my body, I feel whatever power I learned from being in the void has been draining from me. I think I'm going to be back to my normal self soon."

"What is Sight species called?" Bruto asked.

"I am afraid to tell you what I might be," Sight said. "For the obvious answer is right in front of you, and I fear it would cause more questions than answers."

Kaimi stared at him. Like Bruto said, he was blue. He had two eyes. And he had Wings. A tail. It was obvious what he was.

"Sight," Kaimi said, "you're a Zovvler?!"

Chapter Eleven
Scrounger's Return

"Not quite," Sight said. "A distant relative, perhaps? When I was alive, I don't think green Zovvlers existed. Like I said, I am an ancient species. But maybe to keep things simple, by technical terms, maybe I am a Zovvler."

"Bruto meet two Zovvlers! Me so happy!"

Sight stood up. "Sorry, captain. This chair is yours," he said.

"Right," Kaimi said, taking her seat. "We have to turn this ship–"

Something hit the ship, interrupting Kaimi. The ship went flying toward the void, which was now only two seconds away. And somehow, it was getting closer. It was both visible and invisible. Like looking into nothing, but seeing so much of it.

"What is all of this?!" Kaimi said, looking out the viewscreen.

She saw parts of ships. So much debris. Metal. Rocks. Steel.

"This must be some sort of dumping ground," Omar said. "A scrapyard."

"If only," Sight said. "This is more like a last resort. It's ships like us, that tried to get away, and failed for one reason or another. No, this is not a scrapyard. This is a graveyard."

247

"Why is that flying toward us then?" Kaimi exclaimed, noticing a big hunk of an old spaceship hurtling toward their ship.

It slammed into them, knocking them even closer to the void.

"Turn it around!" Kaimi cried, looking over at Omar. "We'll both try to control this ship. Bruto, Guardian, Sight, anything you can do to help with your Zovvler powers? We have to move!"

A rock hit the ship.

"Only one second from the void!" Sight cried. "I am sorry! Please. This is all my fault. With no body, I could not think straight. I need a second chance at life. Please!"

Now, as if someone were targeting them, the ship was bombarded over and over, with all different pieces of everything that had ever been left by the void.

Moments away from entering the void, Bruto, Guardian, and Sight all closed their eyes.

Bruto's eye opened suddenly.

"He is here," Bruto said.

"He has returned for you," Guardian added. "Or technically, you have returned, to him!"

Sight opened his eyes and looked around nervously. "What is happening? Who is here?"

Kaimi looked at Omar, who shook his head in disbelief.

"Where did you send him again?" Omar asked.

"Right by the void," Kaimi said. "As close to the void as I could."

A giant makeshift ship flew into the tiny space that was between them and the void. They saw a creature in the front seat, laughing. But just as quickly as they saw him, he vanished.

"Battle stations!" Kaimi cried. "We are about to be in for a nasty fight!"

The creature appeared right next to Kaimi. It was Scrounger.

"So, captain," Scrounger hissed, "miss me?"

"Scrounger, please," Kaimi begged. "Whatever your plan is, just forget it. You are unsafe by this void too. Can we all just fly away from this dangerous spot?"

"No!" Scrounger laughed. "I like seeing others uncomfortable. You will fight me here. If you beat me, I will allow you freedom. If not, I will throw all of you into the void. Collecting my delicious revenge."

"What made you so angry?" Sight asked.

"Who are you?" Scrounger scowled. "You fools are picking up strays? Don't you know there are dangerous creatures that you can't trust out here?"

He grinned, showing his rows of teeth. He teleported around the ship, as if to taunt them.

"Sight," Bruto said. "Zovvlers protect everyone!"

Guardian, Bruto, and Sight went to rush toward Scrounger, hoping to take him by surprise. Scrounger laughed, and yawned. He teleported away, as they were about to reach him.

"Hello, Omar," Scrounger hissed, landing right by him. "I forgot to tell you earlier. Clory felt responsible for getting his friends lost. So, being the only Elder here, maybe you should try to be just like him and take responsibility for everything. After all, Elders are the worst."

"Bruto responsible," Bruto said somberly. "Me make mistake."

"Like Zovvlers always do!" Scrounger laughed. "Right, Guardian?!"

He teleported next to Guardian.

"Enough, Scrounger!" Guardian said, gritting his teeth.

"Oh, but once they know that green Zovvlers were a mistake, it will be so much more delightful! Imagine Bruto, knowing his truth! He is a mistake! Just like you, Guardian. That's why you were banished out here. That's why Bruto was put up for adoption! Zovvlers decided you two weren't good enough."

"Bruto no believe!" Bruto said.

Scrounger teleported again, landing by Sight. "And you," Scrounger said, staring intently. "You look like the other Zovvlers, but you are so old. You are an ancient being. Oh, Guardian. Is this what your secret meant?!"

"Bruto confused," Bruto said.

"Of course he is!" Scrounger yelled. "Bruto is pathetic. Bruto stranded everyone billions of light-years away from their home. Bruto is the reason you are all about to suffer in the void, forever." Scrounger laughed.

"Bruto try to be smart."

"Bruto fail," Scrounger said, mocking him. "Zovvlers dabbled in magic beyond their comprehension. Your memories are more damaged than your actual brain."

"That is enough!" Guardian screamed. He ran toward Scrounger.

"Remember this trick?" Scrounger said, avoiding him. He slowly raised his body off the ground, and a shield formed around him. "Thanks for teaching me such a neat trick. I used it when I was sent here by your captain. Did you not have the guts to actually finish the job? You could have sent me into the void maybe? But I guess you wanted me to defeat you. That could be why you are here now. That shield trick may have saved my life. Teleporting me into space by this void was cruel. But I immediately saw an opportunity and built my beautiful makeshift ship from all that wreckage."

"Bruto not understanding," Bruto cried, looking at Guardian.

"What is there to not understand?" Scrounger bellowed. "You were taken out by your own species, and then lied to. Zovvlers covered their own tracks. They are actually smart, unlike you. According to Guardian's memories, they are the ones who overtook your home world."

"Home planet overtaken by evil creatures! Not Zovvlers!"

"Bruto!" Scrounger screamed. "Be quiet! Your voice is painful! You need to understand one thing. Many of the different species out there are mutated Zovvlers. Just like you. You are an echo. You are a mutant throwaway that no one wants. The beings that banished Guardian, the things that you thought overtook your planet? They were Zovvlers. True, blue, Zovvlers. Your history has been scrambled and retold. They

251

managed to weave these false stories into your mind. How they convinced you to believe the lies is beyond me. I do love it when history gets messed with. But the truth is, whatever creatures you were describing, whatever you were told, it was a cover story. The greatest enemy of Zovvlers, is actual Zovvlers. So hate this Sight fellow, because it was his kind that took everything from you!"

Bruto looked at Sight. Sight shook his head in disbelief.

"And finally," Scrounger said, teleporting to Kaimi, "captain worthless over here. You were supposed to get everyone home! You can't do anything right, can you? How are you back here, flirting with disaster? It's like you want me to end all of your lives. Well, I am happy to oblige. But ending your lives would show mercy. Whoever wants the blame for this, you can all share it. You will never get home. You will be just as lonely and damaged as me. But you will be sealed in this void for all eternity. While I find every friend, every relative, every living thing that gets in my way, and I destroy it."

Chapter Twelve
Guardian's Gift

"You have a lot to say," Sight said. "And I think you have said quite enough. You think you understand these people, and you use your words to get in their heads. You never answered my question, you coward. What made you so angry?!"

Scrounger huffed, and stared directly at Sight.

"You wanna know what makes me so angry?! Arrogant beings like you!"

He teleported next to sight and picked him up.

"I thought you were smarter than this," Scrounger said, spitting on Sight. "Tell you what. If you do one thing for me, I will spare you from the void."

"And what would that be?" Sight whispered.

Scrounger held back a smile, and simply said, "Destroy yourself."

He threw Sight at Guardian, knocking them both over.

"I'm going back to my ship," Scrounger said. "Have fun in the void. While you are there overthinking for all eternity, remember the name of the creature who divulged all the secrets that will drive you mad!"

Scrounger teleported back to his ship.

Kaimi took a deep breath. "The weapons are a last resort," she sighed.

She pressed buttons to once again reveal the big red button.

"Scrounger has given us no choice, and shown no mercy. As captain, it is my duty to make calls like this. I am sorry, everyone."

She pressed the button. A missile fired toward Scrounger's ship. It blew up. As the smoke cleared, pieces littered their view.

"It is time to leave this dangerous area," Kaimi said, somberly.

"Captain," Omar said. "You did the right thing."

"Why does the right thing feel so wrong then?" Kaimi whispered.

"That creature would have made all of us suffer indefinitely," Guardian said. "You saved us."

Kaimi forced a smile. "Let's get out of here."

As Kaimi began to turn the ship around, everyone stared one last time at the void.

"It's so empty," Omar said.

Sight looked away. "I never want to see it again."

"Why is it even here?" Omar asked.

"It is the space between realities," Sight said. "It is inescapable, well, mostly. Legend says it is here to prevent direct travel to different realities. But other ways were found. It is definitely possible to travel to alternate realities, dimensions, timelines… it's just difficult. And you can't travel through the void. You have to find a way around it."

Now facing away from the void, Kaimi sighed. She tried to fly the ship full speed away, but it wouldn't move.

"Omar?" Kaimi asked. "What's wrong with the ship?"

Omar tried to look into the issue. "Nothing according to diagnostics."

The ship began to fly backwards.

"Are we falling into the void?!" Kaimi asked, pressing buttons.

Omar switched the viewscreen to show what was behind them.

"How is this possible?" Guardian mumbled.

"Something is wrong," Sight cried. "I feel something. An evil presence."

Laughing could be heard.

"It can't be," Kaimi said. "We just destroyed him!"

"Bruto help," Bruto said.

Bruto closed his eye. Guardian did the same.

"There he is," Guardian said. "He is under the ship!"

"How?!"

"He is on a small hunk of his ship!" Guardian said. "Oh no."

Omar switched through the camera angles on the viewscreen. Something caught Guardian's eye, but for the moment, he said nothing about it.

"There!" Omar exclaimed.

On a piece of metal that resembled a surfboard, stood Scrounger. This surfboard had some sort of power source underneath it propelling it forward.

"Do you like it?" Scrounger hissed. "I have seen creatures you wouldn't believe. The amount of abilities you have seen me use? Only a small percentage of

255

what I am capable of. Every single power I have ever witnessed is at my disposal. So it is my honor to escort your ship into the void."

Kaimi tried once again to move the ship forward. It continued to move backward.

"I could teleport out there and fight him," Omar suggested.

"No," Kaimi said. "He is too powerful."

"It has been my job to protect everyone from the void," Guardian said, walking toward the teleportation pad. "I accept what must be done."

"Guardian, what are you doing?!" Kaimi demanded.

Guardian smiled. "Please, Kaimi," he said. "I must. Allow me to save everyone."

"You are a part of this crew!" Kaimi cried. "We can't lose you."

"You also can't allow Scrounger to do this," Guardian said.

Bruto opened his eye and ran toward Guardian. "Bruto need you," he said.

"Yes," Guardian said. "Bruto needs me to save everyone. You are not a mistake. No matter what you are told."

"Scrounger told truth?" Bruto cried. "Zovvlers no like us?"

"I am sorry, Bruto," Guardian sighed.

Bruto nodded and backed away from his friend.

"Bruto make you proud," Bruto said. "Me find Agnor's book."

"You do that, buddy," Guardian said. "Thank you all for accepting me."

"Thank you, Guardian," Omar said.

"I now fulfill my true purpose," Guardian smiled. "I am, The Final Guardian."

Kaimi looked around at the crew, then at Guardian. She threw the switch, and Guardian vanished from the ship. He appeared on the makeshift surfboard next to Scrounger, immediately forming a protective shield around himself. Knowing that Scrounger would anticipate his every move, and his powers, Guardian would try the one thing Scrounger could not understand. This was the only trick he had left up his sleeve. Sacrifice.

He punched the surfboard, knocking it away from the ship. Electricity coursed through it, rendering Scrounger temporarily paralyzed. Kaimi knew this was the one chance they would have of breaking free. But she still could not justify leaving Guardian alone with this monster.

Bruto closed his eye. It was as if he was receiving a message.

"Kaimi need to fly ship away!" Bruto cried. "Guardian say he have one final surprise for crew!"

As the surfboard continued to fly toward the void, Scrounger began to regain his strength. Everyone watched on in confusion. Guardian had been eyeing a piece of debris since he noticed it on the viewscreen earlier.

"Bruto think Guardian save mission!" Bruto cried. "Kaimi need to fly away from void as fast as Kaimi can!"

257

Guardian hovered off the surfboard and caught the large piece of debris.

"What is that?" Omar wondered.

Guardian landed back on the surfboard holding what he caught. He closed his eye, and light shot from the debris. He forced Scrounger to take it. The surfboard was now dangerously unstable.

"Bruto see!" Bruto said. "Guardian using Scrounger like conduit to power up debris! Scrounger can't move from electricity shock! But he hold ton of power!"

Guardian punched the surfboard again, hovering off of it. It began to enter the void. Another electric shockwave forced Scrounger to let go of the debris. Guardian snatched it, and held it toward their ship. Everyone watched, as Scrounger, who was still somewhat paralyzed from the electrical shocks, was taken by the void.

"He defeated Scrounger!" Omar said. "Can we save Guardian now?"

Kaimi nodded, but Bruto screamed, "Now! Kaimi, Guardian says full speed away from void! Quick! He say might be only chance to get home!"

Before Kaimi could react, Guardian landed on what was left of the surfboard, still holding the now highly powered object toward their ship.

"Guardian sorry his journey ends here," Bruto cried.

With the unstable surfboard beneath him, and the highly powered artifact in his hand, Guardian looked toward the ship.

"Guardian say he regret nothing," Bruto said somberly.

The surfboard exploded, as Guardian jumped off of it. The piece of debris Guardian was holding hurtled toward their ship. But Guardian was nowhere to be seen. The object picked up speed, and Bruto remembered what Guardian had said.

"Kaimi!" Bruto cried. "Fly away as fast as Kaimi can!"

Kaimi obeyed. The ship picked up speed, flying away from everything. The glowing hunk of debris was gaining on them, no matter how fast they went.

"Bruto receive phantom message," Bruto cried. "Guardian send final message before disappearing."

The ship flew even faster still, as the glowing object was about to crash into them.

"Guardian say, he find stray teleport device. He power it up to give us chance. Glowing debris is old piece of ship, it teleportation!"

The final gift from The Final Guardian collided with their ship. A vortex of planets, stars, and debris could be seen outside the viewscreen. Kaimi, unsure if this could even work, looked down at the coordinates, as they changed swiftly.

"Captain?" Omar asked.

Everything began to slow down, as the ship came to a sudden halt.

"Where are we?" Omar said, nervously.

"I can't believe it," Kaimi said. "This should be impossible."

"Are we back home?" Omar asked.

Kaimi nodded. "Seven days away from Agnor's coordinates! He did it! We are back on track!"

"But how?" Omar cried.

"Bruto understand," Bruto said. "Guardian somehow guide ship home. Thank you, Guardian."

"Thank you, Guardian," the entire crew said, one after the other.

Chapter Thirteen
Crystal Rain

Kaimi was looking at the screen that showed the coordinates.

"I can not believe it," she said. "The fact that we are back, after all the crazy adventures we had way out by the void."

"I just hope there is a life for me out here," Sight said. "It sounds like the Zovvlers that look like me have done some horrible things."

"But you didn't," Omar said. "Besides, you always have a place with us."

Kaimi nodded.

"What sorts of things are we going to see?" Sight asked.

"Well, so far, we had not seen much before we got thrown across the galaxy," Omar laughed. "There was this derelict ship that basically caused us to get so lost. Do you think that was a trap, Kaimi? I still can not believe the power it had over our minds."

"It was quite alarming," Kaimi admitted. "But Bruto promised to protect us if something like that happens again. Which it will not!"

"Positive thinking!" Omar said.

"Bruto wonder," Bruto said, hovering over to Sight. "Sight have more powers than me?"

"As my memories return," Sight began, "I do think I will discover more about who I was, who I am, and why I was banished in the first place."

"I almost forgot that you were banished," Omar said.

"I wish I could understand more about who I was right now," Sight admitted.

"Bruto help?" Bruto asked.

"Would that be safe?" Kaimi answered. "This readjusting to reality seems like a good idea. Don't get me wrong, finding out would be amazing. But I don't want to risk overloading your newly refound body with a flood of information."

"Fair point," Sight said. "Bruto, if I haven't figured out who I am by the time we find this book you are looking for, then maybe you can help me remember."

Bruto smiled. His smile faded, and his eye closed suddenly. He opened it back up and started to look around frantically.

"Planet taking ship!" Bruto cried.

"What planet?" Kaimi asked.

"There!" Bruto pointed.

Way off in the distance a planet could be seen.

"So we'll avoid that planet," Kaimi said. "It won't take this ship."

"No!" Bruto exclaimed. "Planet taking another ship! Crash!"

"Crash?" Kaimi mumbled. "Buddy, what do you see?"

Bruto closed his eye again. "Me see unknown creature falling and crashing into planet!"

"Can we even do anything about that?" Omar asked.

Kaimi sighed. "We have to," she said. "It is barely out of our way, and if someone is in danger, we have to at least try."

"Wait," Omar said. "What if it's a trick?"

"I don't care," Kaimi answered. "We have to see what's going on."

Omar nodded in agreement. Kaimi turned the ship slightly to head toward the planet. She looked at the screen that showed their current location.

"The planet is called Oasis," Kaimi said, confused. "The population was last calculated in the tens of thousands. All different species."

"So couldn't whoever is down there help us make sure this ship landed safely?" Omar asked.

"Potentially," Kaimi said, pressing buttons on the screen. "It says over the past twenty years, many species have taken their families elsewhere, due to the change in weather patterns."

"Hotter or colder?" Omar questioned.

"Neither," Kaimi said, eyes widened. "It says the crystal rain has become more frequent in certain areas. A tenth of the planet is uninhabitable, but their scientists say it is slowly getting worse."

"Crystal rain?" Sight interrupted. "What is that?"

"Let me see if I can, ah, here it is! Crystal rain is the act of literal crystals falling from the sky?"

"That should be impossible," Omar said. "Right?"

"I think so," Kaimi said. "It also claims that the crystal rain's origin is unknown."

263

"So, you're telling me, out of nowhere, a planet just started having bouts of crystals fall from its skies?" Omar asked. "And there are still tens of thousands of people that just stay on the planet?"

"Yes," Kaimi said. "Unless someone down there is hiding something."

Omar sighed, then smiled. "I guess adventure calls!"

As the planet drew closer, Bruto suddenly fell to the floor.

"Buddy?!" Kaimi exclaimed. "What is it?!"

"Bruto have second thoughts. Oasis dangerous. Secret beyond secrets hidden on planet."

Sight hovered over. "Bruto, may I?"

He reached out his hand to help Bruto stand.

"Bruto dizzy."

"Take my hand," Sight said. "Maybe an old Zovvler and a new Zovvler, together, can bring some clarity to your mind."

Bruto accepted Sight's hand. He closed his eye. Sight closed his eyes.

"Bruto," Sight said. "I can't see anything. What do you see?"

"Bruto see crystal rain," Bruto said. "Bruto see hunks of glass fall from sky."

"Glass?" Kaimi asked.

"Glass, crystal, something scary," Bruto said. "Bruto see scared creatures. Planet not safe."

"If these weather patterns continue at their current speed," Kaimi added, "scientists say a complete evacuation of the entire planet will take place within the next century."

"Less than one hundred years is the life expectancy of this planet," Omar said, shocked, "and there are still tens of thousands of creatures just living their lives?"

"It's their home," Sight said. "Maybe they are taking a stand."

"Against the weather?" Omar questioned. "That doesn't seem smart."

"Sometimes people take a stand in vain," Kaimi sighed. "I don't think the weather cares what anybody stands for."

Bruto and Sight still had their eyes closed.

"Bruto want to save everyone from oncoming storm," Bruto said. "But everyone laugh! Everyone say scientists trick them so everyone leave. Then scientists harvest planet for themselves!"

"Could it be a man-made issue?" Omar asked. "Or is this just nature taking its course?"

"Unfortunately," Kaimi said, "after we save this other ship that Bruto saw, we have to be on our way. We have a mission of our own, and I am sure Agnor will be wondering where we are if we stay off track too long. Don't get me wrong, I would love to stay and help in any way we can, but perhaps after we return Agnor's book, we can revisit this planet."

"Wow," Omar said, taking in the beauty of the planet as they got closer. "Oasis is beautiful."

"Bruto," Kaimi said, "where is this crashing ship?"

"Bruto not sure," Bruto said.

265

He let go of Sight's hand and opened his eye.

"Someone is hailing us," Omar said.

"Oasis," Kaimi guessed. "Answer them."

A colorful creature appeared on the viewscreen. Her two eyes were tinted blue, green, and purple. Her nose was similar to a human's, but oval. She had feathers instead of hair. Her arms were covered in art. Whether that was there from birth, or added later in life like tattoos, was irrelevant. She was beautiful.

"Hello and welcome!" said the creature. "My name is Alora. We invite you to land on our planet to take in all of its glory. Are you visitors or outcasts?"

"Both," Sight said quietly.

"Visitors," Kaimi said. "I am the captain of this vessel. My crew and I are just passing through."

"Please accept our warmest of greetings, and the instructions for where to land that I have just sent to your ship."

"Thank you," Kaimi smiled. "We look forward to discovering the beauty of your lovely planet."

Alora smiled back, and ended the transmission.

"Instructions received," Omar said. "Captain?"

Kaimi nodded. "Oasis," she said, "please be kind to us."

Chapter Fourteen
Oasis

After safely landing on the planet, Kaimi and crew were met by Alora herself.

"Your ship will be safe with us," Alora said. "While you peruse our lovely Oasis, your ship will be waiting for you at this station. Don't forget where you landed. Station fifty-seven."

Omar shot Kaimi I look, who shrugged. That number? Again? Maybe it was a coincidence.

"We can't stay long, unfortunately," Kaimi admitted. "We are on a mission of our own."

"If it isn't imposing," Alora said, "might I ask what this mission is about?"

Kaimi wasn't sure if she should say, but then again, what harm could it do?

"We are looking for a magical book," she said.

"A magical book?!" Alora gasped. "That must be quite the story! So what brings you to Oasis?"

Kaimi didn't want to alarm their new friend by telling her about a crashing ship, so she simply said, "Adventure."

"I can't argue with that," Alora smiled. "I hope you find what you're looking for, both out there on your mission, and right here on Oasis."

"Thank you," Kaimi said.

"Miss, I have a question," Omar said.

"Alora," Alora said. "You can call me Alora." She stopped in her tracks looking closely at Omar. "And what can I call you?"

Omar blushed a little, as he found her very beautiful. "Omar," he said.

"I apologize," Kaimi said. "I am new to this captain business. Yes, that is Omar. And this fellow is Bruto."

"Bruto think Alora beautiful," Bruto smiled.

"Why thank you kindly," Alora said.

"And this is the newest addition to our crew," Kaimi said. "Sight."

"Quite the team you got there," Alora said. "If any of you ever find yourselves in need of a home, you are always welcome on Oasis. Now, Omar was it? What was your question?"

"Well, I just don't understand, Alora," Omar sighed.

Kaimi shot him a look, and slightly shook her head, but Omar didn't notice.

"Don't understand?" Alora asked.

"This crystal rain," Omar answered.

Immediately, Alora's gaze shifted away from him.

"How can everyone stay so content?" Omar asked. "Knowing the planet could be uninhabitable someday?"

"Omar!" Kaimi scolded him.

"No, it is fine," Alora said. "I just don't like to think about that. Besides, given enough time, every planet becomes uninhabitable."

"But no one knows where this crystal rain came from? Or why it happens?"

"There are whispers," Alora said, quietly. "Some say it began when a strange visitor was vacationing here about thirty years ago. But we have no proof."

"But I just don't understand how anybody can stay on a planet, knowing everything could get worse," Omar sighed. "How is that a life?"

"I'm afraid this is where I must depart from you," Alora responded. "Omar, maybe after you visit us, you will understand why some of us can't bring ourselves to leave. This is our home. Our Oasis. Besides, we have ways of warding off this crystal rain. I think this visit will educate you on our past, present, and future. Good luck, friends. And remember. Station fifty-seven."

Kaimi nodded, as she led her crew out the front door of the station.

"Amazing view!" she marveled, as they took in their surroundings. "This planet is already so beautiful."

Just outside the station, they were greeted by colorful trees. The sky was painted with purple, blue, and red blotches. In the distance, they saw magnificent buildings.

"Why don't they mention Oasis back on L-VII?" Omar wondered.

"They are both beautiful in their own right," Kaimi said. "But that is a good question."

Bird creatures flew above, while dark green clouds rolled through the skies.

"Bruto love Oasis," Bruto said.

"It is breathtaking," Sight agreed.

"Hey you!" someone said.

Everyone turned their gaze to the voice.

"Welcome to Oasis!"

As the creature drew nearer, Sight's eyes widened. A smile began to form on Bruto's face.

"Zovvler!" he exclaimed.

It was a blue Zovvler.

"My name is Calixta," the female Zovvler smiled as she got closer. She looked puzzled. "Two different kinds of Zovvlers, together?"

"Bruto find so many Zovvlers!" he beamed. "My name Bruto!"

"Hello, Bruto," Calixta smiled. She looked at Sight.

"It is a pleasure to meet you, Calixta," Sight said. "My name is Sight."

"That is an interesting name," Calixta replied.

Calixta looked over at Kaimi.

"I am Kaimi, and this is our friend Omar."

"What magical force had to be summoned that could allow two different variations of Zovvlers to not utterly hate each other?" Calixta asked.

"That bad, huh?" Sight sighed. "Why do blue and green Zovvlers hate each other so much?"

"Oh, honey," Calixta began, "it is just war. The blue Zovvlers accidentally created the green Zovvlers when they started messing with magic beyond their comprehension. After realizing what they had done, they began to make up stories and lies and reasons to banish not only the green Zovvlers, but every other variation of Zovvler that did not look like them. Like us."

"So why are you here and not with them?" Sight asked.

"Because I disagree wholeheartedly with what they were doing," she said. "No one deserves that kind of treatment. They were, they are us. Zovvlers. Once I expressed my feelings, they banished me as well. So I am a sort of refugee living on this planet now."

"Other Zovvlers here too?" Bruto asked.

"I haven't found them," Calixta answered. "But I haven't searched the entire planet. I landed in station fifty-seven many years ago, just to visit, to take a break from aimlessly wandering through space. And I never looked back. Neverending adventures seem like a fun idea, until they don't."

Kaimi looked over at Omar.

"Neverending adventures are what we are fighting for," Omar said.

"And that is brilliant!" Calixta exclaimed. "Just because it wasn't for me, doesn't mean it isn't for you! I was just so tired. Lonely. And I found a new family here with Alora and so many others!"

"That is wonderful," Kaimi said.

"What is your story?" Calixta asked, looking at Sight. "I never thought I would see a blue Zovvler again. How can you not know of Zovvler history? Were you living in a void?"

Sight stared at Calixta.

"Funny you should say that," Omar interrupted.

"What did I say?" Calixta asked. "I am sorry if I upset you!"

271

"No, you're fine," Sight said. "I was stuck in a void. For a very long time. And I don't even remember the reason I was sent there."

"Not all mysteries need solving," Calixta said. "I do apologize for what I said. I had no idea."

"Of course," Sight said. "No harm done."

"Bruto curious about crystal rain," Bruto said.

Kaimi shook her head. "I don't think the locals like to talk about the rain."

"Actually," Calixta said, "can you keep a secret?"

Bruto nodded.

Calixta looked around, then started walking away. She looked back.

"Well?" she said. "Follow me!"

Chapter Fifteen
Hazard

Sight was the first one to follow after Calixta. Omar looked at Kaimi, who in turn looked at Bruto. The three of them followed. As they were nearly running to keep up with Calixta and Sight, Bruto started to laugh.

"What's so funny, Bruto?" Omar asked.

"Omar run funny," Bruto said, holding back laughter.

"Do I?" Omar asked.

"I wasn't going to say anything," Kaimi said, shaking her head. "But, since you asked…"

"Bruto think Omar running even funnier, because Omar teleport."

Omar held back laughter. "Bruto," he said. "You are absolutely right!"

He teleported close to Sight, scaring him. After regaining his composure, Sight caught up to Calixta. Omar waited for Kaimi and Bruto.

"Where is she taking us?" Omar wondered.

"Bruto want to catch up with Zovvlers!" Bruto said. "Captain?"

"Go ahead, buddy!" Kaimi said.

Bruto hovered off the ground and yelled, "Wait for Bruto!"

Sight turned back and saw him. Bruto caught up, and the three Zovvlers were now ahead of Kaimi and Omar.

As they continued to follow for quite some time, they noticed the amount of trees double. Triple. There were patches of tall grass. Flowers. Piles of rocks. And still they all followed Calixta.

"I think this trip is going to take more time than I anticipated," Kaimi said to Omar.

"Weren't we here for the crashing ship Bruto saw?" Omar replied. "I think we might be off course."

"Just a lot," Kaimi said. "But look at Sight and Bruto with Calixta. They look like a happy family."

Omar smiled. "They do, don't they? I am so glad Bruto is meeting all these Zovvlers."

"I think they have finally reached their destination!" Omar exclaimed.

Calixta, Sight, and Bruto were all standing by an old tree. Kaimi and Omar joined their friends at the tree.

"Everyone is here, right?" Calixta asked.

Kaimi nodded.

Calixta went behind the tree and began to rustle through a pile of leaves and dirt.

"Where is it?" she cried. "It's gone!"

"What are you looking for?" Sight asked.

"It is a remote," she said, nervously. "It gives me access to everything. All my research. If someone found it, I could lose everything!"

"What does it look like?" Kaimi questioned.

"It is a small, chrome device, with buttons on it."

"And you are sure this is the tree you left it at?" Sight asked.

"Yes!" Calixta answered.

"Bruto see device!" Bruto exclaimed.

"Where?!" Calixta cried.

Bruto pointed up. "Bird creature!"

"Is that bird sentient enough to know what it took?" Sight asked.

"I don't know," Calixta said, beginning to hover off the ground. "I don't like flying in public, but I need that device back!"

"Do you need help?" Sight asked.

"You go that way, I'll go this way. Bruto, can you make sure that bird doesn't get away from us?"

Bruto saluted.

Calixta flew toward the bird. It immediately flew the opposite way. It noticed Sight. Compared to everything else on Oasis, this bird was not that vibrant. It was gray. Solid gray. It had small talons that were holding Calixta's remote, and a small beak. It let out a quick, but sharp, noise. It tried to fly yet another way, but Calixta was there to block it. The two Zovvlers were closing in on the bird. There was only one way out, and the bird saw the opportunity. It flew away from both Zovvlers, looking back at them, thinking it was free with the stolen remote. It turned its head back around to see Bruto, who had been watching the entire time from the ground. Bruto snatched the remote from the bird. The bird let out another sharp chirp. It clawed Bruto's wing, and flew away.

Bruto slowly hovered back down to the ground by Kaimi and Omar, holding Calixta's remote. Sight and Calixta joined him.

"Are you alright, Bruto?" Kaimi asked.

"Bird scratch Bruto," Bruto said. "Wing hurt. But me save Calixta's secret!"

Bruto handed Calixta the remote.

"Thank you so much, Bruto!" Calixta said. "I am sorry you got scratched."

"Was that a random event with a wild animal, or do you suspect someone sent that bird?" Sight asked.

"Honestly, as of late, the crystal rain has been making everyone do some crazy things," Calixta said. "That is actually what I wanted to show you."

She pressed a button on the remote.

"What are we waiting for?" Kaimi asked.

Something could be heard from a distance. It sounded like it was rolling its way toward them.

"My robot friend," Calixta said. "He hides out here in the forest. No one bothers him. He bothers no one."

"Hello, Calixta," the robot said, in his mechanical tone. "What knowledge do you seek?"

"You built this?" Sight marveled. "That is so cool."

"After landing on Oasis, I quickly became fascinated with everything about it. It has become my refuge, and I, among many other creatures, do not want to surrender to the crystal rain."

"How were you able to build a robot?" Kaimi asked.

"Parts of my own ship," Calixta said. "Remember, I was banished and left to travel aimlessly. A few months after I landed, I decided that I would need all the help I could get. But I couldn't keep going into station fifty-seven to do my research. I was afraid it might upset Alora. So I took pieces of my own ship to make this simple robot. My ship can still fly, obviously. I needed to make sure I still had a way out, in case, well, you know. But I'd like to introduce you all to Hazard!"

"Calixta," Hazard reiterated. "What knowledge do you seek?"

"Show my friends everything," Calixta instructed.

"Are you sure that is wise?" Hazard cautioned.

"I trust them," Calixta said.

"Accessing crystal rain files," Hazard said. "Access code required."

Calixta looked around, then whispered the code to Hazard.

"Access granted," Hazard said. "Crystal rain files. Summary. Twenty-nine years ago, a strange creature visited this planet."

"Where is this creature now?" Omar interrupted.

Hazard tilted his head toward Omar, then looked at Calixta.

"Answer any and all questions my friends have," Calixta said. "Maybe their interest and insight will help us solve this before total evacuation."

Hazard looked back at Omar.

"Current whereabouts of strange creature unknown."

"Who was he, or she?" Sight asked.

"Identity of strange creature unknown."

"That's the problem," Calixta said. "I have even tried to use my Zovvler powers to figure this out. But any information about that creature, it seems, has been erased from time itself. So I turned my focus onto the 'why', instead of the 'who'. Hazard, tell them what we figured out."

"A disturbance in the crust of the planet began twenty-nine years ago after this visitor crashed on Oasis. Some believe it to be magic. Some think he found a way to use science to slowly harm the planet. But something happened. This is not natural. Someone is slowly destroying this planet."

"Hazard say crashed," Bruto said. "Bruto see crash!"

"What do you mean?" Calixta said, confused.

"Maybe crash Bruto saw was mysterious evil creature," Bruto said.

"Bruto, you think the crash you had visions of today was actually from nearly thirty years ago?" Kaimi asked.

"Bruto not sure," he frowned.

"Calixta tried to use her powers to see anything about the creature," Omar said. "So how could Bruto see something if she couldn't?"

"Wait," Kaimi said. "Calixta, you said information about this creature might have been erased from time itself?"

"Potentially."

Kaimi looked around at everyone as she was processing everything. "Where do you suspect something would go if it was potentially erased from time?"

"Nowhere," Calixta said.

"Some sort of nothing place," Omar guessed.

"The void," Sight said. "The void! If something was erased from time, maybe the echoes of what it was would be sent to the void."

"Bruto was in void!" Bruto cried.

"You too?" Calixta cried. "You all need to tell me that story someday. But if the crash Bruto saw was some sort of remnant from being in the void, maybe he can try to see this creature again?"

"Last time Bruto saw the visions of the crash, he felt dizzy after, as we drew nearer to the planet," Kaimi sighed. "Maybe it was because of the lost void memories. Some sort of mental feedback?"

"Bruto try?" Bruto said. "Please, captain? Bruto try to save Oasis?"

"Remember what stabilized his thoughts and made them clear again. I took his hand," Sight reminded Kaimi. "Maybe my eternities in the void serve a purpose greater than even I could imagine. Maybe the two of us together could try again."

Unsure if it was safe, Kaimi realized she could not stand in the way of potential progress. So she nodded.

Bruto took Sight's hand, and they closed their eyes. Immediately, a shockwave tossed the two Zovvlers in opposite directions, as if something repelled them away from each other.

"Nevermind," Sight said, trying to lighten the mood. "Bad idea."

"Bruto agree," Bruto said. "Me not going to try that again."

"Something wants to stay hidden," Calixta said. "I am sorry, you two."

"Bruto wanted to try," Bruto said. "Sight wanted to help. No sorry, Calixta."

Sight agreed. "No harm done," he said.

Calixta looked disappointed. She looked at Hazard, as if she wanted him to say something.

"As I was saying earlier, this crystal rain is definitely not natural. Something set in motion all those years ago has slowly been destroying the planet. Calixta instructed me to monitor the unnatural weather patterns. I was created to solve a mystery and so Calixta would have someone to talk to."

"Hazard," Calixta scolded him.

"No, it's okay," Kaimi said. "Having a friend to talk to is sometimes the only thing that keeps us sane. Besides, what you have created here is amazing."

"I found more information," Hazard said, looking at Calixta. "Recent storms around Oasis have increased rapidly. New estimate of total evacuation reached."

"You have about one hundred years until that, don't you?" Omar asked.

Calixta nodded. "Plenty of time to try and figure this out."

"I am sorry to inform you," Hazard began, "but total evacuation of Oasis is imminent in approximately twenty-eight years."

Chapter Sixteen
Calixta's Ship

"Twenty-eight?!" Calixta exclaimed. "What happened?!"

"About twenty percent of the planet is now uninhabitable," Hazard stated. "And that number is swiftly increasing. The information I just received, if it hasn't already been discovered by the planet's scientists, will be found out by them shortly. I suspect a lot more creatures will choose to leave once this information is public."

Calixta shook her head. "I thought we had time. We were supposed to have more time!"

Omar was counting out loud.

"Omar," Kaimi said, staring at him. "What are you counting?"

"How many years ago did that mysterious creature crash?"

"Twenty-nine," Calixta said.

"But that's impossible," Omar said.

"What is?" Calixta asked.

"Twenty-nine years ago, the disturbance began. Now there are only twenty-eight years until total evacuation. There it is again!"

Kaimi started adding the numbers in her head. "Oh my," she said.

"Fifty-seven!" Bruto cried.

"Why that number?" Omar said. "Again, it's that number."

"That's the number of the station I landed at," Calixta said. "But maybe it is just a coincidence."

"We were lost," Kaimi said. "Thrown into the depths of space. We were fifty-seven billion light-years away. That number has been following us the entire time. Why?"

"L-VII," Bruto said, closing his eye, having a sudden realization.

"What is L-VII?" Calixta asked.

"The name of our home planet," Kaimi said. "What about it, Bruto?"

"Bruto see knowledge from days gone by. Bruto see letters. Letters as numbers. Call them Roman numerals."

"Oh, I remember learning about those," Kaimi said. "Earth history has done its best to thrive throughout time and space. Roman numerals were difficult for me to get my mind around. I was never really good at figuring out what each letter meant."

"Home planet fifty-seven," Bruto said.

"It is?" Kaimi asked.

Bruto nodded. "Fifty-seven also important to Elders."

"That is significant to our history," Omar said.

"I am sorry," Calixta said. "I have taken up enough of your time. I need to find a way to stop this crystal rain. I can not surrender to it."

Kaimi sighed. "I want to stay and help in any way I can."

"But you have the mission," Sight said. "You must find Agnor's book and return it to your planet."

"Once we return the book," Omar said, "we can return here. I want to help too."

"Bruto help save planet!"

Calixta smiled. "You are all too kind," she said.

"We are about seven days away from the coordinates Agnor gave us," Kaimi said.

"Seven days?" Calixta asked. "Is that all?"

"Seven days at the fastest speed our ship can travel," Kaimi said. "And it is the best of the best."

"Are you sure?" Calixta questioned. "My ship can travel days in seconds. Even after I took some of its parts to make Hazard."

"But I thought Agnor gave us the fastest ship," Omar said.

"Maybe it is the fastest one that he had. But my ship was made by Zovvlers," Calixta said, proudly. "In order to save time, and get back here fast, I would allow you to borrow my ship."

"Really?" Omar said.

"Is that a good idea?" Kaimi wondered.

"Why not? If you want to get this book back to Agnor quickly," Calixta said. "You can put the coordinates in my ship, fly over there, get the book, fly back here, and then take your ship back to L-VII. Just so you don't cause confusion or chaos back on your planet. A random new ship showing up might be alarming at this time."

"It could work," Kaimi said.

"I need to stay here on Oasis," Calixta said. "I would love to go with you, but I have so much work to do."

"Understood," Kaimi said.

"But I do have time to walk you back to the station," Calixta smiled. "I'll tell Alora that you friends are borrowing my ship."

"That is very kind of you," Kaimi said. "I appreciate this."

"We owe you," Omar said.

"Complete your quest," Calixta said, "then maybe you can help me save Oasis."

Omar nodded. "I would love that."

Calixta looked at Hazard. "Hide," she said. "I'll summon you when I return."

Hazard rolled off into the forest. Calixta looked at the remote still in her hands.

"It's getting more and more risky to hide this remote out here," she said. "I fear one of these times I won't find it."

"Just bring it to the station," Omar suggested.

"But I don't want Alora to ask questions," Calixta said. "I don't want to upset her."

"I'll watch it for you," Sight said.

"But what about your friends?" Calixta asked. "Your mission?"

"They are my friends," Sight said, "but this is not my mission. I want to stay here, captain. Time is fleeting. Twenty-eight years is a lot, but it's also not. Please, captain."

"Sight," Kaimi said. "I would love to help when we find and return Agnor's book."

Sight frowned.

"However," Kaimi continued, "although you will always be considered part of my crew, I understand why you want to stay and help Calixta now. And I won't stand in your way. But we will be back. We will help you save Oasis."

Sight smiled. "I won't let you down, captain. By the time you, Bruto, and Omar return, I hope to greet you with good news of significant progress. We will save Oasis. Good luck, captain."

"You too," Kaimi said.

Calixta looked at Sight, and fought back tears. "I appreciate this. I'll be right back."

"Bruto thank Sight," Bruto said. "Me want to stay too, but me promise Guardian me find Agnor's book. So Bruto help find book, then Bruto return. Zovvlers. Family."

"We better get going," Calixta said. "We all have so much work to do. Call Hazard back, Sight. You can start to brainstorm with him."

Sight nodded, and pressed the button on the remote. Hazard could be heard rolling back to him.

"Back to station fifty-seven for us," Calixta said. "Follow me."

It took them about two hours to return to the station. Alora met them at the door.

"Calixta!" she said.

"Hello, Alora!" Calixta said.

"Where is your other friend?" Alora asked, looking at Kaimi.

"He chose to stay on Oasis," Kaimi said.

"Wonderful," Alora said. "Are you off to find your magical book?"

"Yes," Kaimi said.

"I am going to lend them my ship," Calixta said. "It will travel much faster than their ship."

"That's the hospitality we offer here on Oasis!" Alora exclaimed. "Your ship is this way, Calixta."

"I really can't thank you enough," Kaimi said to Calixta.

"It's nothing," Calixta said. "We are helping each other."

"Right this way," Alora said, as she continued to lead everyone to the ship.

"I love my ship," Calixta said. "But I trust you, Kaimi. Take care of her, okay?"

"I promise," Kaimi said.

"Just around this corner," Alora said.

As they all rounded the corner, Calixta's ship met their gaze. It was beautiful. Almost all covered in chrome, the blue stripe across the side gave it just a splash of color.

"Let me give you a quick tutorial on how to fly her," Calixta said.

Calixta showed Kaimi and crew around her ship. First, she walked them around the outside, explaining where all the weapons were, and showing them the engines. Then, she walked them inside.

"How does it fly so fast?" Kaimi asked. "You said it travels days within seconds. Is it just teleport?"

"Yes. No. It's complicated," Calixta said. "This technology is possibly beyond your comprehension. I don't say that to be mean. I don't quite understand the technicalities of how it works myself. I just know how to use it. But technically, there is a bit of teleportation involved."

Calixta reached into an overhead compartment above the captain's chair, and handed Kaimi a bracelet.

"What is this?" she asked.

"It's how you fly the ship," Calixta said. "This, and this."

Calixta reached behind one of her wings, and pulled out a second bracelet.

"Is this safe for a human?" Kaimi asked.

"Do you have a mind?" Calixta said, knowing the answer. "It is telekinetic. You wear one bracelet on your right arm, and the other on your left. You can do this."

Bruto walked over to Kaimi.

"Captain?"

"Yes, Bruto?"

"If Kaimi afraid or unsure, Bruto fly ship to coordinates?"

"Oh, buddy, I am not sure–"

"Of course!" Calixta said. "Yes, Kaimi, you could fly it. But Bruto is a Zovvler. Things will go much more smoothly if he is flying it."

"Bruto remember coordinates," Bruto said. "Me see them on our ship. Me fly us safely to Agnor's book!"

"It is a Zovvler ship," Omar nodded.

"Is it safe for Bruto?" Kaimi asked. "It sounds like Zovvler physiology has changed quite a bit."

"He is still a Zovvler," Calixta said. "And a Zovvler in the driver's seat is your best option here. Yes, Bruto will be safe."

"Okay," Kaimi said. "Bruto, looks like you're flying the ship to those coordinates."

Bruto was elated. "If Guardian here, he be so proud of Bruto flying ship!"

"The ship used to talk to me," Calixta said. "But unfortunately, I took that part of the ship for Hazard. Everything important should still be functional. I took only trivial parts of the ship to help create Hazard. Everything else you need to know, Bruto will take care of. Once he connects to the ship, he will have all the answers. This is where I leave you all. Good luck. Bring my ship, yourselves, and the book, all back in one piece, okay?"

Calixta handed Bruto one of the bracelets. Kaimi handed him the other one. Bruto put them both on, and sat down in the captain's chair, excited to fly the ship.

Kaimi and Omar walked with Calixta to the door of the ship.

"Be careful, okay?" Calixta warned them. "Whatever awaits you when you find that book, be ready for it."

"Calixta," Kaimi said, "you be careful too. This crystal rain is dangerous. We will find a way to save Oasis. But you need to be ready for anything too. If you need to make an escape for any reason, obviously, you and Sight can take our ship."

288

"I appreciate that," Calixta said. "But we aren't leaving. We aren't going anywhere. This crystal rain will not displace me again."

"Bruto ready," Bruto exclaimed.

"Be careful, Bruto!" Calixta said.

"Bruto careful!" he replied. "Me thank Calixta!"

"You two better go sit down," Calixta instructed. "I'll leave you all to your mission. Bruto is about to leave with the ship's door open! Be safe, friends!"

Calixta walked outside and stood next to Alora.

"We will look forward to seeing you all again soon," Alora said, as the door of the ship closed.

"Thank you, Alora!" Kaimi said, waving.

Kaimi and Omar found seats and sat down.

"Well, Bruto," Kaimi said, "Captain Bruto, take us to Agnor's book!"

Chapter Seventeen
Travesty

Bruto closed his eye. The ship began to rumble, as the engines started.

"It is sort of like a telekinetic ship!" Omar whispered to Kaimi. "That is so cool!"

"Bruto telling ship coordinates now," Bruto said.

There was a screen by Kaimi's chair. She began to look at it. Omar looked over to see the same screen.

"Where are these coordinates taking us, anyway?" Omar asked.

"Agnor never said," Kaimi admitted. "And the ship never told us. We were just instructed on where to go. I think it would be a planet? Wherever those shadow creatures were taking his book."

"But how could Agnor know where they were going?" Omar asked.

Kaimi pressed some buttons on the screen.

"There!" she said.

"Is that where the coordinates land?" Omar asked.

"This is where the ship is headed now," Kaimi said. "Bruto told the ship where to go, so now it's telling us."

"It's weird that our ship wasn't given this much information. It's almost as if Agnor wanted to hide something."

"Ship at coordinates in one minute," Bruto said.

"Seven days in one minute," Omar said. "This technology is amazing."

"The planet has no name," Kaimi said. "How can an entire planet exist with no name?"

"This is getting more cryptic," Omar admitted.

"Bruto see other ships!" Bruto said. "Flown by other Zovvlers!"

"Stay focused, buddy!" Kaimi said. "You're flying with your mind, so try not to get too distracted!"

"Bruto understand!" Bruto said. "Ship reach coordinates in thirty seconds."

Kaimi continued to look at the screen.

"Kaimi," Omar said. "What if the book isn't here?"

"Well," Kaimi said, "if the book isn't here, then Agnor was wrong. And maybe, the book isn't magical."

The next twenty seconds, Kaimi tried to find any background on the planet. But there was not much. It was inhabited by creatures. But with no name in the system, Kaimi felt uneasy about it all.

"Landing at coordinates," Bruto said, "in three, two, one."

Now there was no window to the outside like on their ship. Potentially because it was flown by the mind, it could be a safety issue.

"Bruto, what do you see?" Kaimi asked.

"Bruto show you," Bruto said.

The screen by Kaimi's chair showed the current view outside. Omar looked over to see.

"Why does that planet look so dark?" Kaimi asked.

"It's sort of like the opposite of L-VII," Omar said. "Where we have the lights every month, they offer dark skies. Look closely at that."

Clouds of smoke covered large surfaces of the planet.

"And this planet sustains life?" Kaimi wondered.

"Agnor did say shadow creatures stole his book," Omar remembered. "How do we get it back?"

"Bruto fly toward the planet slowly," Bruto said. "Maybe we get answers."

"I don't like this," Omar said. "Something feels off."

"Someone hailing us," Bruto said. "Me answer and project image onto Kaimi's screen."

"Why do you disturb us?" a gray alien asked. "We live in the shadows of the corners of the galaxy. Out of your way. Stay out of our way. You are not welcome on planet Travesty. Leave."

"Can he hear me?" Kaimi asked, looking at Bruto.

"Yes" the gray alien said. "Now hear this: leave, or be destroyed by the shadows of Travesty."

"Agnor's book," Kaimi said. "Do you have it?"

"You will not take it from us again," the gray alien said. "Your kind has committed such burglary many times in the last decades. Agnor's book belongs on Travesty. With Agnor."

"Sir," Kaimi said. "Please. Allow us to land so we can talk this out."

"I will allow no such thing."

The ship came to a halt. Bruto winced in pain.

"Are you okay, Bruto?" Kaimi asked.

"Bruto fine," Bruto said. "But me not get any closer to Travesty."

"What is your name?" Kaimi asked.

"Why do you care? You are not getting Agnor's book. It belongs here."

"It was stolen from my home planet," Kaimi cried. "We are on a mission sent here by Agnor himself to retrieve his book."

"Now that is impossible," the gray alien screeched. "You do not know the great magnitude of the presence of Agnor."

"We are working for him!" Kaimi said.

"Let's find out if that's true," the gray alien hissed.

The screen went off. A tractor beam from the planet's surface locked onto their ship, and slowly pulled them to Travesty.

"Oh, I definitely don't like this," Omar cried.

"Agnor did say it was dangerous," Kaimi said. "But this is kind of terrifying."

"Bruto lose control of ship," Bruto cried. "Me bad captain."

"No, buddy," Kaimi said. "You are a good captain."

Kaimi's screen showed the surface of the planet as it got closer. It was covered in smoke, dust, and dirt. The buildings, though tall, looked decrepit and neglected. This entire planet was, in fact, a travesty.

"Why does it look like that?" Omar asked.

The ship landed safely. They received another hail call.

"You stand by your earlier comment?" the gray alien asked. "Because this is your last chance to tell the truth."

"Of course we stand by it!" Kaimi said. "Agnor hired us to retrieve his book. So we are out here to reclaim what is rightfully his."

"Why do your buildings look so old and worn out?" Omar asked.

"None of your concern," the gray alien hissed. "But since you are about to be destroyed, I'll just tell you that it is part of our society. It is how we hide. They aren't as bad as they look. But everyone stays away because of how they look. And that is all you need to know. For now, I would like to introduce to you, the man himself."

"Who?" Kaimi whispered.

Bruto hovered over to Kaimi.

"Bruto scared," he said.

The door of the ship began to open.

"How are they controlling our ship?" Kaimi cried.

"Everything that touches Travesty, is ours," the gray alien smiled. "We can control ships once they reach our soil. And you refused to leave. Then, claimed to work for Agnor."

"Because we do work for Agnor!" Omar exclaimed.

As the door fully opened, a creature could be seen standing outside the ship. He walked into view, onto the ship. He looked similar to the gray alien on the screen, except he was wearing a crown, and a dark purple robe. He held a scepter in his right hand and a book in his left hand.

"Try anything, and he will destroy you on the spot," the gray alien on Kaimi's screen said. "Although, he will do that anyway. He likes to take care of things personally. I always tell him how dangerous that is, but he says this is our turf, and he wants to be the one who is celebrated after your defeat. He has the victory already. A travesty this is for you. If only you had left when I warned you. Like so many that came before you, your journey ends here."

The screen went dark as the call ended.

"Who are you?" Kaimi asked.

"The man you claim to work for," the creature said. "I am Agnor."

Chapter Eighteen
Agnor?

"That is definitely not Agnor," Omar whispered.

"I most definitely am Agnor!" the creature that claimed to be Agnor reiterated. "How dare you question my word!"

"Bruto see Agnor's book," Bruto said.

"Oh, is this why you're here?" Agnor laughed. "Well, why don't you try and take it from me."

"Just give us the book," Omar demanded. "And we will be on our way."

Agnor laughed.

"For many years, people like you have landed on our planet. Time and time again, we lost this book. But after being defeated so many times, we learned so much. We, ourselves, have gone back out into the cosmos to retrieve this book from many different planets after they stole it from us. I believe L-VII was the last stop we made."

"What do you mean?" Kaimi asked. "Other planets want this book too?"

"Oh simple human," Agnor shook his head. "You don't understand the constant struggle it is for any one planet to keep such a treasure. But here on Travesty, we have no choice but to fight to the death for it."

"Why?" Bruto said. "Why Travesty so special? L-VII need book more!"

"I highly doubt it," Agnor said. "For if my book were to be isolated from Travesty, bad things would begin to happen."

"Bad things?" Kaimi mumbled. "But that's what our Agnor back on L-VII told us."

"Something is wrong," Omar said.

"It is," Agnor said. "But I am about to take care of the problem. So you need not worry, Elder. Many months ago, I believe it was a small band of Elders that actually overtook us. So my revenge will be had."

"What were their names?" Omar asked.

Thrown off by the question, Agnor just shook his head. "Names do not matter! Three Elders, one that was similar to you, and two others, used their chaotic powers to confuse us and take my book. But we understand now. We have done extensive research on not only Elders," Agnor turned to look at Bruto, "but Zovvlers too. There isn't much known about you creatures, but I learned enough to see that you have an interesting history. We studied every species in the database. We are superior to all of you."

Bruto looked at Kaimi, who nodded. She could tell he had an idea. He hovered over to the captain's chair.

"Whatever you think you are trying, I stop thee!" Agnor exclaimed.

He slammed the scepter onto the floor of the ship. It sent out a shockwave of noise that was so loud, everyone was forced to cover their ears. Unfortunately, that did not help with the piercing sound. Agnor stood there, smiling, somehow unaffected. Bruto was right next to the captain's chair, hands on his ears. The sound slowly dissipated.

"Now," he said, "mercy is unfortunately no longer an option. For you have not only trespassed on my planet, you have also defamed my name. You do not work for me. You never have worked for me. And you never will work for me. My book will be staying here on Travesty with me. And you will become one with the planet, as the dust of your bodies joins the very soil of the ground. You will be swept up in the glory of the buildings of Travesty. For that, my friends, is your fate. And it is sealed."

Agnor raised the scepter in the air. He was about to send out another deafening, possibly deadly, shockwave. Bruto had managed to sit down in the captain's chair.

Still wearing both bracelets, he screamed, "Agnor stop!"

The scepter flew out of Agnor's hand, and landed in Bruto's. Bruto seemed to be gaining strength.

"Agnor's book ours!" Bruto screamed.

The book flew from Agnor's hand to Bruto's other hand.

"Leave Zovvler ship," Bruto cried.

Agnor charged toward Bruto. Bruto threw the scepter at Agnor, which broke upon impact, sending Agnor flying out the door of the ship.

"We will be back," Agnor yelled. "L-VII will be destroyed, as every ship on Travesty will join us this time. We will not sneak in and steal the book. We will end your entire planet for what you have done. L-VII will be destroyed!"

The door of the ship slammed shut. Bruto threw the book to Kaimi.

"Guardian proud," Bruto said. "Zovvler ship take Agnor by surprise. Not much known about Zovvlers used to Bruto's advantage. Now Bruto set coordinates to Oasis."

The ship began to take off. A tractor beam halted them.

"Travesty!" Bruto exclaimed.

Bruto's eye closed. He was concentrating on his foes mentally, to give him, and the ship, a boost of power.

"Travesty let us go!" Bruto screamed.

They broke free from the tractor beam. Bruto began to look like he was in distress from all the power he was sharing with the ship.

"Bruto, are you okay?" Kaimi asked.

"No time!" Bruto cried. "Oasis. Coordinates."

The ship left Travesty in the blink of an eye.

"One minute until Oasis," Bruto said. "Bruto see other Zovvler ships again! Maybe they help? Bruto feel sick. Me need to stop."

"Then stop!" Kaimi insisted.

"Bruto must continue on," Bruto said.

"Buddy," Kaimi cried. "We have the book. We can slow down. We'll get it back to L-VII!"

"Travesty creatures on tail," Bruto said. "Me get us safe to Oasis. Zovvler ship faster. Must try."

Omar shook his head. "Be careful, Bruto. You are more important than any of this."

"Me take us to Oasis. Thirty seconds away. Rest is on Oasis."

"What do we do?" Omar asked.

Kaimi, still holding Agnor's book, was at a loss.

"This book," Kaimi said, "has caused so much chaos, so much trouble. I wish we had answers, Omar."

"Fifteen seconds!" Bruto cried, his voice getting quieter. "Watch screen by chair, captain."

Kaimi looked at her screen, as the ship swiftly drew nearer to the coordinates of Oasis.

"Is he going to be okay?" Omar cried. "Look at him!"

"Don't interfere with Bruto," Bruto cried. "Me saving us."

"I am sorry, Bruto," Kaimi said. "I wish I could be in that chair." She looked at Omar. "I don't know what to do," she admitted. "What kind of captain am I?"

Moments away from Oasis, Bruto's bracelets began to spark.

"Five... Four... Bruto... can't... think..."

The ship came to a sudden halt. Bruto fell out of the captain's chair. The bracelets on his wrists looked to be burnt out, as smoke began to flow from them. They fell off Bruto's arms. The lights on the ship glitched off and on. Kaimi's screen went dark.

"Fifty-seven seconds," Bruto whispered softly. "Me tried, captain. Bruto fail."

Three seconds away from Oasis by Zovvler ship, the now inoperable vessel, along with its crew, were helplessly stuck in the middle of unknown space.

Chapter Nineteen
Distant Relative

"Bruto, buddy?" Kaimi cried, running over to him. "Are you okay?"

His eye opened slightly to look at Kaimi.

"Bruto need to recharge mind. Me sorry."

"What can we do to help?" Omar asked, walking over to Bruto.

"Bruto need to rest," he said. "Calixta gonna be mad for Bruto ruining ship."

"Calixta will understand," Kaimi reassured him.

"Can we fly this without the bracelets?" Omar asked. "Maybe we can slowly return to Oasis."

"There is no way," Bruto said. "Maybe bracelets recharge with Bruto. They key to fly ship."

Kaimi and Omar looked at the damaged bracelets on the floor by their friend. They were still sparking and smoking.

"I don't think those are going to be working anytime soon," Omar said softly.

"Bruto fix when he wakes," Bruto said, closing his eye.

Omar picked up a bracelet. He immediately let it fall back to the ground.

"Those are scorching hot!" he cried.

"We are nearly out of options," Kaimi said somberly, still holding on to Agnor's book.

"Captain," Omar said. "We have the book. We are so close to completing this mission. Then, endless adventures await us."

"They have to charge," Kaimi said, looking at the bracelets. "The ship can't move at all. If anybody finds us in this state, all is lost. So we can't let them."

"What do you propose?"

"We open the book," Kaimi said.

"Does it have power?" Omar asked. "Is it actually magical?"

"That's what we have to find out," Kaimi said. "But only if you are in agreement. Maybe it can charge the bracelets or fly the ship or something."

"What if opening it lets off some sort of signal?" Omar said, worriedly. "We might draw an enemy right to us."

"What if it is letting off a signal anyway?" Kaimi sighed. "This book brings nothing to us but endless questions. Back on Travesty, their Agnor was under the same impression as our Agnor. If this book were to be away from our planet, Agnor said we would notice. Then, Travesty Agnor said bad things would happen to their planet if we took it away from them. That is more than just a coincidence."

"It sounds like this book is making the rounds," Omar said. "Agnor, Travesty Agnor, said they themselves have gone out into the cosmos to retrieve the book. They stole it from L-VII!"

"But he also said a band of Elders stole it from Travesty last time," Kaimi said. "What do we even know about L-VII and Agnor's book?"

"Nothing," Omar said. "Absolutely nothing. We have been kept in the dark."

"Is it even part of our history?" Kaimi wondered out loud. "Why was it so important to our Agnor? This band of Elders that Travesty Agnor claims stole it from them last time, do you believe one of them was actually your distant relative?"

"I believe that could be," Omar said. "But if it was, and Clory and his friends brought it to L-VII, only for the creatures of Travesty to return to our planet and steal it back, does that mean our Agnor is just constantly hiring anybody and everybody to fly to Travesty to get the book back?"

"This goes beyond Travesty and L-VII," Kaimi said. "Travesty Agnor mentioned that their species has traveled to many different planets to retrieve the book, after said planets stole it from them. This goes deeper than we could imagine. Everyone wants this book. And I wonder if everyone fears it is vital to their planet somehow. This book is causing a war among everyone."

"Kaimi," Omar said, looking at Agnor's book. "When did you open the book?"

Shocked, Kaimi looked down at her own hands, holding the open book.

"I don't remember!" Kaimi cried.

"Close it!" Omar advised.

They heard a weird noise outside the ship. But with no viewscreen window, Bruto resting, and the screen by Kaimi's chair still dark, they had no way of seeing outside. They were vulnerable. Anything could be out there.

Minutes went by, and they heard nothing but silence. Maybe whatever it was had moved on. The lights were still flickering on and off. Kaimi's screen blinked on and off. Omar noticed something on the screen.

"Was someone trying to hail us?" Omar asked.

Kaimi walked over to the screen, open book in hand. She saw the screen blink on and off.

"I think so," Kaimi said. "But there isn't enough power."

"So maybe we could—"

Someone appeared on the ship. They teleported right through. Omar was about to scream, when he recognized the teleporter.

"Clory!" he exclaimed.

He hugged his distant relative.

"Kaimi! This is Clory!"

Clory looked over at Kaimi.

"Ma'am," Clory said. "You might want to close that book. You guys are letting off a powerful signal."

Kaimi immediately shut the book.

"Oh, so you listen to him?" Omar smirked. "Clory, I haven't seen you in forever!"

"It's good to see you, Omar," Clory said. "What are you guys doing with Agnor's book?"

"Returning it to L-VII," Kaimi said.

"We already did that!" Clory cried. "Agnor hired us months ago. We went to Travesty, retrieved the book, returned it to him, and we were on our way."

"What did he offer you?" Omar asked. "You can already travel wherever you want in the galaxy. Elders have powerful technology, just like this Zovvler ship. After you and your friends saved everyone from the great war all that time ago, he couldn't possibly offer you anything worth risking your lives over."

"Omar," Clory said. "For my friends and I, it is just about answering the call for help. We received a distress signal. Somehow, Agnor sent it out pretty far."

"So you just went out of your way to help a stranger?"

"Basically," Clory said. "But if I am being truthful, my friends and I had a strange feeling about Agnor's book. From the moment it was mentioned, we were intrigued."

"What are you doing out here still?" Kaimi asked.

"After we delivered Agnor's book back to L-VII, we stuck around," Clory said. "This book is not like any other. There is something off about it. When we had it in our possession, Trolk, my friend, was trying to do extensive research on it. But at first, she found nothing. The book was with us for such a short amount of time, the information we finally managed to retrieve wasn't even attained until after the delivery."

"What do you mean?" Omar asked.

"Our smart ship," Clory pointed to the wall, "this ship has no window. I apologize. My friends are on our smart ship, just beyond that wall, waiting for me. Anyway, Trolk opened the book back on our ship before we delivered it to L-VII, releasing its past into the air. I'm telling you, this book is not only magical, but I think it wants us to help it somehow."

"What do you mean it released its past?" Kaimi said.

"Unbeknownst to us, the ship had received information from the book. And it wasn't until days after we gave it back to Agnor that our ship finally decoded and provided us with the information. We managed to trace the book's history, Where it had traveled. It has been to an astounding fifty-seven different planets over the last few decades."

"Fifty-seven again?!" Omar cried.

"The number follows you around now too, huh?" Clory smiled. "You get used to it."

"Every planet is named, except for one," Clory said.

"Ominous," Kaimi replied.

Bruto began to stir.

"Is your friend okay?" Clory asked.

"We fell out of our coordinates," Kaimi said. "The creatures on Travesty have become stronger. They nearly overtook us. But Bruto flew our Zovvler ship with all his mind. And it burnt him, and the control bracelets, out."

"Oh my," Clory cried.

"Clory? Is everything okay?" a voice could be heard.

Kaimi noticed Clory was wearing a watch on his wrist. A woman could be seen on the tiny screen.

"Yes, Trolk," Clory said, "you won't believe who I found."

"It better not be Smedge again," Trolk said, seriously. "He has caused enough trouble."

"Tell me about it," Clory said. "No, I found Omar!"

"Hello," Omar said, looking at the watch. "I don't think we have met."

"Not officially," Trolk said. "But Clory has mentioned you! You are lucky to be a teleporter!"

"Hey Trolk," Clory said, "do you or Gleck know anything about Zovvler technology?"

"Zovvler?" a man's voice could be heard on the watch. "Trolk, remember when we met that Zovvler back on Triad Nine?"

"How could I forget that?" Trolk laughed. "You insulted the governor of Triad itself!"

"How was I to know hats weren't permitted?!" Gleck laughed.

"What noise is Bruto hearing?" Bruto said, sitting up. "Obnoxious noise wake Bruto."

Trolk laughed. "Gleck, your laugh woke someone up."

"It's not that obnoxious!" Gleck defended himself.

"Guys," Clory said.

"Sorry," Trolk and Gleck said in unison.

"Do you understand Zovvler technology?" Clory asked his friends once again over the watch.

"No," Trolk said. "I want to, though."

"Zovvlers are cool," Gleck said, "but their technology is so complex, the only creatures that understand it, if they can even understand it, are Zovvlers."

"Bruto understand technology," Bruto said. "Me no recognize voice. Who talking?"

"Gleck!" Gleck said.

308

"And Trolk," Trolk added.

"This is my distant relative, Clory!" Omar said.

"Bruto feel better," Bruto said. He looked at the bracelets still on the floor. "Bruto recharge," he said, picking them up.

Though the smoke had finally dissipated, the bracelets still looked a bit damaged.

"They were on fire earlier," Omar said. "I tried to pick them up, but I couldn't."

"They cool off," Bruto said. "They recharge."

"But they looked so damaged!" Kaimi said, wondering how they would work again.

"So did Bruto," Bruto smiled.

He put them on his wrists.

"Is that wise?" Omar asked.

Bruto held his arms out. The bracelets began to glow again. But not from being hot. Somehow, Bruto was restoring them.

"Bruto integrated mind with ship to fly earlier," Bruto said. "We both burn out. Now, Bruto integrate mind with ship once again. Me share the healing power of relaxation."

"But you're alive," Omar said. "The ship is not."

"Two things," Bruto said. "One, Zovvlers always have more secrets. Two? Who said ship wasn't alive?"

Now fully functional, the bracelets looked as good as new. Bruto closed his eye.

"Bruto heal ship," Bruto said.

The lights stopped flickering. The screen by Kaimi's chair turned back on.

"We travel to Oasis in approximately three seconds," Bruto said.

"Oasis?" Clory said. "Where is that? I have never heard of such a place."

"We have to land on Oasis and pick up our ship," Kaimi said. "I think we also need to figure out the story behind this book. Even though we were hired by Agnor to retrieve it, even though L-VII is our home, giving it back to Agnor with no answers seems like the worst thing we can do now. Someone would just steal it again. Travesty is about to declare war and destroy L-VII."

"Follow us, Clory," Omar said. "We can introduce you to our friends Sight and Calixta."

Clory looked at his watch to see what Trolk and Gleck thought.

"An Oasis sounds nice," Gleck said.

Trolk nodded. "Maybe we can finally get some answers."

"How will you keep up with us?" Omar asked. "Our ship is super fast."

Clory laughed. "Don't worry about us," he said. "Just lead the way."

Clory teleported back to his ship.

"That was ominous," Omar said.

"Well," Kaimi smiled, "Bruto, are you ready?"

"Bruto ready!" Bruto said.

"Take us back to Oasis, captain!" Kaimi exclaimed.

"Three... two... one... and we have arrived!" Bruto said.

"And look who is right behind us," Omar said, looking at Kaimi's screen.

"I hope that's Clory," Kaimi said.

Someone hailed their ship. Bruto answered it and sent the image to Kaimi's screen.

"I told you," Clory said, "no need to worry."

"How is that possible?" Omar asked.

"One story at a time," Clory said. "Is that Oasis? That planet is beautiful!"

"Clory," Kaimi said, "we should hang up. I think Alora, a local down on Oasis, is going to need to give you clearance. She will recognize this ship, but not yours."

"Understood," Clory said. "We will meet you on the ground."

"Station fifty-seven," Omar laughed.

"Of course," Clory smiled. "Always fifty-seven with us."

"Bruto receive instructions to land," Bruto said.

"I hope Sight and Calixta have made progress on their dilemma," Kaimi sighed.

"Bruto landing ship now! Welcome back to Oasis!"

Chapter Twenty
Connections

Bruto safely landed Calixta's ship. He went to get out of the captain's chair, and he fell to the ground.

"Bruto, are you okay?" Kaimi asked.

Bruto immediately stood back up.

"Yes, Bruto fine," Bruto said. "Just felt dizzy, but me okay now."

Kaimi, Omar, and Bruto were greeted at the door by Calixta.

"Back so soon?" Calixta asked.

"We have the book!" Kaimi said, book in hand.

"Well that's wonderful," Calixta said. "You should return it to your planet!"

"Yeah, about that," Kaimi began, "we might need more answers before we can do that."

"How's my ship?" Calixta asked, joining her friends on her ship.

"Bruto burnt it out," Bruto said. "But me recharge and fix!"

"Oh, maybe I took more pieces than I should have for Hazard," Calixta admitted. "I am sorry, Bruto."

"Bruto okay!"

Calixta looked around at her ship, then walked out the front door.

"Welcome back to station fifty-seven!"

Everyone followed her off the ship.

"Has Clory landed yet?" Omar asked.

"Clory?" Calixta said, unsure of the name.

"We found my distant relative and his friends," Omar said. "Maybe they can help you with this crystal rain issue."

"I'll take all the help I can get," Calixta admitted. "But if they were with you, they may have landed next to your ship. I don't quite know where you guys landed."

"Don't worry," a woman's voice echoed. It was Alora. "I believe your friends are looking for you."

Alora was leading Clory, Trolk, and Gleck.

"Your friends are very kind," Alora continued. "They already expressed their love for our beautiful planet. I reiterate what I said earlier. If any of you would like to call Oasis your home, we would love to have you on our beautiful planet. I have business to attend to. I trust Calixta will guide everyone where they need to go. Nice to meet you, Clory, Trolk, Gleck. Nice to see you again, Bruto, Kaimi, and Omar. Calixta, thank you."

Alora walked away.

Gleck looked around at everyone.

"That is a very loud hat," Calixta said, looking at Gleck.

"Everytime with the hat, Gleck!" Trolk scolded him. "I told you to leave that on the ship!"

"No, I like it!" Calixta laughed.

"Any changes in the weather since we were here?" Kaimi asked.

"The crystal rain is slowly increasing, but we still have twenty-eight years until total evacuation, according to Hazard."

Clory's eyes widened. "Crystal rain?!"

"We haven't mentioned any of this to Clory and his friends," Kaimi said. "Maybe we should catch them up."

"I'll lead us all back to Sight and Hazard," Calixta said. "If our new friends would like to join us."

"Maybe," Kaimi said, looking at Agnor's book, thoughtfully, "maybe something will begin to make sense."

"Connections will be made," Bruto said, eye closed.

"Buddy?" Kaimi said, concernedly.

"You have brought me back," Bruto said.

"That is not Bruto's voice," Omar cried.

"I never thought I would find my way back, but you somehow managed to carry me," Bruto said.

"Who are you?" Kaimi demanded.

Bruto fell to the floor.

"Bruto confused," Bruto said.

Clory stared at Bruto.

"That was not normal," Gleck said.

"That book," Clory wondered. "I will be right back!"

Clory teleported away.

"Where did he go?" Omar asked.

"I'm used to him just vanishing, then returning with relevant information," Trolk said.

Gleck, trying to break the awkward silence, said, "So, crystal rain. I think I used to listen to that band."

Trolk sighed. "Gleck."

Clory teleported back to everyone.

"I had a feeling!" he cried. "You are about to get a lot of answers, and maybe more questions."

"Where were you?" Kaimi asked.

"I teleported to our ship," Clory said. "I checked the history of Agnor's book. Remember how I said that out of the fifty-seven planets this book has traveled to, one was unnamed?"

Kaimi nodded.

"Oasis!" Clory cried. "I had never heard of it. And I am pretty certain that the unnamed planet the book had traveled to, is this planet!"

"But why?" Gleck asked. "Why is Oasis unnamed in the galactic system?"

Clory shrugged.

"Bruto feel funny," Bruto said. "Open book."

"What?" Kaimi asked.

"Open book!" Bruto cried.

He reached for the book. It immediately began to glow.

"Me open book," Bruto cried.

He opened the book, and began to speak in a different voice. The same voice that they heard moments ago.

"I fear, this is all my fault," Bruto said.

"Who are you?" Kaimi asked. "Please don't hurt our friend."

"I have no ill intentions," Bruto cried, in a deep voice that wasn't his own. "I have been stuck inside this book for nearly thirty years."

"Earlier, he said connections will be made," Kaimi said. "Thirty years, you say?"

315

"Allow me to introduce myself," Bruto said. "My name is Agnor, and I think I have a lot of explaining to do."

"I am thoroughly confused," Gleck said. "Is that Bruto or Agnor?"

"Agnor is speaking through Bruto," Trolk answered.

"If you can get me out of this book," Bruto continued, "maybe it will be less confusing."

"How did you even get in the book?" Kaimi asked.

"My ship was crashing, about three decades ago now, onto this very planet, Oasis. I think I upset the locals, as they thought I was invading. But it was an honest mistake. My ship was badly damaged from a fight I had just lost. I was running away from my enemy. I had no idea where I was. Then my engines began to give up. The closest planet was this one. I wanted to answer the hail call when they tried to reach me, but I had no control over my ship. I was crashing, whether they accepted that or not."

"Where is your ship now?" Kaimi asked.

"It fell deep into the crust of Oasis," Bruto continued. "I feared for my life. As my ship somehow continued to bury itself deeper and deeper, I acted on the one option that was given to me. I hid myself in this book. That was only a temporary solution. But then things got out of hand. As days went by, I could not find my way out."

"Agnor," Kaimi said, "what was on your ship?"

Clory shook his head. "I already know the answer."

"Crystals," Bruto said. "The magical crystals I collected from all different planets. Between you and me, and you can tell no one, I had crystals from different timelines too."

"If you hid yourself in this book, then why can't you just unhide yourself?" Gleck asked. "Do the opposite of whatever you did to hide."

"Don't you think I tried?" Bruto answered.

"Where did you find this book?"

"As my ship, along with the crystals, sank deep into the crust of Oasis, I was terrified. Everything was breaking around me. Crystals were cutting through the fabric of the planet. I looked around for some sort of relief or help. There was none. With the magical crystals beginning to change the very structure of Oasis, I was frightened. At first, I thought if I was found, after what I did to their planet, I would surely be held accountable for my actions. So I used what little knowledge I knew of magic to seek help. And that is when this book showed up out of nowhere."

"Is the book's origin from this planet then, or did you create it?"

"I have no idea," Bruto sighed. "I just somehow understood what I had to do. Hide myself in this book. I am not that skilled at magic. But I managed to complete the spell. I had done it! I was hidden away. No one could harm me. I was safe. But locked inside the book with no idea how to escape. After days went by, I felt so guilty for what I had done to Oasis, I began to panic. I tried to send out a distress call. I was afraid that if I wasn't found, something bad would happen. So I projected that thought as far as I could. Heightened by the now magic crust of Oasis, I think my thoughts altered everyone's perception."

"Connections are being made," Kaimi cried. "You projected the thought that you had to be found, or something bad would happen? Everyone that wants this book, wants it because they fear that if their planet is without it for too long, bad things will happen. I think your message was lost in translation."

"Days after sending that distress call, I was found," Bruto said. "But I still couldn't get out of the book. I then began this nearly thirty year journey across the cosmos, going from planet to planet every few weeks, in this never-ending cycle."

"We have to get this information to Sight and Hazard," Calixta said.

"Why now?" Omar asked. "How are you contacting us now? Have you not tried this with anybody else in these decades gone by?"

"No one was as strong as this Bruto fellow," Bruto said. "This is the first time I have had a chance like this. Please. I am begging you. Get me out of this book."

"The crystal rain," Calixta sighed. "It began after you crashed. The planet is angry. It is going to destroy itself. And all the years that have gone by, the magic has been slowly spreading throughout the entirety of Oasis."

"I can stop it," Bruto said. "Get me out of this book, and I promise you, I will stop it. I will save Oasis."

Bruto closed the book, and handed it back to Kaimi.

"Bruto back," Bruto said.

Kaimi looked at Calixta, then nodded.

"Take us to them," Kaimi said. "Sight and Hazard."

Chapter Twenty-One
Zero

Calixta immediately began walking. Everyone followed. While Calixta led the way, Kaimi, Omar, and Bruto began to tell Clory, Trolk, and Gleck about everything leading up to this point. When they mentioned Guardian, Gleck interrupted their story.

"We saw The Final Guardian too!" Gleck cried. "He was scary at first, but I think he saved our lives. He sent us in the opposite direction, away from some sort of void."

"He was an amazing friend," Omar said, somberly.

"Bruto miss Guardian," Bruto sighed. "He sacrifice himself to save us."

"The Final Guardian?" Trolk said, puzzled. "Why would he leave his post? I thought he stayed there all the time."

"He was abandoned by his people," Kaimi said. "Zovvler history is complicated."

"He was a Zovvler?!" Clory cried. "He never revealed that information to us. And our ship had trouble detecting his species. It never gave us an actual answer."

"We also met a vicious beast named Scrounger," Kaimi said.

Clory shivered.

"Don't get me started on that creature," Clory said. "That is one of the most dangerous beings we have ever encountered."

"In some ways, even worse than your brother, Smedge," Gleck added.

"He nearly destroyed us," Trolk said. "If it weren't for Clory's quick thinking and Gleck's ideas, we might not have made it back here."

"Don't sell yourself short, Trolk," Gleck said. "You saved us, and you're too humble to admit that."

Trolk smiled. "It was teamwork. Something Scrounger knows nothing about, the poor creature."

"I hope he never finds us," Gleck said.

"Oh, we sent him into the void," Omar said, nonchalantly.

"How?!" Clory exclaimed.

"Guardian!" Bruto cried. "That when Guardian sacrifice himself. He fight Scrounger on piece of metal. Scrounger taken by void. Guardian gave everything to send friends home."

"How did he move your ship billions of light-years?"

"Right by the void was like a junkyard," Kaimi said. "Guardian found an old teleportation device left by a stray ship. He threw it toward us, and somehow managed to guide us back home."

"I find it weird that we were both flung fifty-seven billion light-years away from our mission," Omar said, looking at Clory. "How did you guys get back?"

"Oh, I would love to tell you that story," Clory said. "But I think we have arrived."

Omar looked ahead as Calixta ran toward Sight. She gave him a hug. Hazard was also waiting for them.

"We have so much information to tell you," Calixta said. "But first, everyone, this is Sight. Sight, this is Clory, Trolk, and Gleck."

"Nice to meet you all," Sight said.

"My name is Hazard," Hazard said.

"This is my robot," Calixta smiled.

"A robot?!" Gleck exclaimed.

"You said you have information for me," Sight began, "but Calixta, I have some alarming news for you."

"What is it?" Calixta asked.

"Ever since you left to greet our friends, now that I think of it, ever since they entered the planet's atmosphere, the readings, they have gone crazy."

"How so?" Calixta wondered. "Worse?"

"No," Sight beamed. "Not by much, but by a noticeable fraction, the crystal rain has lessened."

"Really?" Kaimi said, staring at Agnor's book. "I am beginning to understand somewhat."

Clory looked at her, then noticed her looking at the book.

"The book?" Clory asked.

"Bruto ask Agnor," Bruto said.

He reached for the book and opened it.

"You brought me back to the crash site," a deep voice said.

"Is that book talking?" Sight cried.

He looked at Bruto, then noticed Bruto's mouth moving to the words being spoken.

"I want to be alive again," Agnor said through Bruto. "Get me out of this book, and I will fix this. I am sorry. My curiosity and need to collect those crystals has endangered an entire planet. I have ruined Oasis. I must fix it."

"Close the book," Sight said, somberly. "Close it right now."

Bruto obeyed.

"What is wrong?" Kaimi asked.

Sight pointed to Hazard.

"He scanned the book for life signs," Sight said. "And he projected the number of life signs in that book. But no one noticed."

"Was it fifty-seven?" Omar asked. "Wait, that could be horribly dangerous if there were that many life forms stuck in that book."

"Hazard," Sight said. "Show them."

Hazard projected the number for all to see. It said zero.

"More data recovered," Hazard said. "I was able to scan the past when the book possessed Bruto."

Hazard projected a video onto a tree. It showed Agnor's initial crash. It showed the crystals spilling out of the ship as it burrowed deep into the crust of Oasis. Glowing crystals were seen for miles around as the ship continued to sink into the planet. Small roots formed around the crystals, as the planet accepted them and tried to adapt. Glimpses of Agnor were seen as more crystals were shown. Agnor raised his hands up. It looked like he was calling on someone or something for help. Lightning formed around his arms, and a book seemingly appeared out of nowhere right in front of him. He picked it up, looked around, and vanished.

"What did I just watch?" Kaimi cried.

"You watched a planet transform into something new," Sight said.

Hazard's projection glitched, then stabilized. The book could be seen, stuck miles beneath the planet's surface. Time went by, and the book didn't move. Suddenly, a small glow could be seen forming around the book.

"That must be when Agnor sent out his signal?" Clory wondered.

As they continued to watch, the glow around the book became brighter and brighter. More time passed, until a creature could be seen climbing down into the planet. It was too dark to see what the creature was.

"Does this movie have audio?" Gleck asked.

"I wish," Sight said.

Bruto opened the book back up.

"Sound recorded in book maybe," Bruto said.

"Bruto wait!" Sight cried.

Immediately, sound was added to the projection.

"What will you tell the people of Oasis?" a male voice said.

"Don't worry about them," a female voice could be heard. "I'll make sure this stays buried. Something like this is bad for business. I'll take care of this, you get rid of that book."

"I will take it to my home planet," the male voice said. "I was surprised no one else brought this to your attention. I have been looking for this book. For if I do not get it back to my home planet, something bad will happen."

"Yes, yes," the female voice said. "Take it. You told me of this when you landed here. I was fully aware of the situation. It isn't easy to run an entire planet, you know. Business is business. The more creatures that stay on Oasis, the more profits I will be able to make. Once creatures agree to stay, they will help the economy. Even an Oasis needs to be profitable, my friend. Now leave, take the book. I will erase what I can. The book was never here."

"I will protect my book from harm," the male voice responded. "I will save my planet. For I am Agnor."

"Go!" the female voice cried.

The projection began to glitch.

"Another Agnor," Omar shook his head.

"That's just it," Kaimi cried. "Ever since that book came into existence, everyone thinks they are Agnor. Everyone thinks they need that book on their home planet, or something bad will happen."

"But why?" Gleck asked. "Just because of the original Agnor's frightened thoughts?"

"No," Clory said.

"We are missing something," Trolk added.

The projection disappeared. Hazard began to speak.

"Allow me," he said. "I understand. I took more readings as you were watching the projection. Again, ever so slightly, the crystal rain has begun to dissipate. Full evacuation in thirty-two years."

325

"The book?" Kaimi's eyes widened. "The book being here is slowing the crystal rain down?"

Bruto closed the book.

"It belongs here now," Bruto cried. "Bruto start to see."

Bruto closed his eye.

"Everything begin to make sense," he continued. "Bruto concentrate. Bruto feel crystal rain calming down. Book was created as planet was changing. Planet was attacked by magical crystals. Agnor ask for help to save himself for fear of being alone. But planet misinterpret. Planet help Agnor create book to offer relief. Book belongs on Oasis now. Book acts as mitigation against crystal rain. It offers relief. It needs to stay here. Forever."

"But with everyone thinking they need it to save their planet," Kaimi said, "will there ever be a time when someone isn't trying to steal this book?"

"Maybe Agnor can send out another signal to counter the first one," Gleck said.

"But Hazard said there are zero life signs in this book," Calixta said. "So what exactly is talking to us when we open that book?"

"An echo of time?" Clory asked. "Does he even know he isn't alive anymore?"

"Maybe there is still a way to save him, somehow," Kaimi said softly.

"Talk to Agnor," Bruto said. "Bruto help find answers."

Bruto opened the book.

Hazard began to project more video.

"Thank you, ma'am," the male voice said, picking up the book.

"Don't mention it," the female voice said. "Never mention it, to anybody. This book must never return to Oasis. It will surely destroy my business here."

"Why does she sound so familiar?" Kaimi asked.

"You thought so too?" Omar answered. "I thought I was going crazy."

"That voice," Calixta said. "It can't be."

"Who?!" Kaimi asked.

As they all looked at the projection, they could see the creature with the male voice leaving with the book. They caught a glimpse of the woman's face as he left. It shocked everyone, as they all recognized her.

It was Alora.

"Alora?!" Kaimi cried.

Everyone heard rustling in the forest behind them.

"Is it another bird?" Omar wondered. "Like the one that tried to steal the remote?"

"I don't think so," Calixta sighed. "I think I know exactly who it is."

"What have you done?!" a voice said.

"Alora?" Calixta asked. "How did you find us?"

"I have been tracking that book since you landed with it!" the voice said, as the creature came into view. "Of course it is me!" Alora cried.

Chapter Twenty-Two
Agnors

"You have betrayed us, Calixta," Alora continued. "This book causes nothing but turmoil. The crystal rain began because of that book!" She looked at Kaimi. "You were supposed to take that book directly back to your planet. I never should have allowed this. I was hesitant as we spoke earlier, but I hoped you would just bring it back to your planet without causing drama. You too have betrayed us."

"I am so sorry," a deep voice could be heard.

Alora looked at Bruto, who was holding the book open.

"That is not your voice," Alora said.

"No," Bruto continued, "it is I, Agnor."

"The creature that took this book off my planet originally?" Alora said, skeptically.

"No," Agnor, speaking through Bruto, cried. "I am the original Agnor that crashed into Oasis about thirty years ago."

"You!" Alora yelled. "You have disrupted my business! You have caused my profits to be at an all time low!"

"You never even tried to understand what happened!" Bruto screamed. "You just gave me to the first creature that walked on by!"

"I don't need to understand," Alora said. "You messed with magic on my planet without my permission! The crust has been altered! My planet is slowly dying because of you."

"It was an accidental crash," Bruto sighed. "I begged anybody for help as the crystals and I were taken by Oasis. The only help I received was this book."

"And who answered your call?" Alora said. "What magical being sent you that book?"

"We might have the answer to that," Kaimi interrupted. "We think that maybe the planet itself created the book."

"That's preposterous!" Alora said. "Why would Oasis create such a harmful thing?"

"Alora," Calixta said. "When Agnor crashed, it changed Oasis. He reached out for help, and he received it. This book appeared out of nowhere, but we think the planet created some sort of remedy or form of alleviation to the crystal rain."

"How could Oasis create a remedy from the sickness that plagued It?!" Alora screamed. "This can't be, that would mean that I sent away the one thing that could quell our imminent evacuation. That would mean so many creatures leaving would be my fault! That would be a bad business decision!"

"If you find a way to get me out of this book," Bruto said, "I promise to dedicate my life to finding an actual cure for Oasis."

Everyone got quiet.

"What is it?" Bruto asked.

"Agnor," Kaimi sighed. "We have reason to believe that you are no longer alive."

"I am!" Bruto cried. "I can hear you! I am speaking with you. How else would that be possible? I have been aware for nearly thirty years. I am alive. I am!"

"No," Hazard said. "You are not."

He scanned for life signs again.

"It says zero, Agnor," Calixta said.

"Oh no," Bruto said. "Please. Save me."

Noise began to fill the sky, as a ship came into view.

"They can not land here!" Alora yelled. "Go back to station fifty-seven for clearance!"

Another ship appeared. And another.

"What is the meaning of this?" Alora exclaimed.

"They have all arrived," Bruto cried.

"No way," Clory said.

"All of the wannabe Agnors have come to Oasis to lay claim to Agnor's book," Kaimi said. "Wait, I recognize the look of that ship."

She pointed to one of the ships.

"I think that is one of ours," Omar said. "Do you think our Agnor actually left L-VII? He said he was too old to travel!"

"If that is him, he may not be happy with us, and the decision we have to make," Kaimi said. "This book is not going back to our planet. It needs to stay on Oasis. It's literally a matter of life or death."

"If everyone believes they need this book, or bad things will happen on their planet," Omar said, "I have a feeling we might not want to be here when they all land their ships."

"There is nowhere to go," Calixta said somberly. "We won't make it back to our ships. And even if we tried to leave, they would just follow us. And we can't just take the book off Oasis again. It belongs here."

The ships began to attempt a landing. Trees were taken down, and flowers were crushed, as the first ship successfully landed. It was the one Kaimi and Omar recognized as being from L-VII. The door of the ship opened.

"Agnor!" Kaimi said, confirming that it was, in fact, their Agnor from L-VII.

"You have completed your mission," L-VII Agnor said. "Hand over the book, and you will be rewarded. Kaimi. Omar. Bruto. I knew I could count on you three. Whatever snafu had you stuck on this planet for so long, is forgiven, no questions asked. Hand over the book, before the imposters all land. You know who I am. I hired you. I am Agnor. No one else is."

Bruto looked over at L-VII Agnor. "Sir," he said, "I am Agnor."

"No, you are Bruto," L-VII Agnor said. "Why do you sound different?"

"I am the original Agnor, owner of this book," Bruto said. "This book was created when I was in distress."

Another ship landed, crushing more of the forest around them.

"My Oasis," Alora cried.

This ship was also recognized.

"Travesty," Kaimi said.

Four other ships landed right by it. They all looked the same. The door of the lead ship opened first. A familiar face walked out. Travesty Agnor.

"Well, well, well," Travesty Agnor said. "Guess we won't have to attack and destroy L-VII like we promised. If you hand me the book, I will rescind every word I said earlier. L-VII will be safe from the wrath of Travesty."

"Don't listen to him!" L-VII Agnor yelled. "I am your boss!"

More ships landed. The forest around them was completely destroyed.

"You have all declared war on Oasis!" Alora cried. "You have desecrated a beautiful forest. You have brought destruction upon my beautiful planet!"

As more creatures exited their ships, they all stated one common thing.

"I am Agnor! I am here to collect my book!"

"What do we do?" Kaimi said, looking at her friends.

"Could we teleport the book out of here?" Omar asked.

"No," Clory said. "They will destroy this entire planet looking for it if we try that. There has to be something we can do to break whatever is making them think they are all Agnor."

"Destroy the book," Alora said.

"That could destroy any chance your planet has of surviving!" Kaimi said.

"Does it matter?" Alora asked. "I have already caused so much damage to the planet when I sent that book away thirty years ago. I was trying to save face, I was trying to be strong and save my business, but I think it is time to find a new business endeavor elsewhere. We have to save ourselves. Better yet, give them the book. Any of them. This planet has become more of a nuisance than anything. I can't run a profitable business here after everything. What creature is going to want to stay here after they hear the very well-being of Oasis is based on a book? This has gone too far. I hereby resign. The following act solidifies my resignation from the Oasis project."

Alora ripped the book from Bruto's hands and closed it, severing the original Agnor's connection to Bruto. He nearly fell over, but caught his balance.

"Bruto need to help!" Bruto, now himself again, said. "Alora, we save Oasis!"

"Oh Agnors!" Alora said, taunting, "I have your book! Who wants it?"

Alora threw the book high into the air. Everyone else, all the wannabe Agnors, Kaimi and her crew, Clory and his friends, Sight, Calixta, everyone, in a frenzy, rushed over to where the book was about to land. Alora sneaked away, unnoticed, with plans of reaching her ship, flying away, and leaving Oasis forever.

Chapter Twenty-Three
Time Stop

As the book was still flying higher, the entire crowd had their eyes trained on it. Way up in the air, it began to twirl slightly as it would begin its fall back to Oasis. Everyone was now standing where they thought the book would land. Bruto looked at Sight.

"Sight," he whispered. "Time stop!"

Bruto closed his eye and put his hands on his head. He began to hover off the ground. Sight followed his lead.

Everything was silent now. The crowd was frozen. A woman's voice could be heard.

"I forgot about time stop," she said.

Confused, Bruto and Sight looked over to see Calixta. The three Zovvlers were now hovering off the ground.

"Bruto not sure what to do next," Bruto said. "Once book lands, surely war will break out."

"No, I don't think so," a deep, booming voice filled the sky.

"Who said that?" Bruto asked.

Sight pointed up. Calixta, Bruto, and Sight, were amazed at what they saw. Agnor's book was frozen in time, open. The pages were facing the crowd, as the book was planning to fall back to Oasis.

"Time stop," the deep voice said. "That's a good way to buy us some time."

"Agnor?" Sight asked.

"Of course!" Agnor said. "Now do you believe that I am alive?"

"I really want to!" Sight said.

"What is the plan here?" Agnor asked. "Once time begins, I am afraid chaos will overtake—"

The ground beneath began to shake.

"It is time the truth is revealed," someone said.

"Bruto looked around. He counted everyone that was currently able to speak.

"Bruto, Sight, Calixta, Agnor. Four. Who is voice five?"

"I am using Agnor's book to amplify, and to do the impossible," the voice said. "I should not be able to do this, but ever since the crash about thirty years ago, I have been changing. I need to go back. Please, listen to me. I am dying."

"Who are you?" Bruto asked.

"The crystal rain has been destroying me. Even though the presence of the book has slowed it down, I need a cure, not a temporary solution."

"Oasis?" Bruto cried.

"Yes," Oasis said. "Through the magic crystals that invaded my crust all those years ago, I have found a way to speak to you. When you paused time, and the book was frozen in the air, I found a way to channel my feelings through the crystals and to the very book that brought me healing."

"Oasis," Agnor said, "I am so sorry. I never meant to crash."

"I understand," Oasis said. "I believe you. But we can't dwell on the past. We have to look to the future. Agnor. I think it's time."

"Time for what?" Agnor asked.

"The reason the distress call was originally sent out," Oasis said. "The reason you went on this journey of decades. Do you not remember?"

"I am confused," Agnor said.

"A side effect," Oasis said. "Time is stopped, so I will remind you, before you make the great sacrifice. All those years ago, you crashed into my crust. The crystals began to spill and alter my core. As you were sinking deeper, you cried out for help. Now, as I was becoming sentient because of those magical crystals, I had a way to offer you help. But I needed help too. You would have died had nothing been done."

"They say I died anyway," Agnor interrupted. "There are no life signs in this book."

"I am sorry," Oasis said. "Since you knew your choices were to die in vain, or have a chance to right the wrong caused by the accident, you chose the latter choice."

"So I am dead?" Agnor said, softly.

"If you aren't already," Oasis said, "the sacrifice you are about to make would ensure your demise."

"What was the plan?" Agnor asked. "And why can't I remember it?"

"Perhaps it was too agonizing to remember," Oasis said. "Maybe you found a way to bury the truth.

And maybe you could save yourself and get out of that book. Maybe whoever tried to read your life signs was malfunctioning. But if you leave the book now, I will die. I surely would be overtaken by the crystal rain."

As silent as they could be, Sight, Calixta, and Bruto were in shock and awe at everything going on around them. A planet talking to a magical book? If only their friends could join the time stop. No one would believe such a tale.

"Can you bring back my memories?" Agnor asked.

"I can try," Oasis said, "but I will continue to tell you the story. That should remind you."

"Planet telling book a story," Bruto whispered.

"Shush," Sight said, trying not to laugh at him. "This is serious."

"As you cried out to anybody for help," Oasis continued, "I heard you. I called back to you. I created this book as a sort of cure. But the cure needed time. And information. In those moments, you and I understood each other immediately. I could not physically talk like I am now, but I whispered into your soul and you heard me. The mission was simple. I was sure that if nothing were to be done, I would surely be destroyed. I felt the magic changing me. And the crystal rain was imminent. Crystals from different places and timelines, all trying to rewrite who I am. I am an oasis."

"I remember seeing the book and finding refuge in it, but then it gets hazy," Agnor sighed.

"Once you were safely inside the book, the mission began. We sent out a signal. Again, this was

337

dangerous, but we had to get information to find a cure. The distress signal we sent out made anybody who heard it think they needed this book on their planet, or something bad would happen."

Bruto wanted to say something, but he managed to remain quiet.

"That is when the first creature arrived to take the book away," Oasis said. "And thus began your journey. You flew around the cosmos to many different planets on many different ships. You were able to download and obtain information from different species, different places, different ships, enough information to save me. I understand what has to be done now. And without you, this would have been impossible. Without a soul attached to the book, this may not have worked."

"When Bruto had visions of crash," Bruto whispered, "that led to Kaimi and crew discovering Oasis and collecting Agnor's book."

"That is right," Oasis said to Bruto. "And without the soul of Agnor connected to the book, reaching out to you, this mission may have failed. So thank you, Bruto. I owe you and your friends my everything."

"Everywhere I have been in the last three decades," Agnor cried, "I have been collecting information to save you?"

"Search through the information," Oasis said. "Look for your own thoughts from years gone by. I promise you, Agnor. You agreed to help. I am forever indebted to you as well."

A moment of silence was followed by Agnor's voice.

"Oasis," Agnor said, "I believe you. I am so sorry for what I have done to you. And I am sure that I would give anything to right such a wrong."

"You even found information on alternate timelines," Oasis said. "Clory and his friends have quite the history. So much information you have brought, Agnor. But, I fear I need to make you one final offer before we complete this mission."

"What is that?" Agnor asked.

"I may be able to use all the magic coursing through me to free you from the book. Your soul is clearly intact. Maybe we can save you, Agnor. Would you like me to do that for you?"

"Oasis," Agnor said, "I would love that. However, if you do that, this entire mission could be jeopardized. As you said, without a soul attached to the book, this may not work. I will not put you in danger a second time. I found the information, Oasis. I remember our agreement. You saved me to save you. I would have ceased to exist otherwise. I survived decades longer than I would have, because of you. Maybe the reason they couldn't pick up my life sign is simple. I am no longer alive. By their terms. By their scanners. But these past thirty years I have learned so much. I have seen so much. I thought I was lost. I thought I needed help. But I was wrong. I am found. I am where I need to be. Oasis, with my final moments, I pour out my soul, and all the information we have collected, to right the wrong I accidentally created. I am Agnor. This is my legacy. This is my story. This is my book!"

The Zovvlers ended the time stop. Time began to move forward.

Chapter Twenty-Four
Wisps

Everyone had their eyes on the book. The pages were still facing the crowd. The book began to glow. Even though time was moving forward again, Agnor's book was frozen in the air. Something magical was about to occur.

"We just missed something important," Kaimi said looking at Bruto.

"What happened?" Omar asked.

Clory, Trolk, and Gleck, looked a bit confused as well.

"It was a time stop," Sight said.

"Agnor's book went on adventure," Bruto said. "Gather information from every ship, planet, and species it visited. Tried to find cure for crystal rain."

"Zovvlers," Clory said. "You haven't even unlocked your full potential, yet you're already so powerful. That book was collecting and storing information to save Oasis, huh? It must have found a ton of information from our ship. I hope Agnor found what he was looking for."

"Attention visitors of Oasis," the real Agnor's voice echoed from the book above. "For the last three decades, you have all been part of something greater. You have all had the lingering thought that you were Agnor."

"I am Agnor!" L-VII Agnor cried.

"No, I am Agnor!" Travesty Agnor bellowed.

The entire crowd of Agnors began to argue.

"Enough!" Agnor said. "I am Agnor. And I am here to bring peace. No more shall you believe your name is Agnor."

Wisps of light began to descend from Agnor's book.

"What is that?" Omar asked.

"Healing," Bruto answered.

"I have searched the galaxy," Agnor continued. "I have been to over fifty different planets. I have garnered enough information to save multiple worlds from so many scenarios. But you were all in the crossfire. For your help, I am forever indebted to you."

Wisps of light continued to fall from the book.

"Help?" Travesty Agnor cried. "I would never help anybody! Except my people! I need that book, or something bad will happen to my planet!"

"No!" L-VII Agnor yelled. "That is my story! I need the book to save my planet! Do you accept my challenge of battling to the death, imposter?!"

Travesty Agnor, holding L-VII Agnor's gaze, nodded.

"It was never true!" Agnor shouted. "L-VII was never in danger. Travesty was never in danger. All of your planets were fine. Haven was safe. Triad was safe. The only danger was here, on Oasis. And the knowledge that has been bestowed upon my book, after traveling for so many years, is what shall save this planet."

The wisps of light began to increase. They began to reach the crowd of wannabe Agnors.

"Healing begins here," Agnor said. "As the magical light washes away all of your false thoughts, as the magic sinks into Oasis itself, healing begins here. Information alone can be powerful. But knowledge mixed with magic is quite miraculous. Because of all of you, Oasis will finally have the peace it has needed for decades. The crystal rain will no longer plague this beautiful planet. My initial crash was unfortunate. It was an accident. But I now right that wrong. Healing, for me, for you, for all, begins here."

"It looks like rain!" Omar said, as the magical wisps of light began to wash over everyone, sinking into the ground beneath them.

"But a good kind of rain," Sight said, elated. "Hazard, where are you?"

Hazard rolled up next to Sight.

"What do the readings say now?" Sight asked.

"Full evacuation in fifty-seven years," Hazard said.

Omar smiled at Clory.

"Oasis," Agnor said. "This cure begins right here where my ship crashed. It will spread throughout the entire planet swiftly, annihilating every ounce of harmful magic the crystals have tormented you with. My destiny has arrived. Thank you for saving me, so I could save you."

A downpour of larger strands of light poured out of Agnor's book. The light washed over the crowd, then sunk into the ground.

"Full evacuation in seventy-five years," Hazard said. "Ninety-nine years."

"Agnor," a voice echoed, shaking the ground beneath everyone. "The torment of the magic crystals has left me."

Everyone looked around to see who was talking.

"It's Oasis," Bruto said.

"Oasis?" Kaimi asked. "The planet can talk?"

"Yes, and no," Calixta said.

"I bet Oasis talked during the time stop," Clory said.

Bruto nodded.

As Agnor's book was still suspended in midair, the crowd watched as the glow around it slowly began to dissipate. The final bits of light fell from the book and vanished into thin air. The book immediately began to descend upon the crowd.

"Oh no," Trolk said. "There is going to be a riot for that book!"

"I don't think so," Kaimi said. "Look."

All of the wannabe Agnors began to walk away as the book was landing. Bruto caught Agnor's book.

"Magic is completely depleted," Bruto cried. "Just normal book now." He flipped through the pages. "No words. All empty pages."

"Are you sure?" Kaimi asked Bruto.

"Hazard?" Bruto asked, showing him the book.

"No magic detected," Hazard said.

"Life signs?" Kaimi asked.

"No," Hazard said. "No life signs detected."

"Agnor really had to pour his soul into this mission," Omar said.

"His sacrifice will not be forgotten," Calixta said. "I promise."

"Agnor?" Kaimi said, yelling after her boss. "Agnor!"

"That is not my name," he answered. "That is none of our names. We were pawns in someone else's game. And for this, I am enraged. Thirty years I was under that spell."

"We have a lot of cleaning up to do," another wannabe Agnor said. "I must explain all of this to my people."

Travesty Agnor shook his head and led his people to their ships. They all began to fly away. Even though a good thing had happened, everyone that was caught in the crossfire, as an Agnor, was visibly upset. One after another, every single creature left, until the only one left was the one from L-VII.

"What is your name?" Kaimi asked.

"Kaimi," he answered. "This is not your fault. But I have a lot of explaining to do back on L-VII. For Oasis, this is a good day. But for over fifty other planets, we have damage control to take care of."

Bruto walked over with Agnor's book. He tried to hand it to his boss.

"I don't even remember my name," the distressed man from L-VII admitted. "I must return to L-VII, and hope my people forgive me. Maybe they have the answers I need."

Kaimi, Bruto, and Omar watched, as the man that hired them walked away from them. The engines of his ship fired on, and he flew away, confused and upset.

Clory, Trolk, and Gleck looked at their friends. Kaimi wasn't sure what to do.

"Oasis saved," Bruto said. "We have Agnor's book. Captain Kaimi, now what?"

Kaimi looked around at the destruction caused by all the ships landing in the forest around them. The ground began to have a slight glow to it. The trees that were damaged magically healed themselves. The flowers that were crushed were reborn.

"Agnor like guardian angel now?" Bruto asked.

"Either that, or it was one final act of kindness from him," Omar answered.

"Guys," Kaimi said, somberly. "I am sorry. I do not think our boss will be offering payment for this mission. I think we are on our own."

"I think seeing our faces on L-VII might be too much for Agnor, I mean, whatever his real name is," Omar sighed.

"Bruto agree," Bruto said.

Omar saw Kaimi's face. Realizing she felt like a failure to her crew, he tried to offer words of encouragement.

"Thank you, captain," Omar said. "You brought us to victory. We were able to help save this planet because of your leadership."

"Captain," Bruto said, "original mission was to find book, and save planet. We have done both!"

"That's right," Omar said. "We were misguided, as was our boss. A planet was in need of saving. And it is saved now. You are not a failure to us, captain."

Bruto nodded.

Kaimi smiled. "Thanks, guys. You are an amazing crew." She sighed, and looked at everyone around her. "Thank you, everyone."

Chapter Twenty-Five
Farewell

"Oasis is healed," Calixta said. "I want to throw a celebration of sorts. The danger of the harmful magic and crystal rain is gone."

"With Alora absent, are you going to take over running the planet?" Omar asked Calixta.

Calixta looked around at everyone and nodded.

"I want to stay on Oasis," Sight said.

His friends looked at him, and understood.

"So you two will be running Oasis," Kaimi said, smiling. "Running station fifty-seven. Monitoring and welcoming visitors. Maintaining the well-being of the inhabitants of Oasis. I wouldn't want to leave this planet in anybody else's hands."

"Captain?" Bruto said, looking nervous.

"What is it, buddy?" Kaimi asked.

"Remember how goal for Bruto was to find more Zovvlers?" Bruto asked.

"Of course!" Kaimi said. "We found so many!"

"Can Bruto stay on Oasis with Calixta and Sight?" Bruto asked. "Me help run entire planet, with Zovvlers."

Although this question broke Kaimi's heart, she knew she couldn't ask Bruto to give everything up just so he could travel the skies with her and Omar.

"Of course, buddy!" Kaimi said. "We will miss you so much, though."

"Kaimi and Omar stay too!" Bruto exclaimed.

Kaimi looked at Omar. Without speaking, they both knew in their hearts that traveling was for them. So they wouldn't want to settle down on Oasis.

"Omar and I want to travel the stars," Kaimi said, somberly.

"You'll visit Bruto?" Bruto asked.

"Of course!" Kaimi cried.

"Always," Omar added.

Bruto hugged Kaimi.

"Should we head back to station fifty-seven?" Kaimi asked.

"Maybe. There is no need to hide out here anymore," Calixta said. "But it is beautiful, isn't it?"

"It really is," Clory said. He looked at Trolk and Gleck. "Do we have anywhere else to be?"

"No," Trolk said. "We have nothing on the schedule."

Clory nodded. "We would be glad to stay here for a day or two and help out wherever we can with your celebration."

"All the people of Oasis," Calixta said, "they need this good news. And this will help get the word out that the crystal rain is no more."

As discussion began among everyone, some time went by. No one noticed the minutes go by. The minutes turned into about an hour. Fifty-seven minutes, in fact, had gone by. When out of nowhere, a loud noise could be heard off in the distance.

349

"What is that?" Calixta asked.

"It sounds like a ship," Clory said.

"From where?" Sight wondered.

"From the direction of station fifty-seven," Hazard said.

Before anybody could say anything, the ship could be seen in the sky above. It was getting closer and closer to them.

"No," Calixta said. "No, it can't be."

"Who is it?" Gleck asked.

Trolk shook her head. "I have an idea of who that is. I want to be wrong."

As the ship drew closer still, Calixta sighed.

"Whatever is about to happen," Calixta said, "I thank you guys for everything."

Kaimi looked around, then at the ship. Her heart sank. She realized who was in that ship.

"Attention, Oasis," a female voice said.

"Alora?" Bruto asked.

"Hello again," the female voice said. It was, in fact, Alora. "So, we have a problem."

"Alora, just leave," Calixta said. "This planet is under my protection now. I will not allow you to exploit the planet, or the people, anymore. You have used us all long enough. No more profits. Your business endeavor is over. Leave."

"So the problem is," Alora continued, her voice echoing from the ship above, "even if I were to give up this planet, any of you could destroy my name throughout the cosmos. Thus preventing any future business endeavors. Alternatively, on my way to my ship, I overheard what was going on. The planet is healed? Maybe I was a bit hasty earlier. Allow me to take back my planet, and continue on with my business here, and I'll spare you all. Defy me, and you will all be destroyed. Right here. Right now."

"Alora," Bruto said. "You look beautiful on outside. But you have ugly soul."

"Then you shall be destroyed first," Alora said, angrily.

Shots were fired from her ship, directed toward Bruto. Bruto hovered out of the way, and flew straight toward Alora's ship.

"Bruto!" Kaimi cried. "Be careful!"

Sight looked at Calixta, and they both immediately took flight with Bruto.

"This planet is ours now," Sight said. "We will protect the people of Oasis at any cost."

"Final chance, Alora," Calixta said, sternly. "Leave us right now. We are a powerful species. Do not make us fight you."

Alora laughed.

"Okay," Alora said. "I will leave. Thank you for showing me the error of my ways."

Kaimi shook her head. "Something is wrong."

"I agree," Clory said.

"Enjoy Oasis!" Alora said.

She fired a shot directly at Bruto. He fell straight to the ground. Calixta and Sight stared after him. All of his friends on the ground rushed over to him. Alora fired another shot, nearly hitting Sight. She fired again, clipping his wing. He fell to the ground. Unable to fly currently, he stood up and ran over to Bruto.

"Oh," Alora said, "the element of surprise is fun! I guess allowing you all to live would have been a liability. So thank you for not accepting my offer. I am sorry for destroying you all."

Alora began to recklessly fire at everyone below. Hitting trees, the ground, burning up the grass and flowers.

"You have become the very thing that made you want to abandon Oasis!" Calixta screamed, still hovering in the air. "Do you want to save this planet, or destroy it?"

"I wanted to destroy you last," Alora admitted. "Calixta. The brave little Zovvler refugee. Hiding on Oasis. Don't think I didn't know. Don't think I didn't see. I was aware of what you were doing. I was aware of your little robot friend. I allowed it all because you were doing research that could save Oasis. Something I had no time for. I was focused on damage control. So thank you. Thank you for saving Oasis. Give it back to me. I'll allow you to live. You have my word."

"You shot my friends!" Calixta cried. "No!"

Alora sighed. She fired another shot toward the ground, nearly hitting Omar. He teleported away, and appeared again near the same spot.

"No?" Alora said, disappointedly. "Calixta, I am sorry."

Alora fired at Calixta, who managed to evade the shot. As Calixta flew through the air, Alora continued to fire, hitting more trees around the area, knocking them down.

"Just let me destroy you!" Alora screamed.

As shots continued to decimate the area around them, another tree, the biggest tree in the forest, began to fall. It was right by Bruto and his friends.

Wounded from the shot, Bruto, in a haze, closed his eye. His friends were still standing over him.

"Move," Bruto cried. "Tree fall and crush everyone. Please."

"Clory, can we teleport Bruto away from here?" Omar asked.

Before Clory could answer, the tree fell directly toward Bruto and his friends. No one had time to react. No one had time to run. Teleportation might work, but in the chaos, how could they teleport everyone away safely in time?

In the moments to follow, although there was no time to react, everything flashed before Kaimi's eyes. From being hired back on planet L-VII, to acquiring Agnor's book, to where they were now, everything. Kaimi sighed, realizing all hope was lost. There was nothing humanly possible that she could do to save her crew. The Elders couldn't react quickly enough. The Zovvlers on the ground were incapacitated.

Calixta watched from the sky in horror, as the massive tree fell on top of everyone below.

"I could have done something!" she cried. "Alora, why?!"

"Why?!" Alora hissed. "Money! That's why! My business will thrive here on Oasis. I don't care who I have to destroy to get everything back up and running. I don't care who has to die so I can profit. I never cared about anyone or anything, except making a profit! Don't you see?! That's all that matters! None of this, none of you, matter. Now join your friends in the sweet mercy of death. Don't worry, I'll take care of Oasis. Just like I always have. Oasis loves me."

Alora was about to fire at Calixta, who was in tears over the loss of all of her friends.

"Goodbye, Calixta," Alora said.

The shot fired from Alora's ship. Calixta watched, as it was about to hit her. She slowly hovered down to the ground by the tree that had crushed her friends. Alora fired more shots at Calixta as she landed. One hit the downed tree, setting it on fire.

"I am so sorry, Sight," Calixta cried. "Bruto. I let you down. Kaimi. Clory. Everyone. I am sorry."

"All is not lost," a hushed voice said.

"Hello?" Calixta said, confused.

"My final gift to you, and your friends," the voice whispered.

"Who's there?" Calixta asked.

"Who are you talking to?" Alora yelled. "You're insane. Zovvler. You may rest now with your friends. I offer you mercy. Death."

A final shot was fired from Alora's ship, headed directly toward Calixta.

"Thank you, Calixta," the hushed voice whispered. "Thank Bruto for me. Thank everyone. I release these final wisps of magic, to save you all. Just like you all saved me."

The ground beneath began to glow once again. The trees began to heal. The grass and flowers flourished. The destruction began to turn into beauty. As the shot was about to hit Calixta, it dissipated. The ground shook. The tree that presumably crushed Bruto and everyone to death magically returned to its original spot. Underneath, a shield could be seen, protecting everyone from harm.

"It worked," Sight cried. "Bruto, you saved everyone!"

"Bruto try to use Zovvler shield," Bruto cried, coughing. "Sight help. Sight and Bruto save everyone."

"I could do this all day," Alora sighed. "I won't allow any of you to take what belongs to me. Oasis. This is my home. This is my endeavor. This is my planet. This is my business!"

The ground beneath stabilized, as the healing process was once again completed. The ground still had a slight glow to it. The light began to fade all around, concentrating itself in one spot. A single beam of light shot up from the ground, hitting Alora's ship.

"Oasis rejects you," a loud voice echoed through the skies. "Oasis is not your home. It is not your planet. And it is definitely not your business! To the void you will be banished, for you are not worthy of this universe. Or any universe."

Alora's ship imploded instantaneously. No destruction was caused as a result. Alora was defeated.

"Bruto are you okay?" Kaimi asked.

"Captain," Bruto said, "Bruto see shiny hat."

Bruto pointed to the sky. Kaimi, and everyone, looked up. A glorious display of lights similar to the display back on L-VII could be seen.

"The events that took place here," Hazard said, "the magic that has coursed through this planet for decades, whatever is left of it after all of this, is safely being discharged. I expect this light show to continue for the foreseeable future."

"Oasis managed to be more beautiful than it already was," Kaimi cried.

"Bruto will be okay," Bruto sighed, standing up. "Just need to heal. Calixta. Sight. Friends. Celebration time!"

As the conversation about the celebration once again continued, Calixta led the way back to station fifty-seven. With the help of everyone, the following day, an event so grand took place. There was not a soul on Oasis that was unaware of the victory. The crystal rain was gone. All current threats were no more. And Oasis was saved. It could thrive and be what it was meant to be. Not a business. An oasis.

Creatures from all around the planet showed up for the celebration. And some that had left to relocate returned in the following days.

After about a week of celebration, Kaimi, and all of her friends were gathered together in the building next to station fifty-seven. This building was where Calixta, Sight, and Bruto would assemble in the future to discuss everything Oasis. A sort of base of operations for them.

"Well, we must be on our way," Clory admitted. "But it was such a great time. I'm glad we decided to stay more than a day. Thank you, Calixta."

"Thank you, Clory," Calixta said. "Thank you all for your help here. This planet is thriving once again."

"And it will continue to do so under your guidance," Clory smiled. "You, Sight, and Bruto."

"Our other friends may be wondering where we are," Gleck laughed, obnoxiously. "Quo is going to love this story. I wish he were here for all of this!"

"Quo and Glor have a lot to take in," Trolk admitted. "After what happened at their wedding all that time ago, their lives have been one adventure after another."

Bruto was holding Agnor's book.

"Words appeared," Bruto admitted. "It tells story of Agnor's book."

He handed it to Gleck.

"Give book to friend Quo," Bruto smiled. "He can read story of Agnor's book."

"Is that safe?" Gleck asked. "This entire time, that book was destined to return here. I don't want to cause a disturbance on Oasis."

"Turn to last page," Bruto smiled. "Bruto read book multiple times after words appear. Magic completely depleted from book. Book is normal book now."

Gleck turned to the last page. Clory read over his shoulder.

"What does it say?" Kaimi asked.

"'Share the story of Agnor's book'," Gleck read aloud. "'Let this book soar across the stars, as the tale of Agnor, and his sacrifice for Oasis, reaches all the corners of the universe.'"

"How?" Omar wondered.

"I think Agnor, or more likely Oasis itself, added the words somehow," Clory smiled. "Quo is going to love this, Bruto. Thank you."

Bruto smiled.

"Hey Clory," Omar said. "Can we travel with you?"

Kaimi shot Omar a look, then realized what an amazing adventure that could be.

"Imagine," Kaimi said, "our ships flying side by side, searching for endless adventure."

Clory looked at Trolk and Gleck.

"I love that idea!" Gleck exclaimed.

Trolk nodded in agreement.

"Just drop me off at home first," Clory laughed. "I'll make sure Quo gets this book. But I need a break from adventuring."

In the following moments, a farewell of sorts began. Calixta, Sight, and Bruto said goodbye to their friends. Clory, Trolk, and Gleck entered their ship. Kaimi and Omar entered their ship. Both ships were currently parked next to each other in station fifty-seven. Bruto followed Kaimi and Omar.

"Bruto love you guys," Bruto said. "Me never forget this. Please do not forget Bruto."

"We love you too, buddy!" Kaimi said. "There is no way we could forget about you."

"We'll see you soon," Omar said. "Maybe once you're settled, you can join us for an adventure or two?"

"Definitely," Bruto smiled. He saluted Kaimi. "Captain."

Kaimi smiled, saluting him back. "I am so proud of you. Bruto. Protector of Oasis. Farewell, Bruto."

Bruto joined Sight and Calixta outside the ship.

As the engines of both ships roared, the three Zovvlers watched on, as their friends took off to the sky to find endless adventures.

About the author

Massachusetts-based Keith Imbody is a musician, writer, and the author of The Elders' Chronicles series. After many years of writing songs and stories, Keith decided it was time to start self-publishing. He has a passion for science fiction and fantasy, which you might find out after talking with him for just five minutes. His other passion is singing, though these two passions probably wouldn't work well together. Would anybody enjoy a Science Fiction musical?

Made in United States
North Haven, CT
31 May 2025